Mensa, Magic, and Mayhem

A DragonEye, PI Story

Karina Fabian

LASER COW PRESS

Laser Cow Press

MERRITT ISLAND, FL

Laser Cow Press
Merritt Island, FL
https://fabianspace.com

Cover art by Dawn Grimes
DragonEye Logo by Len Fabian

Book Layout © 2017 BookDesignTemplates.com

Mensa, Magic, and Mayhem/Karina Fabian -- 1st ed.
ISBN 978-1-956489-24-8

Dedication

New Edition:
To Suzanna Linton: A good friend and a great writer and critique partner who makes me better.

Old Edition (Magic, Mensa, & Mayhem):
To Rob: For wit, for wisdom, for love. I'll be your sidekick, anytime!
To my kids and godchildren: Who always want to hear another Vern story.
To Terry Pratchett, Douglas Adams, Robert Asprin, & Jody Lyn Nye: When I want to laugh, you're where I turn. Thank you. (And Piers Anthony, just for pun.)

Why am I getting déjà vu? Anyway, thanks to all my fans who make even a rewrite possible. You won't be disappointed.

Contents

List of Characters

Who let all these people in here? Vern and Sister Grace deal with a lot of people, so Vern wrote a glossary you can refer to.

Vern (Vurnerrah): The Eighth Day Creation, a dragon, and your hero.

Sister Grace McCarthy: My business partner; a Faerie nun and high-powered mage.

Gapman (aka Ron Engleson): A Mundane superhero under Vern's tender mercies...er, mentorship.

Agarrabarresheh: Secondkin of dragons.

Al'Beah: Genie Wish Artist *If Wishes Were Dragons*.

Baby Irby (Baby Dragonrider): Tried to ride me.

Barry Welles: Hotel manager of Citrus Stars.

Bert Loogan: Her husband, ex-sheriff, and friend.

Betanna: Princess Galinda's lady-in-waiting, friend and unconscionable gossip

Bill Reed: Thinks he's National Geographic and I'm his study. Zoologist specializing in Faerie.

Bishop Aiden: Bishop of the Faerie Archdiocese of Peebles-on-Tweed, and the duke's brother.

Brunhilde: Valkyrie, body builder, and small businesswoman.

Buddy Irby: Teenage son of Clyde Irby and just as stupid.

Cambridge Ramada: PI of sorts. We have history.

Cardinal Graystone: A Faerie cardinal

Casey: Purser on *Cloudskater,* in charge of luggage and supplies.

Catarina: Neice of Pope Pius. Was being harassed by a demon.

Charlie Wilmot, Herald: Duke Galen's favorite herald for working in the Mundane.

Clyde Irby: Father of Baby Dragonrider.

Cory Delastrade: Hotel security.

Coyote: Faerie empyrum. Just like the trickster of Native American fame.

Dr. George Alistarre: Mundane sociologist.

Duchessikins: Duke Galen's pet name for his wife.

Duke Galen of Peebles-on-Tweed: His duchy is where the Faerie end of the Gap appeared. Bishop Aiden's brother.

Durrehkeh: Eldestkin of the dragons.

Eliza Smithing: Coordinator of Mensa World Gathering. It was her idea to invite the Faerie.

EnviroGuy: Leader of the environmental protestors.

Euterpe (Terpie): Muse of Music. She and Grace have history.

FAE (Faerie Acoustic Enchanters): Band playing at World Gathering.

Father Rich: Priest in Los Lagos. I don't know if he's a Mensan, but he was smart enough not to come.

Frank Cisneros: Mensan. We had dinner with him and his wife, Lucy.

Frederico SanGermano: Faerie expert on Magicals—like a zoologist, if zoology included sentient beings. Works for the Tavendors.

Garn: A dwarf way too fixated on his pickax.

Garrett: Made fun of Siegfried and regretted it.

Gary Spade: Hotel security.

Gator Louie (Sinclair Jones): MeTuber who specializes in swamp creatures.

Gozonvabosomofic of the House Eternal Winds of the Shores of the High Elves (Goes-on-verbose-some-more-fic): Speaker of the Winds for the House Eternal Winds

Grislakeh. (Griss): My twinkin. We used to get into mischief together.

Heather Haskel: Rhoda Dakota's real name.

Higgenbo: Hobgoblin.

Inspector Logeston: Taught a forensics seminar.

Isaac Monroe: Mensan teenager gets into mischief.

Janey Taylor: Hotel Security. Native American, so she knows all about Coyote.

Jason Haskell: Little brother of Heather (aka Rhoda Dakota).

Jean Pierre Bargedecurie: Faerie French gourmet chef who runs the Con Café.

Jeeves: Princess Galinda's rented butler.

Kaliope: One of the Muses. Muse of poetry. Finicky editor.

Keiko: Japanese Mensan. Bought an enchanted purse off the internet, Nekosan.

Kenjo: Head of the hobgoblin tribe that is squatting in Tokneo.

Kent: A dwarf actor with stars in his eyes and ambitions.

Kevin Olson: Mundane. Owns a soda bottling company that wants to do business in Faerie.

Kitty McGrue: "Intrepid" reporter for the *Los Lagos Gazette*, known for getting the facts, then drawing the wrong conclusions.

Leesi: Kenjo's loving wife.

Lilly: Leader of the naiads.

Lucy Cisneros: Mensan. We had dinner with her and her husband, Frank.

Marisol: Mundane. A maid at the Citrus Stars and a "friend" of Coyote.

Maurena: Mundane. Host of *The Maurena Show*, which guested Princess Galinda and Galendor.

Melchoir Rawlings: High-strung Mundane artist.

Michael Santry, Captain: Los Logos' Chief of Police, and a pain in my tail.

MOUS: Moles of Unusual Size.

Natura Logan: Aging hippie, restauranteur, friend.

Nekosan: A kaminigi, a cat spirit taking the shape of a purse. Adopted by Keiko.

Pampaserrbahgh of the House Eternal Winds of the Forests of the High Elves (Pompous Airbag): Keeper of the Artifacts for the House Eternal Winds and a member of the Forest tribe.

Penelope Granger: Mensan kid, likes dinosaurs and dragons.

Percival, Aaron: A local lawyer I work with.

Pinjal: A hobgoblin known for reckless bravery...in other words, a hobgoblin.

Plinsina: Female hobgoblin. Crushing on Pinjal.

Polyhymnia: One of the Muses.

Pope Pius of Faerie: The pope in charge when St. George and I fought. He named me "Vern d'Wyvern."

Princess Galinda Tavendor: A human princess in Faerie.

Ray Rojas: Mundane who was given the ability to play any song he learns.

Rhoda Dakota (Heather Haskell): A teenage singer and actress.

Rita Irby: Tried to put her baby on my back and stick a quarter in my ear.

Roger: Receptionist at the Citrus Stars. Poor guy.

Roxanne Lewis: TV reporter for WCWG. I like her.

Sam Nix: First Officer on *Cloudskater*.

Shirley Starke: Mensan. Invited Euterpe and Grace to discuss the magic of music.

Shogzallie: A proto-empyrie (demigod) in the form of Godzilla-meets-Cthulhu and attacked Tokneo.

Siegfried: Faerie historian of Scandinavia, crushing on Brunhilde.

Sinclair Jones: Gator Louie.

Sister Eloise (Sister Fangirl): A member of Grace's order who specializes in shields spells and magical beasts. Helps Gapman and the hobgoblins.

SkinnyZits: Mundane hotel worker. Brunhilde likes him because he's "minty."

St. George: Yep, we had one, too. He brought me low and put me under the care and charge of the Church.

Starflower: Pixie: one of the artists working with Templegrass.

Templegrass: A pixie artist who runs a coop out of my old warehouse lair.

Tex: Insults Jean Pierre by asking for his steak well done.

Theodore "Led" Zepplin: Airship pilot for *Cloud-skater*.

Watkyndahydiottaru of the House Eternal Winds of the Shores of the High Elves (What kind of idiot are you): A stickler for etiquette, he insisted on calling me by my full name every time until I lost my temper.

Chapter One: The Trouble with Hobgoblins

As an immortal being, I value novelty—and living in the Mundane has given me more than my fair share of it. In the many years I've lived here, Mundanes have asked if I was housebroken, tried to put me in a zoo...and risked their lives for me—me, who cannot die! I've learned to use technology, which to a Faerie creature is far more amazing than magic. I've made friends, enemies, and—a new concept to me—frenemies. I have a nun for a partner in my private investigation business and a superhero for a sidekick. Now that Sister Grace and I have a nice place for our home and offices, and the people of Los Lagos have come to accept me, I can't complain. Much.

Nonetheless, my exploration of the Mundane has not gone outside of Colorado. Between the magic-deprivation illness that affects Magicals like me when we stray too far from the Gap and *my being needed near the Gap to solve mysteries and protect both universes from baddies both Faerie and Mundane, I'd not had the opportunity or inclination to venture further afield.*

All that was about to change.

I stood in the doorway of the abandoned office in a Tokneo building, my wings spread wide and tail swinging to prevent any of the hobgoblins we chased in there from escaping. Inside the office, Gapman was moving around the room, trying to use his superhearing to locate each one while he also tried to reason with their leader.

"Please, Mister—"

"You assume gender?" came a deep, gruff voice from behind the file cabinet.

True to his Mundane American upbringing, Gapman paused. "I, I apologize. I—"

"Leesi," I called out to the hobgoblin's wife, "You got any doubts about his gender?"

They had eight kids and another on the way. She responded with a giggle. Three of the others in the room also responded with catcalls.

"Quit playing games, Kenjo," I said. "We need to talk."

"No!"

I sighed. Once upon a time, dragons, the Eighth Day Creations, were treated with respect and even reverence. Now, I was a private detective dealing with unappreciative Mundanes and acting as accidental landlord to the fairies and hobgoblins who decided to settle in the land I'd been hired to protect. The only reason the hobgoblin tribe was there was because I convinced Tokneo Corp. that they were useful. And they had been until now.

The least the ingrates could do was stand still and listen to me.

Kenjo popped his head out of the bottom drawer. It was a flat oval, mostly mouth and eyes, with a shock of wiry black hair. The beady eyes glowed maliciously. "You'll never take us alive, Copper!"

I should never have let them tap into the Internet. "For the last time, we're not—"

Suddenly, Gapman pounced, reaching for Kenjo. For a moment, I thought he might actually catch him, ending a frustrating hour of chase.

At the last minute, Kenjo leaped. The file drawer closed on Gapman's hand. Gapman yelped and instinctively tried to pull his hand back.

The filing cabinet wobbled.

Kenjo, now on the top of the cabinet, pushed it, then rode it like a snowboarder as it fell on Gapman. The top drawer smacked my superhero padawan on the head. Laughing and soaking up the cheers of his tribesmen, Kenjo hopped off the toppled file cabinet and bounced off Gapman's Lycra-swathed behind.

Unfortunately, for him, he underestimated my padawan.

From under a stack of folders, Gapman whipped out his other arm and caught Kenjo's feet out of the air. While the hobgoblin leader wriggled and swung and kicked, Gapman extricated himself from the mess and stood, shaking out his other hand.

"Gotcha!" he said, remembering his Mid-Atlantic accent even in victory. "Now, Mister Kenjo, if you'd just calm—"

Kenjo ceased struggling just long enough to do an upside-down sit up and bite Gapman in the fleshy part below his thumb.

"Yeow! Stop it! Let go!" Gapman released his grip and shook his hand. Kenjo clenched his jaw and held on for dear life, his eyes flashing triumph and spite while his body flopped like a ragdoll in a tornado. Gapman moved to pull him off, but Kenjo batted away his attempts with stinging blows. Hobgoblins had incredible strength; even through his thick gloves, Gapman must have felt it.

The moment I moved to help, they would escape, and we'd be chasing them all over Tokneo again, so I used my words. "Kenjo—quit playing, and let's talk. This doesn't have to—"

"You'll never take us alive, Copper!" the hobgoblins shouted over my words. His mouth full, occupied with holding off a Mundane with super-speed, Kenjo only grunted agreement. Then he made a sucking sound.

Gapman shouted, "Are you...? Stop drinking my blood!"

Finally, my padawan lost his patience. He ripped off his cape—it's held on with Velcro—and in the blink of an eye, had the belligerent bauchan swaddled like an indomitable infant. Still, Kenjo refused to let go. He hung there like an oversized chrysalis, thwarting Gapman's every attempt to pry his jaw open. Had to hand it to Gapman; despite everything, he was exercising a lot of restraint.

Finally, though, Gapman growled with frustration, reached into his utility belt, pulled out pepper spray, and gave Kenjo an eyeful. When the headstrong hobgoblin opened his mouth to scream, Gapman jerked him away at superspeed and held him at arm's length, facing me.

"Are we done, now?" I asked Kenjo.

He gave me a wide grin of pointy, bloody teeth, and nodded.

I didn't quite trust the gleam in his eye. I tried again, "You're lucky, you know. He could have crushed you more easily than I."

"Nah. He Gapman, Defender of Los Lagos!"

The tribe rushed from their hiding places, cheering, "Gapman! Gapman!"

"Really?" Gapman gaped at them as they laughed and patted his legs.

One of them reached up and ran his finger along Gapman's palm, then stuck it in his mouth.

"Oi!" Gapman yanked his hand away and stared at the holes in his glove. "I'm still bleeding!"

He had superhealing. He expected to be fine by now. I reassured him. "That's the anticoagulants in their saliva. Nothing to worry about."

"Are you certain?" Gapman looked askance at me, then at the hobgoblin who had just tasted him.

Pinjal smacked his lips. "Superblood taste good! Like *ceimigeach dearglit*."

"'*Ceimigeach dearglit*'?" Now, Gapman's persona cracked and Ronnie Engleson, insecure Mundane freelance writer, peeked out. "What's *ceimigeach dearglit*?"

I didn't know, but since it was in his blood, I was sure it was fine. What was not fine was his growing discomfiture and how it was getting in my way.

"Why don't you go have Sister Grace patch it up, *Gapman*? I'll be along in a bit."

Sister Grace was my associate at DragonEye, PI: a Faerie nun and a powerful mage thanks to her part-Siren heritage. We'd started working together after she convinced me—almost too late—

that a nonsense song, "Mishmash," that was making the charts was actually a summoning spell. Together, we'd taken out the proto-empyrum (think Titan or elder god). After, she joined me in my private investigation business. We do solve mysteries, but we also seem to save the universes on a far-too-regular basis. She was the one who thought we could use help and suggested I train Gapman.

I decided to go one further and take him on as a padawan. I'm a better master than Obi Wan. Certainly, more enthusiastic. Grace always patch Gapman up after training.

Said padawan took the hint and got a hold of himself. He nodded and passed me the wrapped-up hobgoblin leader, then turned his attention to the gaggle of followers at his feet. "Ladies. Gentlemen. Those who choose otherwise." He had to pause for the giggles. "I hope we can meet again under better—less violent—circumstances."

And he flew out the door and was halfway to my mountain lair before they had finished their "awwws" of disappointment.

Kenjo struggled under Gapman's cape. Had to hand it to my padawan; he knew how to swaddle. I wonder if he ever babysat?

"Don't even think about gnawing through that material," I warned him. "Just because Gapman can crush you quicker than I doesn't mean I won't do you damage if you cross me again."

Kenjo responded with a heavy sigh and sniffled loudly. "Don' wanna go. We like it here."

The others called out their agreement.

I sighed. This was my fault. I should have talked to them before the real estate agents came.

Tokneo was originally built as a shopping district/amusement park area, designed by Japanese investors—who, incidentally, had high regard for dragons. They'd made me the unofficial mascot of the park, hired me to help with security, and given Grace and me a fancy new lair in the artificial mountain. Unfortunately, another proto-empyrum that we hadn't realized had been summoned by the Mishmash spell had hidden itself in a nearby lake. There, it had grown in power and form thanks to the belief of gullible Mundanes—including one of Tokneo Corp's Japanese employees. Even worse, it had taken shape based on

Mundane attitudes (Godzilla, naturally, with a dash of Cthulhu), so it attacked Tokneo seeking revenge. Can't blame him; he got dubbed "Shogzallie" by the Mundanes; between that and the appearance their belief thrust upon him, he had a right to be angry.

Grace and I stopped it, with a lot of help from other Faerie mages and the Colorado National Guard, but not before it had done a lot of damage to the commercial center and the mountain—*my* mountain. On opening day, too!

The amusement park was in shambles, and without it as an anchor, people didn't want to drive there for the few specialty stores that remained. Tokneo decided a life-sized Godzilla with supernatural powers was too much for its investors to stand behind. They abandoned the project just as it was starting. While Grace and I got to keep the mountain in return for my continued patrols, the entire area was left languishing.

Until Ad Gappum Productions decided they needed production facilities closer to the Gap in order to hire actual Faerie actors. CGI could not compete with real-life magical creatures, but few would last long so far from the Gap and the trickle of magic that suffused Los Lagos and the surrounding area. Ad Gappum had brought out their evaluation team and decided this was the perfect spot and that it could eventually rival Disney or Universal Studios.

"This our home!" Kenjo's wife, Leesi, chimed in. "Our children born here. You can no make us leave. You promised!"

Kenjo added, "We have rights, Copper!"

Kenjo's tribe had emigrated from Faerie and settled here. Yeah, squatters, but I'd turned a blind eye. Or, more accurately, I'd made a deal: They could stay as long as they didn't wreck any property and kept the shopping center clean and vermin-free. They'd kept their part of the bargain, too. Stray pests from roaches to raccoons found themselves on the hobgoblin menu; the main buildings stayed mostly dust-free... They'd even cultivated the garden, replacing the decorative flowers with vegetables, but the realtors seemed charmed by it.

They'd made my life easier up until now. One of the tribe had seen the realtor talking with the Ad Gappum rep and saw eviction papers in their future. However, I had a better idea—if I could get

Kenjo to sit still and listen. And, thanks to Gapman's cape, I had my chance.

"Squatters' rights don't come into effect for eighteen years—you haven't been here even one. However, I did make you a promise, and I intend to keep it. I've had a couple of conversations with the Ad Gappum Productions people and the realtor, and I think there's a way to keep you on here, doing exactly what you're doing."

A cheer went up.

I with my tail, I pulled out the proposal the movie company sent me. "But there are some rules."

The cheers died into "awwwws."

Chapter Two: A Conventional Calling

After 30 minutes of fist-shaking and teeth-snapping, we settled upon a counterproposal I could take to the movie company. From there, they would probably have to go to lawyers; fortunately, I knew an excellent contract lawyer with experience with the Faerie. If Percival could negotiate an equitable deal between Baba Yaga and the fairy that had renovated her house, he could handle the hobgoblins, and with the might of Youngman & Associates behind him, he should be fine with the movie company, as well.

So the hobgoblins would get to keep their home in the Mundane, and Ad Gappum Productions would have free pest control and light groundskeeping, with an option for catering and housekeeping. And I had to help them with their mole hunt. They were strangely adamant about that point.

Still, not a bad deal...as long as the hobgoblins stuck to the contract and no one annoyed them.

Concerns for another day.

For now, I could relax in my triumph and enjoy the flight home. It was a beautiful July day, one perfect for a dragon. We were having an unexpected heat wave, with temperatures reaching into the low 90s—enough to make some townspeople grumble about "global warming" but just enough to keep me comfortable. Personally, I'd give just about anything to be somewhere tropical, or even subtropical, where the temperatures at least flirted with triple-digits and the humidity was enough that I didn't need to expend magic to keep my scales from itching. Why God had to put the Gap in the middle of the Colorado Rockies, I had no idea.

However, I told myself sternly, today was a good day: warm with a gentle breeze that played over my wings as I flew from the wreckage that was Tokneo to the somewhat-better-repaired mountain that was my home. I wondered if Ad Gappum was going to do anything with the amusement park at the summit. It and the restaurants built into the mountain had been a main attraction for Tokneo—at least until Shogzallie decided to smash them like a movie monster on holiday.

Our lair was mid-level and had borne the brunt of Shogzallie's ire, which made sense since we were in the middle of an epic battle. That was over a year ago, and while it was livable, we were still a long way from its original glory. I missed Tokneo's deep pockets. Still, it was a far sight better than the leaky warehouse we used to call home, especially now that that had been converted into a Faerie artists' co-op. Know what's worse than living in a run-down warehouse? Living in a run-down warehouse full of pretentious artists going on about their "process."

I'd been so relieved when we could move back to the mountain.

When Tokneo built the lair, it had had the façade of a Shinto temple—much to Grace's ire. Now, the front looked more like something from *The Hobbit* with windows and doors peeking out from an exterior of stone, dirt, and plants. The door was square, not round, and large enough to allow for me to grow...if God ever decided to reward me with greater size. At this point, I was not eager to go back to my original fighting weight. It'd be hard to hang around humans. If I needed size, I could use MechaVern, my personal giant robot ride...once we got it running again.

The windows were open, and delicious smells wafted from them. Was Grace feeding Gapman? I supposed it made sense; along with superpowers, Ron Engleson had also gained a super metabolism; there was actually a fund to help pay for his meals. I'd be jealous, except he shared with us. Still, this smelled too good—and too Faerie—for anything Grace would whip up for my hungry padawan. In fact, the smells brought to mind the Duke's feasts. The Duke...or his brother, Bishop Aiden.

Yep—there was the official diplomat car, the coat of arms of the Archdiocese of Peebles-on-Tweed magnetically attached to the doors, a bored chauffeur playing on his phone in the driver's seat. I buzzed the Town Car, giving "Jeeves" the scare of his life, then made my way in.

I found Bishop Aiden, his attendee, Grace, and Gapman sitting at the table as if it were some kind of social visit. In fact, Grace and the bishop were chatting while Gapman ate steadily and answered questions only when asked. I knew it was hunger rather than nervousness—despite his insecurities, Ron was a well-known entertainment reporter. He was actually pretty comfortable with celebrities.

Even so, I knew better than to assume this was a casual visit. Most people expect blessings when a bishop walks into their homes, but after eight hundred years of working for the Faerie Catholic Church, I'd acquired a healthy dose of suspicion.

"What do you want and how much is it going to hurt?" I asked as I bent over his ring. I didn't kiss it, of course. Dragon lips don't pucker.

Gapman almost choked on his energy drink.

Bishop Aiden, however, laughed. "I think you'll be pleasantly surprised this time. You do not have any cases currently, I hope?" As he asked, his hand slid into his pocket. At first, I thought he was fingering his rosary, a habit of his, but I heard his thumb brush against paper. Slick paper. Mundane paper. Curious.

Grace and I exchanged glances. For the first time in a long time, we were comfortably busy. I had a regular job keeping watch over Tokneo (which essentially guaranteed our right to live in the mountain) and I was training up my padawan. Grace had regular work at Little Flower Parish. We got the occasional PI job. Most even paid.

Still, Grace and I were agents of the Faerie Catholic Church, here by the grace of the diocese and the Duke—and despite his casual tone, I didn't think he was casually asking. I replied, "Nothing we can't work around. What do you need?"

Aiden pulled out a paper and handed it to Grace. I peered over her shoulder. What could be so dire and still advertise itself with a glossy full-color brochure?

"Mensa World Gathering," she read.

"What's Mensa?" I asked.

"It's a club for persons of high intelligence," Gapman answered in his signature Mid-Atlantic accent. "The top two percent of the population. You should fit right in, Vern."

"I'm not a 'person,' remember? Ask the U.S. Immigration and Naturalization Service," I growled.

When I'd first arrived, the Mundane American government sent a...representative...from the immigration service to investigate my presence in the Mundane. Agent Fischer decided I didn't fit the definition of "person," and no amount of protests to the contrary has changed that decision.

I have more brainpower in my tail than Stephen Hawking had had in his entire head. I've forgotten more facts and stories than your Library of Congress holds. I can read, write, and pun in more languages than your above-average United Nations delegate. Yet I'm not humanoid enough to be considered a "person" by American law. Speciesists.

Gapman rolled his eyes, Grace closely echoing the move. He said, "Mensa isn't a government entity. Bet they'd love to have you on their rolls."

"Are you a member?" the bishop asked.

Did my padawan blush a little at the implied compliment? But he shook his head. "I'm really quite ordinary."

Grace flipped through the brochure. It had the usual exaggerated promises of fun and adventure, and photos of smiling people doing, well, conventional stuff: sitting in uncomfortable chairs listening to people talk, eating, mugging it up for the camera, and playing in an amusement park that anyone—Mundane or Faerie—who has lived in this country for a while would recognize right away. I looked at the photo of what I assumed were Mensans standing by the park mascot and grinning.

Do geniuses really wear cone hats with lace and feathers?

Meanwhile, the bishop explained. "You'll be attending. Both of you. Their international organization has invited a number of Faerie citizens—humans and Magicals—and we feel someone should be there to help keep order, supernaturally speaking. It's only for four days, so it should not be an issue being so far from the Gap. You should enjoy it, Vern. I understand Florida is hot and humid this time of year."

Grace beamed, but I saw where this was headed. "Hold on. You want us to be *chaperones*?"

My brain flooded with visions of enforcing curfews or telling pixies they could not bathe in the hotel fish tank.

"Nonsense. You are welcome to enjoy the conference. Simply be available in case things get out of hand."

"Oh, right," I said. "So, no real authority to enforce any rules, but be ready to clean up after the chaos? Supernatural HAZMAT. So much better. We're not getting paid for this, are we?"

"The Church and the duchy will cover your travel expenses, convention fees, and accommodations. All Faerie citizens will be staying at the same hotel as the convention. It's near someplace called Fanny Flamingo's Fantasyland; I'm told you should fit right in."

Gapman snorted, then tried to cover it as a cough. Even Grace smiled. Aiden, however, kept a guileless expression. At moments like this, I remembered just how much he was like his brother, the Duke.

Ignoring the mirth he'd inspired, he continued, "Grace, we've arranged for you to speak on the theological and stylistic differences between Faerie and Mundane liturgical music."

I suppressed a groan of defeat. Grace had made a study of Mundane religious music and how it differed from that of Faerie. He knew she'd love the chance to share her research and that I would support anything that made her happy.

Of course, she took the bait. "I'd love to! Gapman, you can hold the fort for a few days, can't you?"

For a moment, Gapman's façade slipped, and Ronnie flashed through. "Alone?"

"You're ready to fly solo." I shrugged. "Things seem pretty quiet right now. Just fly a few extra patrols, make sure the local gangs know not to get bored and frisky. As long as no proto-empyrie attack, you'll be fine."

"Of course. Not a problem, then." Gapman's smile looked a little sickly. The last time we'd taken on some proto-empyrie, he'd had to destroy a shed to kill the thing. At least it was his mom's shed. "I mean, what would the odds be, right?"

Grace set a comforting hand on his wrist. "I'm sure if there's anything magical amiss, the bishop would bring in reinforcements—right, Your Excellency?"

"Of course."

I whipped out my phone and texted Gapman the diocese's emergency number as well as Aiden's personal one. "Don't be afraid to call them," I said. I grinned at Bishop Aiden, daring him to contradict me, but he nodded amiably enough.

Gapman's phone chimed, and he checked the text. I saw his shoulders relax, but just slightly. It was one thing to lunch with a celebrity, another to call them asking for help—or more likely, begging, maybe screaming. Gapman could get excitable in a crisis.

"That takes care of that," I said before Gapman or the bishop could discuss conditions for calling. "So, what's my presentation?" I had plenty of great ideas, from common Faerie scams to the proper treatment of Eighth Day Creations. Maybe a condensed history of Faerie or the theory behind Magic in our dimension.

"You'll simply accompany Sister Grace," Bishop Aiden said.

"I'm a *sidekick*?" I exclaimed. I glared at Gapman before he could snicker or make a snide comment. He'd bitten his lip and turned his face away.

"We thought it best that you be free to move about the convention as needed," Aiden said blandly, then rose. "I must be off. I promised Father Rich I'd join him for lunch before Adoration.

Someone will get you the details tomorrow. Gapman, it was a pleasant surprise to have met you today." He made the sign of the cross over us and made a quick but dignified exit.

I resisted the temptation to blow a stream of fire at him. I definitely had to go to Confession now.

Once, I'd held the Knowledge of Eternity and the Wisdom of the Ages and had enjoyed respect, even reverence, from humans and Magicals alike. Now, I got to be the sidekick and a babysitter at a Smart Humans' Convention.

Chapter Three: Pixies in the Program

The next morning, Herald Charlie Wilmot called saying he had the details of our trip. We decided to meet him at Natura's Restaurant for an early lunch. We had some loose ends to wrap up in town, anyway.

"I want to get a few Saint George's medals and have Father bless them so I can imbue them with magic for you, just in case," Grace said. She paused as we went through a particularly bumpy patch of road. My battle with Shogzallie had wrecked a lot of the roadway between our mountain and Tokneo, but lately, even the untouched roads in the commercial center were getting pot-holed. If all their construction was so cheap, it was probably a good thing we'd had to rebuild our lair.

Grace continued, "You've never been outside Colorado. I don't want to take a chance that you depend on magical energy more than other Magicals."

"That would be bad," I agreed. I already knew I depended on magic for my flight and a large part of my eyesight. Maybe my fire. I'd hate to be at the Smart Humans convention and discover that magic contributed to my intellect, too. I had a vision of getting there and suddenly being the stupidest being in the room.

Suppressing a shudder, I changed the subject. "We can drop off the Ad Gappum memorandum on the way, and I've got the research for Percival, too." Percival had agreed to handle the negotiations between me, the studio, and the hobgoblins in return for some PI work. Fortunately, thanks to the Internet and some nifty PI tools, I got that done quickly.

Grace nodded. "And Templegrass called. She's going to the convention, too, and wants our help before we go."

"When did I become a fashion expert?"

Grace laughed. "No—with repairing the roof before we go. There are some leaks, and she wants you to melt some more plastic plates over them, 'to keep the motif.' We are their landlords, after all."

"Are we? They aren't paying rent." Faeries in the warehouse. Hobgoblins in Tokneo. How'd I end up the caretaker of squatters, anyway?

Speaking of...

We found our way blocked by a siege line of Scottish hobgoblins.

Grace lowered her window.

Kenjo stepped toward the car, but stayed dead center in the road. "Vern, you come hunt moles nextday, yes?"

Nextday meant tomorrow. We were leaving before sunrise. I stuck my head out the window to answer. "I can't nextday. We have an assignment. We'll be out of town. We can hunt when I return next week."

Kenjo slammed the butt of his spear on the ground. "No. Moles too big then. Nextday, just right. Maybe day after nextday. Next week—too long. Too big. Too mean. Too many."

Why were hobgoblins such drama? "I'm gone nextday. We'll be back next week. You are brave hunters. I'm a dragon. Sister Grace is a mage. We can handle oversized moles."

"You're bringing me into this, now?" Grace asked me, but she was over-shouted by Kenjo.

"You promised! Nextday!"

The others took up the chant. "Nextday! Nextday!"

I sighed. "I can't nextday."

But they kept chanting.

"Do you really need the help?" Grace asked them. Her brows knit with concern.

With the chanting as his chorus, Kenjo said, "Many moles. Right big. Not enough hunters. May take days even with you, dragon."

I opened my mouth to argue, then had a lovely idea. This is what padawans were for! "How about I send Gapman to help?"

That earned a cheer from some of the hunters and squeals from some of the females. The chant went from "Nextday" to "Gapman." Kenjo silenced them with a look.

"He has superspeed," I wheedled.

"Gapman nextday?" Kenjo asked.

"Sure." He could forego the usual patrol for a day of trapping ground rodents.

"Deal. Start early. Many moles. Take long time."

"I'll let him know."

I waited until we were past the gates of Tokneo and on the two-lane road to the highway before rolling my eyes at Grace, who chuckled sympathetically. Hobgoblins made such a big deal out of everything. Then I pulled out my phone to give my padawan his new assignment for nextday. Who knows? It might be a good bonding experience for them.

Gapman surprised me by being okay with it. "Yeah, Kenjo hailed me as I was flying home and apologized, and Leesi mentioned the moles when she gave me some peas and beets from her garden. No hard feelings. Besides, they're moles. Kind of cute, actually, with their pink noses and big paws. It'll be fun. It seems a little late, though. Last month, we could have got them before the babies left the nest. But I guess if they're just now messing with their garden... Anyway, I got it. Enjoy Florida."

I snorted. Enjoy Florida. Between hunting moles and babysitting Faerie creatures on vacation in the Mundane, I think I'd rather choose the hunt.

Natura looked up from her phone where she was reading the Mensa conference schedule and rolled her eyes at me like I was "so much drama." "Oh, Vern, why are you so hacked? This conference looks like a gas."

I was hacked—and not just about the conference. The warehouse roof had finally progressed beyond what melting some plastic plates and dragon-breath-welded supports could fix. Percival didn't think my research was going to satisfy his client—and if the client didn't pay him, he didn't pay me. So we'd be coming home to more bills and more work. When we went to the police station to tell them we'd be gone for a few days, Captain Santry had been even more sarcastic than usual. It should not have irritated me, but it did.

Nonetheless, I didn't bother to answer Natura. When she made up her mind about something, there was no arguing with her. Instead, I opened my mouth and poured half a bottle of beer into it. Not that beer can get me drunk. It takes about five gallons of ethanol to do that, and now that I've got my fire back, it's not the smartest idea. One wrong belch and I could make a dragon-sized hole in the pavement. But I liked the taste, and this was Bert's latest brew.

Bert, Natura's husband, took a pull from his beer and leaned closer to his wife to look at the program while Grace and I ate. We were sitting at one of the low tables in the Safe Space Lounge of Natura's restaurant. When she'd seen my irritated expression as we'd walked in, she'd immediately escorted us to the lounge, where I had free rein to "express my feelings in an accepting environment" and had told a waiter to bring me a big platter from the buffet in case I was just hangry.

It was India Day, and Grace loves Natura's *dahi vada*. I liked the fact that between the accepting nature of the lounge and the low tables, I could stick my face in my bowl and eat like a dragon while I complained.

Of course, just because I could express myself didn't mean everyone had to agree with me.

"I gotta agree with Natura, Vern," Bert told me. "That polygraph lecture looks interesting."

"I want to go to that one," Grace said, carefully wiping a piece of fallen rice off her habit. "We have a spell for compelling the truth based on the Eighth Commandment, but detecting the truth has always been trickier. People can make themselves believe the most unlikely things."

"We've had the same problem," Bert started, but I cut him off. We were talking about me and my misgivings, after all.

"It's not the Mundane speakers I'm worried about." With one claw, I pointed to one of the Friday lectures.

"*Helreið Brynhildar*—Bryndhilde's Ride to Hel. Faerie Valkyrie Brunhilde talks about her near-death experience in this magical multimedia event," Natura read. "Like, wow!"

Bert looked at me thoughtfully. "In our legend, she had to slay a dragon."

I shrugged. Faerie dragons are immortal. Stab us, we heal. Burn us, we rise from the ashes. Chop us to little bits and whatever's most alive will grow back into a full dragon. It's not easy, and it's often painful, but a Faerie dragon cannot die.

I said, "Ours, too. Formurrgradurr grew back. It's not the dragon slaying I'm worried about so much as the 'multimedia' aspect."

Grace merely shrugged. "We just have to tell her to keep the presentation to sound and visuals. She's surprisingly reasonable."

I grunted, not willing to be comforted, although I was feeling better. Maybe I was hangry. "And Goes-on-Verbose-Soporific of the Eternally Long-Winded? How reasonable is he?"

"Gozonvabosomofic of the House Eternal Winds of the High Elves," Grace chided lightly.

"Potato-potahto. The name fits, and yet they chose him as keynote speaker for the closing ceremony." Gozon was the Speaker for the Winds of one of the largest clans of Elves in Faerie, once a great warrior, now a scholar, and always a pontificating airbag. Worse, I am comparing him to other High Elves, who, unlike the general elf population, are long-lived, and thus, also long-winded. In their native language, it takes half an hour to ask where the bathroom is. I know from experience that Gozon's never been able to figure out the brevity of human speech, no matter how many human languages he's learned. Folks attending his speech risk missing their flights home, and I mean the ones scheduled for the next day.

"We'll figure something out," Grace said, though she, too, looked concerned.

"Hey! Elvis Meets the Dalai Lama!" Bert chuckled.

"Not ours," Grace and I chorused. Elvis was one legend that didn't parallel in Faerie.

"Oh, look! One of the Muses is going to be at the poetry workshop." Natura's delight dissolved into confusion at the look on Grace's face. "What?"

Grace shrugged. "It's just that Kaliope is a notoriously finicky editor. Lots of 'happy' to 'glad.' And of course, she's always right. Compose a poem or a song with a Muse and it'll be perfect, but, well, it's not yours anymore."

"Oh. Like the individual voice is lost..." Natura's eyes glazed for a moment. Then she shook herself. "Bummer. But—wow! Alright, look at this. 'Nude Photography—A Practical Guide.'"

Her husband almost choked on his flatbread.

"Oh, Bert, don't be so conventional. It's art."

"Yeah," he managed to gasp. "Amazing how many teenage boys discover art that way."

Natura elbowed him. "C'mon. It's a celebration of the beauty of the human body."

Grace held up her hands. "The only body I celebrate is Corpus Christi."

"Vern?"

"Seriously? To me a human without clothes is like an apple without skin."

Bert looked confused, but both ladies groaned and explained: "They both lack appeal!"

Chapter Four: Extra-Curricular Assignments

Before Bert could howl his protest, the door to the lounge swung open, causing Natura's meditation chimes to send their rich sounds into the air, and in stepped Charlie Wilmot.

He wore the livery of a herald of the Duchy of Peebles-on-Tweed: a large, green, blousy shirt that hung to mid-calf and orange-and-green striped tights. Over that, he wore an orange tabard bearing the crest of the Duchy of Peebles-on-Tweed: a particularly ugly boar's head with over-large tusks that had been messily severed from its body and spiked onto a spear. The Duke's family has never been known for good taste.

It's even funnier when you consider that a herald's oath as a new pursuivant says they promise to be "sober in dress."

Compared to the calm, muted colors of the Safe Space Lounge, Charlie's uniform was a clanging bell to Natura's gentle chimes.

You might think a herald would have trouble on the Mundane side dressed in a medieval monkey-suit like that, but actually, he takes surprisingly little heat. There were exceptions, of course, but they soon learned that heralds have diplomatic immunity, a strong sense of honor, a sharp wit, and even sharper daggers.

The Duke's herald stopped at our table and drew himself to full attention. In a booming voice, he started, "Vern d'Wyvern and Sister Grace of Our Lady of the Miracles, Greetings from His Grace, Galen, Duke of Peebles-on-Tweed...yadda, yadda. You know the drill." Charlie relaxed into a smile, and we smiled back.

I liked Charlie's style. Even at 16, he'd had moxie, which he showed by slicing the tie of my least favorite police detective after Vialpando challenged him to a gun-vs-knife fight. He'd also tricked the Duke's Seneschal into buying him a vintage 1964 Ford AC Cobra with a V8 engine. It's in the Duke's colors and needed magic to run in the snow, but it's a sweet machine—and totally paid for from Duke Galen's coffers.

Yeah, he had my kind of humor.

"Yadda-yadda, and don't call me 'd'Wyvern'," I said, thus dispensing with the honorifics. "So, Charlie, what's Duke Galen want?"

We scrunched ourselves a little closer together, and the hostess brought water and a table setting for Charlie. Natura excused herself to get him a plateful of food from the buffet. (She charged it to the Duke's account, of course.) Charlie bowed his thanks to both ladies then settled onto the cushion with the athletic ease of youth. On the other side of the lounge, a couple of female students looked his way, and not because of his outrageous uniform. He was the most eligible bachelor of Peebles-on-Tweed, and the duchess and his mother were aching to get him hitched, but like the car, he had very particular ideas about the kind of woman he'd marry.

He pulled out some documents from his satchel and passed them to us, careful of the food that crowded the table.

"Travel arrangements from the Ministry. You'll be joining the other Faerie conventioneers at the

Los Lagos Airship Field to take the *Cloudskater* to Citrus City. Lucky sods—beggin' your pardon, Sister!"

Grace smiled sympathetically. "That's all right, Charlie. I'm looking forward to being a passenger on *Cloudskater* this time."

Airship construction was one of the first Faerie/Mundane industries. Despite the legends of your world, most Faerie cannot fly—not even the Magicals, and certainly not the humans. A few folks have flying carpets—I set one on fire myself, back in the day—but let's face facts: Do you really want to soar up to thirty feet—much less 3,000— on something flimsy enough to roll up? Then there's the weather, flocks of birds, flying insects... Aladdin notwithstanding, there's nothing fun about a magic carpet ride, in either universe. And brooms? Please—I don't know where you Mundanes came up with that. A washtub makes more sense. It'd be more comfortable.

However, your legends about iron and silver do contain some truth. Not only are elves and some Magicals allergic to iron, but they have a special sense about it. Kind of like a shark's ability to sense electrical impulses or my ability to sense magic. Being around certain metals irritates elves like too much static in the air or a high-pitched buzzing might irritate a human. They can tolerate it for a short time—"short time" meaning several hours to an elf—and will, if necessary, in order to travel about the Mundane world. Naturally, however, they'd prefer to avoid such unpleasantness.

A whole slew of industries geared toward non-metallic items have developed. Fiberglass cars, for example, reinforced by Faerie ironwood with engines made of faerimet, a non-magical metal unique to our dimension, are taking over the automotive market, as are airships—airplane/dirigible hybrids that allow folks to cruise in metal-free comfort.

Grace and I were familiar with the airships from a previous case. Someone hadn't liked Dayton-Sybal Industries making it easier for the Faerie to travel around the great U.S. of A., and they'd employed magic to make trouble. D-S then hired DragonEye, PI, to foil the case of sabotage on *Cloudskater*'s maiden voyage.

Cloudskater was one of the bigger airships in the LagosLines fleet and had accommodations for us large four-legged Magicals to travel in comfort.

I had to admit, I was pleased about the travel arrangements. Someone was thinking, and thinking of me.

"There's also a complete list of everyone attending, your hotel reservations, and a prepaid debit card. His Grace said what's on the card is all ye get, so don't go crazy at the markets. Oh, thank ye kindly, Natura." His grin widened as she set the plate in front of him, and he immediately dug in.

I watched him enviously. A human eats like an animal and people chuckle and say, "He's still a growing boy." If I ate like that outside places like the Safe Space Lounge, those same people would be edging slowly toward the door while calling animal control on their cell phones.

Charlie asked, "Hey, Natura, got any Ping Extra?"

Bert cringed.

Natura wrinkled her nose at Charlie. "I will not allow that commercially made poison disguised as a beverage in my restaurant. It totally causes cancer and obesity in lab rats, you know."

Bert huffed. "Feed anything four hundred times its body weight in something and it'll contract obesity and cancer, too. Lab conditions cause cancer in lab rats."

Natura rolled her eyes. "Want an Organacola? Or a beer?"

Charlie sighed. "I'll just have water; I'm on duty."

"That reminds me—have you remembered the recipe for Egyptian beer yet?" Bert asked me.

I shook my head. "Guess God hasn't decided that's knowledge I need."

"Maybe we can get Grace to pray a novena?"

On occasion when we needed specific knowledge, she has prayed a novena for me to remember it.

"I don't think that knowledge will serve God or Man," she scolded.

"It'll serve me good," Bert teased.

Grace shared an exasperated look with Natura, then turned her attention to the pile of papers Charlie had given us.

"Oh, that's the latest intel," Charlie said through a mouth full of food as Grace pulled out a newsletter.

Heralds do carry secrets, but in this case, "intel" consisted more of news and gossip. Grace and

I put out our own weekly report; we get paid a pittance for it, naturally. Maybe I ought to look into getting it published, hiring some local boys to hawk it or do one of those paid newsletter gigs. My padawan, as Ron Engleson, is making money off his online newsletter on Fairie arts and entertainment.

Grace interrupted my publishing fantasy with a hum of concern. "Tensions within House Eternal Winds are rising."

"Oh, I was there for that!" In his excitement, Charlie set down his fork and leaned away from his plate. He'd pretty much cleaned it, anyway. "It was at a trade meeting with some of the Mundane industries and the representatives of the Faerie territories. Gozonvabosomofic and Pampaserrbahgh bumped into each other in the hall—and all they said was 'Excuse me, sir.'"

Grace crossed herself, but Bert snorted. "What's wrong with that?"

"Remember what I said about Gozon? Elves have ritualistic responses for everything," I answered while Grace read on. "It's kind of like the Japanese tradition of bowing—how low and how long you bow depends on the person's age or rank above or below you. Only, Elves apply it to language; plus they also consider family, tribe, and house—and the relationships between those. 'Excuse me' in Elvish consists of a fifteen-minute exchange of recognition, obeisance, and compliments. They usually dispense with it when dealing with humans, but to ignore it with their own kind..." I twitched my tail.

"Funny Bishop Aiden didn't mention any of this," I said to Grace. A small frown was her answer.

"Oh, the bishop's tried to talk to them, he has," Charlie said, "but they won't discuss it. They said, 'It's within the House.' I think he's contacting Cardinal Greystone."

Bert understood enough about the Faerie Catholic Church to know what that meant. "Are we talking about a war?"

"Don't worry," I said. "Elves don't operate on human timetables. About the only thing they do fast is fall in love, and that's only with humans. Even then, it took my friend Galendor an entire weekend to propose to Princess Galinda—and he can speak Human."

"A whole weekend?" Bert exclaimed. His proposal had been, "So, uh, wanna get hitched?" It had taken him longer to convince Natura to have a wedding instead of "shacking up."

I answered, "Sunup Saturday to sundown Sunday. Anyway, there's been something brewing in the House Eternal Winds for seventy-five years or so, and they're just now getting to rudeness. You'll probably be six feet under before they get to yelling at each other. Still, I'd like to know what this is all about."

"Well, we can satisfy your curiosity after the conference," Grace said, reading on. "For now, I'm just glad Gozon is the only Elf from House Eternal Winds we have to worry about. Looks like he's been a busy boy, too. London, Paris, a couple of places in Australia, Norway, Egypt—the Faerie ones, of course. What could he want there?"

Charlie swallowed the food he'd started chewing. "If you ask me, I think the Elves want to corner the faerimet market, and that's what they're fighting about."

"Faerimet?" Natura asked. "So it's back to corporate greed, even in the Faerie. Bummer. Is that stuff really, like, environmentally friendly?"

Bert rolled his eyes.

"It's like a Faerie non-metal metal," I said. "Elves and other iron-sensitive Magicals can tolerate it. Nothing volatile or toxic about it, but it's not the easiest of substances to mine or work with, so no one bothered with it until we met you Mundanes and got a taste for technology."

"It's good for us, too," Bert said. "It works better than metals for some things, like temperature extremes. Supposed to increase engine efficiency by ten percent. Ford's incorporating faerimet components into the new Kobold." Bert had been trying to get Natura to let him buy that SUV since he saw the billboard on I-25.

She handled it like she had for the past three months—by changing the subject. "War over metals?"

Grace said, "More likely, as Speaker for the Winds, he went to visit the Houses in those territories before their conference to get key discussions started; after all, they could never make a decision during the conference otherwise." She had a point: Elves would consider a decision made in two weeks rash. They were the original experts at the pre-meeting meeting.

Charlie shrugged and helped himself to some of the naan from the center of the table. He was making me hungry again. I've got a competitive stomach.

"And what's this?" Grace pulled out a scroll from the stack and broke the seal. Although narrow, the scroll unrolled down to her lap.

"Oh, that," Charlie gulped down his food and followed it with a quick drink of water. "Well, some of us were hoping, seeing as ye were going there and all..."

"You gave us a shopping list?" I exclaimed.

"We've all pitched in some money to yer bank card—"

"We're on assignment. We're not going to shop!"

Grace intervened. "We'll see what we can do." She started to roll up the list.

"You can order stuff online," I griped, then something caught my eye. I stopped Grace by using a claw to pin the list to the table. "Wait a minute. Rhoda Dakota's autograph?"

Charlie blushed. "I read that her family are all Mensans. So, well, you know, if you can find her. She might be in disguise."

I rolled my eyes. Television shows—the Achilles heel of our intrepid herald. "Charlie, she's—"

Grace nudged my flank with her toe. "She's probably very busy—but we'll see what we can do," Grace finished.

Once Charlie had left, I turned to Grace. "So now we're babysitters, damage control—and you know there'll be damage to control—and we're hunting down autographs?"

She just shook her head at me with a bemused grin. "Oh, lighten up, Vern. It'll be a gas."

Chapter Five: For Your Safety and the Sanity of the Dragon...

The trip, at least, would be a gas. About 250,000 cubic meters of it.

As we approached the airport, we could see *Cloudskater* looming large and majestic against the sunrise. Longer and flatter than your typical Goodyear Blimp, she also boasted four wings—two tiny ones in the front and two longer ones in the back—and twin tails. The oblong gondola, I'm told, is about the size of a luxury yacht, but it's built more like a barge with two decks for cabins and common areas and a lower level for the cargo hold surrounded by an observation deck with room enough for forty sightseers at a time. The back side lowered to drive cargo in—or push something out, as I'd learned the hard way. With luck, I wouldn't be getting into any scuffles this trip.

Cloudskater was built for domestic flights, so she only had ten private cabins, a restaurant/lounge, and train-style seating for ninety. She was quite a beauty, too, with the pink light of the sunrise reflecting off her silvery balloon.

"Vern!" Bert called from the driver's seat. He'd offered to drive us so we could leave our car at the lair. He'd even agreed to come extra early so we could avoid any hobgoblins haranguing me about joining their hunt. "Would you please put your head in? I hate it when you do that."

"I wanted a good look," I said as I slunk my neck back through the front window, carefully avoiding bumping Grace in the front seat. I enjoyed riding in Bert's SUV, with the back seats down, I had plenty of room to settle comfortably without kinking my long neck. I was on Natura's side about not replacing it.

"Don't give me that. You stick your head out the window every time I take you somewhere. You're as bad as a dog."

"Dog?" I harrumphed with exaggerated dignity. "I keep my tongue in my mouth, thank you very much. It's just easier for me to see."

"Vern likes the double takes from the other drivers," Grace teased. She knows me too well.

"Well, someday, some out-of-towner's going to double-take himself right into oncoming traffic, and it'll be your fault," Bert scolded.

"Yes, Bert," I said. I tried to sound chagrined, but I didn't fool anybody. I did keep my head in the rest of the way to the airport, though.

The security guard greeted us with a smile and waved us right onto the runway area. Bert parked as near *Cloudskater* as allowed. He opened up the back to grab Grace's bag so I could climb out. We pack light; her carry-on held religious items and magical supplies for non-humans, a fingerprint kit, lockpick tools, and a spare habit. I suggested a swimsuit in case we got to go to the beach, but she insisted she didn't have one she'd feel comfortable wearing in public, especially among Mundanes.

Grace also brought her harp, which she slung across her back before taking her carry-on from Bert. Everything I carried was in my pouch. Yes, dragons have a pouch. How else would we carry treasure? A dragon walking upright and carrying a suitcase would look even sillier than a dragon sticking his head out the car window.

We were heading to the ship when we heard someone shout our names.

Grace winced.

I glowered.

Bert audibly groaned.

"Want me to handle that?" he asked. He wasn't sheriff any longer, but he knew how to act the authority.

"Do you want to get stuck with her interrogating you?" I countered.

With a smirk, he gave us a false salute and left.

"Didn't think so," I said to Grace. She chuckled, but it was a tired sound.

Figured we wouldn't be able to leave without being harassed by the *Los Lagos Gazette*'s own "investigative" reporter, Kitty McGrue. Kitty's incredible investigative skills and ability to sniff out a story were matched only by her ability to misinterpret those facts and get the story wrong. She made up for that by sensationalizing everything to meet her own personal slant. She must have jumped a fence somewhere and had been lying in wait to ambush us.

We didn't slow down or acknowledge her, but that didn't stop her. She caught up with us. "Off to hobnob with the self-proclaimed elite? Or does Aiden expect trouble?" She didn't call him Bishop. She believed he was some kind of spymaster and always dropped his religious title when she thought he was in his secret role.

"No comment," we chorused. One day, I'll get Grace to teach us how to really chorus that and won't Kitty be amused?

She was learning, though. She tried a new tactic: changing the subject instead of clinging to the original like a gluttonous dog with a bone. "Fine. What about the talk of war between the Elves? Will it spread across the Gap? Will Galendor of the House Eternal Winds of the Forests get his human in-laws involved?"

Elf war in this generation? Ri-ight. Gotta get her a copy of *Uncle Vern's Guide to Faerie*. 'Course I'll need to write it first. "No comment."

"Dammit, Vern!" Kitty rushed ahead and stopped in front of me. "This is important! I know you don't like what I do—"

"Wrong. I just don't like how you do it." Fewmets. I'd engaged. I should have stuck to "no comment." That would have been a better zing, too.

But she just huffed. "It might help if you give me something to work with."

I tried not to laugh. Like anything I'd ever "given her to work with" didn't end up warped beyond its original meaning. Work with? Or twist?

"Come on," she wheedled when I didn't answer. She posed and pouted. "For old time's sake?"

What had gotten into her? The last thing I ever wanted was to be reminded of "old times" with her and she knew that. Usually, she played the guilt card since she got hurt when I was fighting Shogzallie last year. Had Gapman spurned her advances again?

I slunk around her, careful to keep my tail from touching her, though I really wanted to swat her like the pest she was. Grace stuck close to my other side.

She yelled at my retreating back. "You were a lot more fun as a human! You know that?"

I saw Grace clutch her cross.

"No comment!" I hollered back. I wanted to tell her to get over me, but that would egg her on and bother Grace. Instead, I slid my tail onto Grace's shoulder and just kept walking.

Halfway to the boarding ramp, we passed some security guards heading the other way. I looked behind me as they grabbed Kitty McGrue by the shoulders and hauled her to the gate. Guess they knew her pretty well, too.

The porter hurried to meet us and took Grace's harp and bag. The Captain waited for us at the top of the ramp. He made quite an impression in his ascot and leather bomber jacket with the company logo emblazoned on the pocket. He stood about five-foot-ten with wavy blond hair and the kind of strong jaw that made girls sigh. I knew because I'd seen that before, too. The cheesy oversized mustache only added to his charm. Just what you'd expect from an airship pilot with the name of Zepplin.

Zepplin's family was related to the original airship creator through some cousins who emigrated in the 1920s. He liked to say they lost an E at Ellis Island. When he heard about the airship project, he left the U.S. Air Force where he flew C-130s and joined LagosLines.

He greeted Grace with a courtly bow and took her hand to help her onto the deck. Then he turned to me. "I had a parachute made just for you."

"Funny," I snarked back. "Stay up all night thinking of that one, Led?"

He just laughed and slapped my flank as I got aboard. Led—not his real name, but the call sign he'd picked up as an Air Force pilot—was an all-right guy. He'd taken a bullet trying to stop the baddies from dumping me overboard on that sabotage case.

"I'll just make sure Grace checks my food before I eat it," I added. I meant it, too. No one was going to catch me like that again. Slipping me a Mickey. I'm still embarrassed.

Led chuckled. "We haven't had a problem since you two put those lowlifes away. How's your wing?"

I unfurled them both as much as I could without upsetting the display cases that lined the reception hallway. "Good as new. How's your shoulder?"

His grin turned rueful. "Aches in the altitude and humidity. I tell people I can sense the weather with it. Adds to the image. So, where do you want to start, and what can we do to help?"

I jerked my head to the scene of Kitty struggling against the security guards as they dragged her away backward. "That's a good start, right there."

"And we can continue right here," Grace said. She pulled out a smaller bag while she explained. "I'm going to make this entrance sensitive to malignant magic—kind of like a metal detector. Anyone carrying an item of dark magic or who has been dabbling with it or is under the influence of an evil spell will set it off. It's similar to the one they use at the Gap."

Led snorted. "You'd think that would be enough."

Grace smiled sympathetically. "Nothing's perfect, which is why redundancy is a good idea. Plus, I'll be more subtle. No one will notice it. Can we make sure everyone enters through here?"

"Not a problem," Led said. "We got told that the one troll canceled."

I nodded. "Yeah. When he found out the Bridge Special Interest Group had to do with cards and not construction, he decided it wasn't worth the trouble."

We left Grace alone to do her thing—which involved a lot of concentration, prayer, and song—while I and Led did a walk-around of the ship and did our thing—which involved a lot of careful looking, listening, and sniffing for anything that might indicate sabotage or pre-staging for magical mayhem. I also set out various talismans that Grace had prepared over the past week. Like her threshold detector, these would alert us to any evil magic or malicious intent. We really didn't expect anything on the flight, but after our last experience on an airship, we weren't taking any chances.

We finished our inspection just as the bus from Faerie drove up. I and Led went to the bridge. I was surprised he didn't want to watch. Elves and dwarves, Valkyrie, Greek empyrie... It looked like Brothers Grimm on parade—or the opening scene of just about any Fanny Flamingo Animations film.

Those passengers who'd sprung for First Class tickets got private rooms; everyone else settled themselves into the compartments. Airship compartments are styled more like those of a sleeper cabin of a train, with room for four. *Cloudskater* also hosted a half-dozen special compartments for those Faerie of non-humanoid form: two room-sized tanks—one for fresh water, one for salt water—deluxe stables, and some oversized cabins. Grace should have already claimed one that had only one row of seats and a large floor cushion for me. I had something to do before I could join her.

On the bridge, the flight attendant smiled nervously at me as she grabbed the microphone to deliver her FAA-required message. "Hello, ladies and gentlemen, creatures of all races and species. On behalf of Captain Theodore "Led" Zepplin and all the crew of the *Cloudskater*, I'd like to welcome you to this specially chartered flight from Los Lagos, Colorado, to Citrus City, Florida. As the captain and bridge crew prepare us for takeoff, I'd like to direct your attention to the video screens in your cabins for some important safety announcements." She keyed off the mic and ran the film, leaving it on for me to watch as well.

It contained the usual stuff. First the features of the DS-7: the cafeteria and lounge, where the cuisine more closely resembled a cruise line's than an airline's, observation port complete with telescopes, etc. You know the drill. I let the infomercial slide over me.

Then it moved to the safety information: Exits are located here, here, and here...in the event of loss of cabin pressure, air masks of varying sizes will be released from the compartments around the passenger areas... The entire airship is a float-ation device, so in the event of a water landing, make your way to the interior of the ship... Passengers are prohibited from entering restricted areas...

"Please do not inhale the helium," Led's First Officer Sam Nix quipped to the bridge crew, then changed his voice, "because it makes you sound ridiculous!"

Then came the Faerie-specific rules: "The DS-7 hybrids like *Cloudskater* not only combine the best aspects of airplanes and dirigibles," the beaming model in the video said brightly, "but also combine Mundane know-how with Faerie materials. Our engines were some of the first to be built with faerimet, enabling LagosLines airships to travel at greater speeds and efficiency than those with engines of Mundane steel. The entire framework is constructed from specially grown cedar-ironwood from the forests of Faerie Leba-non. While lighter, tougher, and less flammable than Mundane nonmetallic materials, *Cloud-skater* is nonetheless potentially magic-sensitive. Therefore, for safety reasons, the practice of magic, except in specific approved situations, is prohibited. Please refer to the card tucked into your door pocket for a list of approved spells and occasions. Elementals are asked to stay in their designated areas at all times, and nymphs of all categories are asked to refrain from communing with the ship."

I rolled my eyes. Nymphs aren't interested in dead wood, but some Mundane in the FAA must have seen a movie or something and decided it was a possible danger. No one consults Uncle Vern.

"Finally, our passengers, both Mundane and Faerie, human and nonhuman, are reminded to please keep their heads, hands, feet, tails, wings, and other extremities within the passenger areas at all times. Thank you and enjoy your flight."

The video faded, and the flight attendant handed the mic to me.

"This is Vurnerrah," I announced. I did not identify myself further. There was only one Vurnerrah, only one dragon, and if they didn't know it, they should. "As I'm sure most of you know, Sister Grace and I have been 'hired' by the Duchy of Peebles-on-Tweed and the Church to ensure your safety at this conference. However, you've probably not been told that we are not getting paid for this. Now, Sister Grace may not mind, but not getting paid makes the dragon cranky. Therefore, to make our job and your lives easier, I'd like to remind you of a few facts.

"Citrus City is not Los Lagos. Most Mundanes have not seen a Faerie except on social media or in the movies. The people at the convention supposedly rank in the top two percent of the Mundane population as far as intelligence, but intelligence does not always equal common sense, especially in Mundanes. Further, you will encounter other Mundanes, and since they don't teach from *Uncle Vern's Book of Faerie Safety*, you're going to have to practice prudence.

"If you venture outside the convention area, do so in groups. If you should find yourself in a confrontation with a Mundane, exercise restraint. You are dealing with an ignorant race that grew up with stories in which captured fairies give treasure. Cut them some slack. Do not use harmful force—physical or magical—unless your life is in danger. Even then, I suggest flight before fight. Think hard about what you do, or I guarantee: If your life wasn't endangered and I find out you used magic on a Mundane, it will be.

"If someone asks you to grant a wish, do not do so, even if it's in your power. You'll just make more trouble for the rest of us. Don't try to sell anyone magic beans or old oil lamps. It's been done on eBay. And *do not* use this as an opportunity for practical jokes. I do not want to find any parents dunking their children in the Withlacoochee River because some Faerie joker told them it'd make their child invulnerable. And if you get the bright idea to send a Mundane on a stupid quest, it'd better be for an asbestos suit because you'll need it.

"Most importantly for you empyrie who are thinking the Mundane world offers a golden opportunity for new worship: Don't Go There. America may have its own laws and ideas about the practice of religion, but Faerie follow the authority of the One True God and the Faerie Church. Both Grace and I have been officers of the Inquisition, and if you try to set up religious housekeeping on this side of the Gap, we will hunt you down.

"To summarize: If you have any doubts about something, don't do it. If you think I might get mildly annoyed by your behavior,"—I snapped my teeth and the sound echoed across the ship—"don't do it. You want the dragon to be your friend."

As I handed back the mic, Led asked, "Think that'll work?"

"I think it depends on the Mundanes."

He laughed. "Well, unless you want to be here for takeoff, you've got about five minutes to find your cabin and strap in."

"Sure you don't need me to get out and push?"

"Get to your cabin or I'll give you a push!"

I found Grace in our cabin and settled in. They'd improved the pad, covering a large area of the floor with that special playground rubber. Comfy and easy to clean. I had to be a little more careful with my claws, but it was at least as comfortable as the pile of pillows and blankets that I had once made my nest when we lived in the warehouse. I had the option of requesting large cushions if I wanted bedding.

Grace looked up from her lecture notes. "Nice speech. Sure you didn't just give them ideas?"

"Why do you think I didn't mention that I didn't want to see humans starting to cart around doggie doo because some leprechaunish comedian said he'd turn it into gold?"

She snorted. "Aye, that would hae' been too great a temptation, indeed."

"For the humans or the leprechauns?"

Led's voice came over the intercom. "Good morning, gentle creatures, and welcome to *Cloudskater*'s chartered flight to beautiful Citrus City. I'm Captain Theodore Zepplin, and my crew and I'll be getting you safely to your destination. The weather looks calm and clear for the entire trip, so once we've reached cruising altitude, you are welcome to move freely about the passenger areas of the ship. Please take advantage of the view."

"No thanks," I muttered aloud. Beside me, Grace nodded. We'd both had enough of views our last time on an airship. They say it's a view to die for, but take it from one who knows: No view is that good.

Chapter Six: High Flight

Led knew his stuff and had years of experience, so liftoff went as smoothly as Grace's singing. In fact, she was humming to herself as she went over her notes. Thanks to Grace's unusual ancestry, a lot of her magical talent is tied into her singing. Used correctly, she can express the Word of God with a beauty you've never experienced, or she can channel the Power of God with the skill to take down empyrie.

Currently, her song harmonized with the wards we'd set, but that didn't make it any less enjoyable. I settled myself down to listen while I went over our assignment papers more closely—starting with the shopping list. Just because the Faerie folk didn't understand online ordering didn't mean I couldn't just buy the stuff and have it waiting at home when we got there.

I quickly learned, however, that they gave us a list of vague requirements instead: "Something unique to Florida," asked the Duke's cousin, who liked to present himself as more of an adventurer than he really was. "Something for my dowry." I didn't recognize the name, but probably one of the duke's staff who needed something to increase her value. Why would someone think a dragon and a nun would be the people to ask?

The next one made me snort. "Something Mundane that's been in space?" I said aloud.

Grace brought her song to a close and set her notes aside. "Aye, that could be a challenge, but if anywhere, Florida would be the place to look."

"Would they even sell that? And *where* would we look?"

She shrugged. "We'll be in a hotel full of smart Mundanes. I'm sure someone will know. But scroll up." She paused for me to cock my head at her pun. I glanced from the paper scroll in my paws to her raised brows. She shrugged. "Just look. You'll see."

I scanned the usual dreck—an authentic Fanny Flamingo ball cap, a seashell from the actual Florida beach—until I got to the top. "Something to make my dear duchessikins laugh."

"Isn't that sweet?" Grace asked. Nun or not, she had a soft spot for love.

I was more jaded. "And dangerous. The last time he was determined to make his *duchessikins* laugh, he blew a hole in the universe."

Duke Galen had wanted to gift his wife a pair of cantaloupes (probably stuffing them down his shirt first to make her laugh before presenting her with the exotic fruit.) He'd hired mages to build a portal to the Faerie New World where they grew. Unfortunately, that spell resonated with a nuclear plant in Los Lagos, Colorado, Mundane. The resulting explosion caused the Gap, a stable interdimensional gateway between Faerie and the Mundane.

When the terrified mages reported what had happened, the first thing he'd asked was, "Do they have cantaloupes?"

"It's a good thing he asked us instead, then, isn't it?"

"I wonder if Florida grows some large, exotic fruit he can stuff down his shirt," I muttered.

Grace laughed, and I realized how much she was looking forward to this trip—shopping, babysitting and all. It had been a hard couple of years, what with saving the universes from proto-empyrie, solving murders, not to mention having our home destroyed. I resolved to handle the worst of the chaos I knew had to be coming so she could relax.

She said, "I've been thinking about the schedule, and I have an idea. What if we convince Gozonvabosomofic to deliver the traditional Farewell Blessing instead?"

"That's a terrific idea. If we can get him to deliver the abbreviated version, even better. That one only takes about forty-five minutes." I stuck out my front legs and stretched like a cat, then arched until my back legs got a good stretch, too. "May as well go ask now, while he's easy to corner."

On the way, we saw Brunhilde in her usual Valkyrie dress, though she'd left off the helmet. We exchanged a few pleasantries and made sure she didn't have any plans to make her "magical multimedia event" into a virtual reality tour. Like Grace said, she was surprisingly reasonable for someone who had to put up with drunken dead Norsemen for millennia on end. Maybe we'd have an easier time on this trip than I'd anticipated.

Gozon had one of the private compartments all to himself. Top of the line, of course; in addition to a comfortable couch, it had an actual bed that folded into the wall. When folded, the bed's supports made a long table, where piles of paper suggested he was working on his speech. The décor was dark woods—literally. Had Gozon brought half the forest with him or was this his "weird ask" as the keynote speaker? How ironic for a member of the Shores tribe. Nonetheless, when he bade us enter, I saw that he'd left a reasonably clear area for guests.

Faerie High Elves are a cross between Tolkien's imaginings and anime: tall and lean, ears sweeping to graceful points, eyes a little too large, and noses a little too small. However, Tolkien and anime both failed to imagine that High Elves are fashion-challenged. They prefer to blend in with their surroundings for the most part, and when having to deal with outsiders, they adopt the dress of the people or creatures they're dealing with. Easy enough—until the Interdimensional Internet introduced them to a bewildering array of styles.

Gozon had had enough experience with Mundanes to pick out reasonable outfits to wear in public, but in private... His orange long-sleeved T-shirt stood out like a hunter's safety vest. Over that, he'd tossed a neon-green bathrobe. Light blue plaid pants and argyle socks completed his look.

He was reading *A Tale of Two Cities*, and while we waited for him to finish the chapter, I toyed with the idea of trying to draw an analogy between him and the long-winded character, the Attorney General. Perhaps then he'd understand the effect his usual speeches had on Mundanes. The more circuitous a route I took to get to my point while still staying relevant, the greater my chances of succeeding.

Of course, that also meant that after we'd made our goodbyes an hour and a half later, Grace and I had to go back to our cabin and decode the conversation.

"He said, 'No,' didn't he?" Grace asked. She shook her head, trying to dislodge the tangles of adverbs, modifiers, and conversational asides that littered the exchange worse than a landfill after Spring Cleaning Week.

I nodded. "Definitely a 'no.' He's got plans for that speech. That worries me."

"What was he saying about plans? 'Four score years in the making.' Surely, he didn't mean this speech."

I circled my mat three times to push and flopped into a comfortable curl. I did enjoy the accommodations. "No, I think he's going to use this speech to brag about some scheme he's been up to. It's a time-honored tradition to reveal your great projects to a third party. But what has he been up to? He's supposed to be on the road to retirement."

"That's right. He's not 'keeping up with the times.'" She pulled out the dossier Charlie had prepared for us and started to go through it again, hoping for clues.

A knock on our door interrupted our musings. I sniffed, then called, "Enter, Friend," in Welsh Dwarvish.

Dwarves have a distinctive scent, especially to my nose. I won't go so far as to say "earthy," but strong and clean, and somehow appropriate for a race of underground creatures. It was the scent of home, both the abandoned dwarf mines where I'd taken residence in Faerie and now in our mountain lair.

Dwarves also had the distinctive body type noted in your Mundane legends: short, stocky, barrel-chested, and bulbous-nosed. Their skin was pale, and most had light blue eyes. The thick choroid layer in their eyes made them reflect green, like a cat's (or mine for that matter). They generally preferred their beards trimmed close to the face and their hair styled like your American military.

This dwarf, however, wore brown contact lenses, sported a beard that hung to his chest with hair to match, and had a tan. Kent was an actor, not a miner, but I still didn't understand why he was in such a clichéd getup.

Before I could ask, he said, "Sister? I was wondering if you had a tonic to calm the nerves."

She smiled and reached for her kit. We'd been expecting something like this from the dwarves. Nonetheless, she told him, "You seem to be doing well, Kent."

"It's not for me. It's Garn. He's in a bad way, like pumice under pressure. He needs a good bracing. I thought you might have an elixir of courage."

Grace and I swapped a glance. "Elixir of courage"? Kent was a method actor, and his stilted vocabulary suggested he was preparing for a role.

"Or could you sedate him?"

We followed him to their cabin. Halfway there, however, I stopped. "Do you hear that?"

The dwarf stared at me and shook his head, but I expected that. Dwarves have great vision and smell, but their hearing and taste fall below the human norm. Grace, after listening hard for a moment, shrugged.

"I could have sworn I heard laughing." It was gone, so I shook it off, and we continued to the cabin.

We found Garn on the floor, in the fetal position, stroking the head of a pickax he held cradled against his chest. The other dwarves had pulled the cushions out of the couches and surrounded him with them. Smart move, giving him the comfort of a tightly enclosed space. Plus, if he went the dwarvish version of postal, they could smother him.

I listened to him, but couldn't make sense of what he was saying. *Get the mine and protect the bull?*

Grace knelt beside him and spoke gently, but he refused to move and continued to mutter. She reached for his pickax, but he jerked it closer to himself. He ignored his friends, who were looking grimly unnerved by their friend's anxiety attack. He didn't seem to understand Faerie Common, and Grace's Dwarvish wasn't particularly good.

The dwarves had predictably chosen one of the smallest cabins, so the best I could do was snake my head in. Fortunately, I have a long neck, and Dwarvish was one of the languages God had returned to my knowledge.

"Yo! Dwarf!" "Yo!" was a standard Dwarvish greeting and profession of peaceful intent. It really irks them when they hear it misused by Mundanes.

His eyes wandered unfocused until they came upon my face. I suppressed a grin as they cleared to some semblance of sanity and his hand instinctively clutched the handle of his pickax, ready to defend his "turf" against me. Good.

"Yo!" I repeated. "You are in a nice, compact cabin with friends and food. What is your problem?" Grace would have handled it more gently. I'm not Grace.

Nonetheless, it seemed to work. He roused himself enough to mutter, "It's not natural, dragon. Dwarves were meant for the ground, not the air. To have agreed to fly in this, this—"

"You're safe here. Quit acting like a gherk." It was a terrible insult, something like weakling-baby-pansy times one hundred. Plus claustrophobe.

Around me, dwarves started reaching for pickaxes. I didn't bother to look at them. They were fancy replicas worn to show off to the conventioneers; they'd probably break on my scales before they did me any damage. I noticed our Gimli cosplayer (a.k.a Kent) in the corner, grinning.

My insult did the trick. "Gherk" sat up, his eyes shooting pale fire. "Take it back, dragon, or feel my pickax. I don't fear you."

"So I see. I'm surprised you fear anything. Feel better now?"

He looked around and saw the pillows and his companions watching anxiously. He swore. "Why did we have to take this aerial monstrosity? Why did the Mundanes deny us the subway? They have it—we have seen their movies."

I ground my teeth. Fine. If I didn't have time to write a book, I should at least create some pamphlets to answer the stupid questions and give weird facts about the Mundane that only Faerie would ask. Maybe I could augment our newsletter, which was more news and intel. "Only in a few big cities. They don't have an underground that stretches across their country."

All the dwarves but Kent gasped. They really were new to the Mundane. I wondered why the Shieldforger clan wasn't invited instead. They had lived in the Mundane for years—although maybe that was why. Did the Mensans want novelty?

"Savages! We weren't made for this. We belong on the ground! I belong down under!" Garn's eyes began to take on a wild look, and he started to get friendly with his pickax again.

If he needed more motivation to get a hold of himself, I could certainly give it. "Okay, I'll fly you down. Why don't you leave that pickax here?"

He swung his pickax over his head. "Leave me, wyrm."

"Yo!" I pulled my head back and let Grace take over. As I backed out of the crowded compartment, I heard his shaky sigh, and a thunk of metal on wood as he lowered the pickax. That one sounded real. Were we going to have a problem with him?

I hung out in the hall as Grace gave him a calming "elixir" and assured him that the airship was perfectly safe and very stable.

Of course, at just that moment, the ship dropped about six inches. I heard shrieks from all the compartments.

Chapter Seven: Flight High

"Stay with them," I called to Grace, then I dashed to the bridge. As I headed back down the hallway, Led announced that we were experiencing "minor turbulence" and for everyone to buckle their restraints. Through that, however, I again heard what sounded like laughter, but exceedingly high and faint. Where was it coming from?

"Have any of Sister Grace's wards been tripped?" Led demanded as soon as I had poked my nose onto the bridge. He was leaning over a console while his chief engineer was typing at the computer. At the cockpit, his first officer did his best to keep the ship steady while the navigator fussed over some kind of readout and spoke into a headset. The chief flight attendant was running through a checklist with the support crew. Unlike the many television shows I've seen, this crew did not wait for its captain to tell them how to do their jobs.

"No. What's going on?" I eeled my way around so I could see the computer screen. It displayed a graphic of the airship envelope with the individual gas cells. In each cell, a table tracked statistics. Three of the cells looked fine, but the air pressure in the fourth was lower and going down.

"We have a leak," Led said unnecessarily. "And that shouldn't happen."

"Security cameras didn't pick up anything," the engineer added. "It was nominal at first, then a big drop—which is when we dropped—now it's nominal again, though at a lower pressure. I don't get it. Why would the leak slow again?"

"I'm more concerned about preventing any sudden losses like we had," Led told him. "Get a team up there. Vern, mind providing some security, just in case?"

"No problem. In the meantime, you might want to get some of the flight attendants doing a head count."

The chief flight attendant replied, "Already on it."

From the pilot's seat, Nix said, "You know, Vern. If this keeps up, we're going to start a new legend about dragons being unlucky on airships."

"Very funny. Have you had any threats lately?" I asked Led.

"No. What about your passengers?"

"Pressure's dropping!" the engineer called.

"Compensating!" Nix replied. The drop was noticeably less severe this time.

Then I heard that noise. "Do you hear that?"

"Hear what?" Led asked.

Suddenly, I understood what I'd heard. I growled. "I know what caused your leak. Come on."

I led the way up the midship tower and along the neutral beam to the gas cell. As I'd suspected, I found them littered across a couple of support beams: Pixies from the art co-op, sucking helium out of a straw they'd punched into the balloon. The straw divided into twelve thinner ones; they sucked in all at once, then giggled and laughed at each other in voices too high for most of God's creatures to hear. Could they be more cliché? Behind me the repair crew stopped and stared.

Altogether, a dozen pixies don't mass as much as my tail, yet they'd managed to suck about a fourth of that cell's helium. A couple had inhaled so much they were hovering slightly.

"The helium will settle into your lungs. You could kill yourselves," I scolded.

"Oh, no, Vern," one of them said. He spoke his own language. Not that it mattered; the humans couldn't hear him. He must have been the ringleader, because the others just smiled and nodded—except for one who was laughing so hard she rolled off the rail. I caught her with my tail. "We just do this!"

They all turned toward me and yelled.

It felt like an icepick going through my skull. My ear flaps closed in defense. "Stop that."

"But—"

"Exhale without screaming!"

"But, we're expressing our existential rage," one protested, and the others laughed as they agreed.

"Keep it up, and I'll be expressing some *essential* rage. What are you doing here, anyway? Don't you know we need that gas to fly this crate?" I, too, spoke Pixie, so none of the engineers objected to my words.

"We'd put it back."

"How, exactly, and would you have done it before we crashed? Never mind. Your judgment's impaired. You're confined to your cabin for the rest of the flight. We're all high enough without you getting a helium rush. Hop on."

With groans of disappointment, they climbed onto my back, and I leapt over to the other gangway to let the engineering crew get to work.

As I neared the midship tower, I heard the engineers laughing. Squeaky and high-pitched laughter.

Yet again since living with humans, I was glad dragons didn't slap their foreheads. I had the feeling mine would be a whole new shape by the end of this assignment.

I got the pixies to their "cabin," a rather deep broom closet holding cat trees decorated with pouf-style cushions and an artificial jungle with plaster vines and exotic flowers. I thought about finding some clothespins to hang my mischievous passengers by their wings until they breathed out the last of the helium. I'd already had to burp one of them to keep her from as-pixiating. A dragon burping a pixie—even if someone were paying me, it couldn't be enough. Plus, they all decided belching was great fun. I guess that was an improvement. Each whistley giggle felt like a needle in my skull.

Acupuncture through my eardrums. I needed that like a hole in the head.

Templegrass looked ready to explode. Apparently, they'd said there were going in search of snacks. I left her expressing her essential rage at their antics, smacking them in the gut Doctor-Strange-style to expel the gas every time one dared to laugh at her. Fortunately, the door muffled the noise as soon as I shut it behind me. I headed back to my cabin. I figured Grace would find me there if she needed me.

Turns out, I found her standing with a porter in front of our cabin door, waiting. Just my luck.

"We have a problem in the luggage compartment." She spoke in Esperanto so no nosy passengers would understand us. Few Faerie had ever heard—or heard of—Esperanto, a wholly Mundane language made up of bits of different human languages. It has the advantage of being easy to learn yet totally incomprehensible to Magicals who didn't know it. We threw in some Klingon and Tolkien's Elvish to make it a true mishmash, and it had served us well.

"Wards go off?"

She shook her head. "But Casey here says there's something weird about the luggage area."

I sighed. I hated "weird."

We followed Casey to the luggage compartment, and he unlocked the door with his porter's keys. He swung it open and we saw—

—well, luggage. Rows of nicely organized luggage of both Faerie and Mundane style. Samsonite hardsiders with wheels and collapsible handles stacked neatly next to Elvish carryalls of bleached leather. All held secure by stiff webbing that hooked into the walls and floors.

Grace and I exchanged shrugs, but Casey lingered at the doorway, unwilling to enter. I poked my head in first; even if anyone or anything succeeded in lopping it off, I could grow it back. Nothing approached me, either with felonious intent or otherwise. I listened and heard only our breathing and heartbeats (and a distant "Worth it!" still beyond human hearing). I sniffed: clean clothes, some native foods, Mundane plastic, and Faerie wood. Nothing out of the ordinary—if anything, neater than I'd have expected. I mentioned that to Casey.

"That's just it," he said, befuddled. "It didn't look like this when I locked it."

"You mean someone cleaned it up while you were getting us?"

"I mean someone did this after I locked up for takeoff and before I came to check after we had that turbulence. What happened, anyway?"

"Gremlins." Not really, but close enough. The compartment was plenty big, so I moved on in to let the others through. Grace went to the far corner, knelt, folded her hands in prayer, and began to sing softly—standard surveillance spell.

While she did her work, I did mine. "How did this look before?'

"Well, everything was secure, but come on. Look at this!" He pointed to a long shelf where the luggage was neatly stowed and organized by color. If you unfocused, it made a rainbow flowing into a puffy white cloud.

"I did think you'd gotten a little creative."

The look he gave me was the dirtiest thing in the room. "Look, I have four duties on this ship. The baggage handlers bring everything up here and get it loaded, and I check to make sure it's secure. Today, we had to scramble because everyone checked in at once and we had about thirty minutes to stow all the stuff for takeoff. Plus, I have to make sure all the meals are loaded and engineering supplies are locked down. That took extra time because we had a last-minute shipment of soda from the Chase Bottling Company. Then I start my flight duties. We pile up the luggage in the order we get it, lock it up, and leave it alone. I just came down here for a post-turbulence check. I mean, there's always a chance some webbing might come undone or something, you know? I expected to see the usual mishmash of stuff pushing against the nets or, worst-case, on the floor. Instead I find..." His voice trailed off and he waved his arm at the room.

"A random act of tidiness?" I offered. Did vandalism have an antonym?

I asked the usual questions and found out the place was locked and supposedly unoccupied from ten minutes before takeoff to twenty minutes ago, when Casey opened it up and found the aftermath of the Attack of the Happy Housekeepers. The alarms hadn't gone off, obviously, and the compartment didn't have a surveillance camera was disabled but immaculately polished. The only thing "missing" was that a case of Ping Cola had only empty cans, but that could have been an error at the bottling plant.

Next, we started to look over the luggage for any signs of tampering, but from all that my enhanced senses could tell me, everything was clean. Literally. Plastic shined, metal buffed, leather polished, not a scuff to be seen. I'd have more luck trying to seek out the scent of cleaner on a passenger's hands than finding prints on their bags. Meanwhile, Casey pulled out his scanner and started taking inventory. He moved quickly; our anal-retentive redecorator had thoughtfully left the shipping tags sticking out and smoothed down.

Grace sighed and crossed herself, then stood. "Well, there's been no evil intent, but whoever was here covered his tracks pretty thoroughly."

"I'm not surprised. Anything missing, Casey?"

"Not so far."

I unhooked the webbing on one of the shelves and pulled out a pink suitcase at random from the edge of the clouds. "Let's see if the inside is as neat as the outside."

It wouldn't open.

"Thought the FAA forbade magically locked luggage." I said to Casey.

"They do."

Grace squatted down in front of the case. "It's not bespelled. Give me a moment." She muttered something, and it snapped open.

Casey whistled. "How'd you do that?"

"A simple cantrip developed by the Faerie Saint Zita. Like your own saint, she's patroness of locks—and of housekeepers, ironically." She pulled it open to reveal folded clothes and toiletries. "If it's been tampered with, there's no way to tell by looking at it." She pulled out a pencil and poked at the clothes.

"Who does this belong to?" I asked Casey.

He knelt to look at the tag, but Grace beat him to the answer by pulling up a brass brassiere—size 42 EE. "Brunhilde, I presume?"

"But this is Mundane luggage!" Casey protested as he knelt down to look.

"American Tourister," I read off the label.

"Come on!"

"At least someone knows how to shop on the InterdimNet," I muttered. Grace poked me with her elbow.

"She sure does." Casey chuckled as he pulled out something silky and lacey. The tag read, "Valkyrie's Whisper."

Grace snatched it from his hands. "Shame on you!"

"Shame on her." He snickered.

Grace sighed heavily as she folded the negligee and put it back under Brun's "working" attire, then shut the case. "You know, after wearing metal on her chest all day, she might just appreciate having something soft," she said severely.

"Yes, Ma'am," Casey replied, though from his smile, I could tell he didn't believe it.

We checked out a couple more cases at random—again, all locked but not bespelled, which is also against FAA regulations—but we couldn't tell if they had been tampered with or tidied up.

"So what do we do?" Grace asked me.

"Nothing. Wait and see if anyone reports anything missing."

"What if they come back?" Casey asked.

"I doubt if they will, but just in case—Grace, can you put a spell on Brunhilde's to let us know if it's touched again?" She did so, and I stuck it in among the line of reds. "There. If they come back,

I'm betting they won't be able to resist that little bit of disorder. Then we catch them."

"That's it?" Casey asked.

"You want to pay us to do more?"

"You're not going to stay here, guard the luggage?"

"From what? The maniacally neat? There's no law against compulsive organizing."

Grace set her arm on his shoulder. "It'll be fine. If whoever did this was just having fun, it's been had. If they were searching for something, they've either found it and won't return or didn't find it and are looking elsewhere. We've only got about forty-five minutes before landing."

Casey shrugged, and I took that as our cue to head back to our room. I was perfectly glad not to see—or hear—a single Faerie on the way.

I flopped into my cushion while Grace took her seat. I griped, "'Just be available in case things get out of hand,' he said. 'You're free to enjoy the conference,' he said. So far, we've had one minor incident, one that could have become a major problem, and a small mystery. What's next?"

"Something mundane, I hope," Grace answered. "With a small M."

Chapter Eight: The Bottom Two Percent

What we got was mundane, all right. That didn't make it any less annoying.

"How do you lose fifty reservations?" a voice behind us shrieked. I think it was a Muse, but at the moment, she sounded more like a harpy. Secretly, I was glad she'd said it. Spared me the need to voice my own dismay, and from the way the receptionist was eyeing me, any strong emotion on my part would probably make him faint.

Couldn't say I blamed him. We'd overflown the Orlando amusement parks, and I'd seen the animated dragon on the tower breathing fire over the heads of the tourists. If that's the kind of dragons this kid grew up with, no wonder he looked like he was wishing for an asbestos suit.

Even so, I didn't intend to move from Grace's side; he'd been giving her the administrative runaround until I showed up and treated him to

The Grin. Unfortunately, now he was so flustered, I wondered if he could control his bowels, much less find our lost reservations. And if he apologized once more, I just might give him a reason to be sorry.

"Not all of them," he replied quickly as his fingers tapped a nervous staccato on the computer keyboard. "See? I have a King suite for the...Naiad Family?"

I snorted. "Unless we're talking king-sized bathtubs, that's not going to work. That'd be like putting a goldfish in a hamster cage."

Grace sighed. "There's obviously been a mistake, but at least we're making progress. Let's just reassign that room—"

"Oh, but I can't. It's in their name—"

"They can't use it," I repeated. "They're *naiads*. Water creatures. In fact, they're in your garden pond right now, happy as clams—"

"I'm sorry!"

"That they're in the lake or that they're happy?"

"Vern!" Grace hissed, then glanced at the receptionist's name tag. "Listen, Roger. Vern and I are designated representatives on behalf of all the

Faerie guests at the conference. We can authorize you to reassign the room."

"Unless you'd like to jump in the lake—" I started.

"Vern!" Grace snapped.

"—and ask them yourself," I concluded with my best innocent look. Grace didn't buy it, of course.

"I'll need to speak to my manager—" Roger started, but I cleared my throat, and he blanched. "But let's see what else I can find. Um, um... Would you take a smoking room, Mr. Dragon?"

"Only if I can smoke in it," I quipped, and let out a puff from my nostrils.

Roger's eyes started to roll into the back of his head. Grace reached out and grabbed his wrist, whispering a prayer, and he steadied.

At this point, Gozon muscled his way to the desk. Even Elvish patience had its limits, it seemed. "Roger, O Most Esteemed Keeper of the Keys of this regarded hostel, the Citrus Stars, that three star-hotel (and we know you deserved four had it not been the unfortunate incident in the kitchens—the one of last October, of course—which your fine manager, Barry Welles—no relation to Orson Welles, though they share a similarity in facial features—has assured our travel agent was remedied and besides, the inspector was at least sixty percent at fault, having stuck his finger in the pot..."

Roger's eyes glazed, and Grace turned to us with a beatific smile that I knew covered frayed nerves. She spoke sweetly, "Gozonvabosomofic, *Vern*, why don't the two of you check on the naiads while Roger and I work this out?"

Gozon started to protest, and I wrapped my tail around his shoulders and steered him away while he was still sputtering out the Elvish equivalent of "But—" It wasn't the most diplomatic thing to do, but I'm an Eighth Day Creation and I breathe fire; diplomacy is what people should use with *me*.

Still, I was a representative of the Faerie Catholic Church, so once we got outside into the sunshine and warm humid air, I apologized. In High Elvish. For all my griping, I actually enjoy a nice long Elvish discourse, well-done. When I have the time, of course; and it seems that in the Mundane world, there's never enough time. Certainly not for High Elvish, anyway.

At the moment, however, we had nothing but time, so while we meandered over to the pond, I indulged myself with the honorifics (mine and his), a summary of our relationship and the relationship between dragons and elves and how that applied to the apology, the nature of working with Mundanes... The whole Elvish enchilada with a side of rice. I had him pretty well mollified by the time we'd settled over by the bank. The naiads came by to let me know they, at least, were happy with their accommodations.

"It's so warm!" one enthused.

"And clean!" added another.

"And pretty! Look!" The third one had picked a Japanese water iris and twisted it into her hair. She'd woven two others into her coontail-and-muskgrass dress. She ducked a hand quickly into the water and pulled out an orange-and-black spotted koi. It wriggled in her grasp, and she tickled it.

"Don't be eating those!" I warned them to leave the koi alone. Naiads may be the size of petite preteen girls, but they ate like teenage football players.

From the guilty-but-not-ashamed looks they shared, I figured we had a penalty fee coming.

Still, the first one said, "Oh, okay. We promise now."

"We'll play with our pet," one suggested and dove away before I could ask. I shrugged to myself. As long as they didn't think they could bring it back with them.

I settled myself down, Sphinx-like, facing Gozon, who sat on a stone bench beside the water, his profile to me. He had listened to my apology with respectful silence, and now I waited quietly as he composed his reply. I hoped he remembered what side of the Gap we were on. In Faerie, politeness dictated that I wait at least three hours before so much as clearing my throat.

Couldn't say I minded the wait, at least for now. My scales soaked in the Florida midday sun, soothing muscles long abused by tough cases and life in a world better suited for bipedal life forms. I curled my tail around my legs to keep it out of harm's way, but even so, I could feel the kinks baking themselves out. The humidity thickened the air, and after the thin stuff on the airship, it made for easy breathing.

Moments later, Gozon began: "Hearken to my tale, Vurnerrah, known among the humans as

Vern d'Wyvern (but who does not like the surname and henceforth I shall mention it not, for well is it known the restraint you showed in not eating Watkyndahydiottaru after he—in great inconsiderateness and puerile humor—did insist upon addressing you by full name). Vurnerrah, Eighth Day Creation, Fellow Citizen of the Golden Land, Land of Magic and Beauty, where the Eternal Winds blow gentle o'er the softly blooming meadows of Caraparavelenciana, where once you flew with grandeur and strength..."

As Gozon recounted my life before my famous fight with St. George, I relaxed. My muscles melted in the heat. Gozon's words took on the cadence of a Faerie epic. Under it, the sound of the naiads chasing the fish in the pond made a soothing counterpoint.

He moved on to post-George: my capture, my losing everything, my work to regain my former glory through faithful service to God and His creatures. "And thus, Vurnerrah, once the grandest of God's creations—yea, created from God's most glorious imaginings—who was brought to the humblest of stations and who has labored so assiduously to retrieve what is his by right; you, of all creatures, shall understand. For I, too, share such a predicament, an insult to the pride and a paining of the psyche, that they whom I had served so long and so well..."

My phone buzzed. Manners dictated I ignore it, but it could have been Grace saying everything was taken care of. Ha. Right. Most likely, it was someone with some kind of emergency. Either way, Gozon was still staring unseeing in the general direction of the pond, his mind on his tale and his mouth on automatic. I could chance a look.

It was from Gapman: *Ha ha. You could have warned me!*

I clenched my jaws against a longsuffering sigh. He was supposed to be mole hunting with the hobgoblins by now. I sent back a single question mark, waited, and when I didn't get an answer, I put the phone away. Guess they figured out whatever it was I was supposed to warn him about.

Meanwhile, Gozon had progressed to his tale of woe and how he'd been unappreciated and undervalued, and how his people planned to retire him from his position in order to replace him with someone younger.

His tale encompassed decades of twist and intrigues, but it wasn't anything new: Upper Management (in this case Queen Imdaboz'ndonchafuggeditt and her consort) decides the old guy can't keep up with the times, so they plan to "creatively reassign" him. Old guy fights it as best he knows, but not by actually tackling the problem and getting with the times. In this case, Gozon was mighty circumspect about his plans, other than his confidence of great success. Didn't stop him from going on about it, and I had to admit, a part of me admired his ability to talk for so long, nonstop, and say nothing.

The rest of me, however, just took in the soothing cadence of Elvish longspeech. I remembered a time, millennia ago, when I'd listened to another Speaker of the Winds voice a similar complaint. Sometimes, an elf just needed to talk it out.

That one had taken three days. Gozon had an hour, maybe two, before he had to get past it enough to make nice with the Mundanes. But I could indulge him until then. Grace had things under control; if not, she'd call and I'd answer, manners notwithstanding.

I was tired. Was it the heat or the distance from the Gap? My eyelids got heavy and I didn't fight them. Gozonvabosomofic was "in the zone": staring straight ahead and focusing at a distance, mind somewhere in the last century as he recounted yet another snub and the hatchings of his plan, so caught in his own tale that a marching band could pass in front of him and he wouldn't realize it. He wouldn't notice if I closed my eyes for a few. I could still listen...

I don't know how long I'd been dozing, or when I lost awareness of my surroundings, but I was jerked back to full consciousness when I felt a sudden weight plop itself on my shoulders and little hands grab onto one of my back spikes. I may have been half-asleep, but after years of babysitting the Costas, I knew that feeling anywhere. Someone had just put a kid on my back.

I opened my eyes but otherwise didn't move as I took in the scene. The last thing I wanted to do was start a panic or move too quickly with an unharnessed innocent on my back. In front of me, a couple of Mundanes were circling Gozon, waving their hands in front of his eyes, making faces and generally doing all the stuff obnoxious tourists do to try to make the guards at Buckingham Palace react. They looked like father and son, based on their relative ages, similar bone structure, and identical buffoonery.

Just like the beleaguered British guards, Gozon didn't so much as twitch, but continued with his speech, caught in the Elvish Toastmaster Trance.

Junior glanced my way and turned, his mouth falling open in a fairly good imitation of the picture of Rhoda Dakota that adorned his T-shirt. "Whoa! Look! Its eyes opened!" Almost on top of his exclamation, a woman—Mom, I guessed—said something about not seeing where to put the quarters.

Gozon, oblivious, continued his soliloquy. "...of my epic adventure ends, yet this was only the merest step of a plan whose complexity is like that of the caves of Rivaldebahn, where once, O Vurnerrah, terror and grace of the Medsea skies, you had made your home..."

Slowly, so as not to frighten them, I twisted my head and spoke. "Please remove your child from my back."

Slackerboy laughed while Peewee rocked and kicked his heels into my side. "Did you hear this thing?"

A middle-aged copy of Slackerboy went to stand by his son. A 35mm Nikon hung by a wide strap from his neck and rested on his potbelly, covering the face of Fanny Flamingo on his T-shirt. He wore plaid golf shorts, tube socks, and black shower shoes. And I thought elves were fashion-challenged. "Amazing! What they can do with animatronics!"

Great. The hotel apparently forgot to inform all the non-Mensa patrons about the Faerie. After the speech I gave on the plane, Grace would flip if I overreacted (or, rather, reacted in the way I thought was appropriate.)

I spoke calmly. "I'm not a machine. I'm a living creature. Please remove your child from my back."

Clueless and Son laughed while Baby started to whine for the ride to start. The mother was standing near my flank, holding a quarter, but clearly hesitant. Since she seemed to be displaying more intelligence than the men in her family, I turned to her. "Madame, I am a member of the Faerie delegation here for a convention. While I generally like children, I do not give free rides."

Despite my suave voice and patient manner, she took a step back. "Clyde…"

Clueless Clyde, however, was chortling. "Oh, come on, Rita! It's obviously a hoax! Remember that Leno stunt with the talking photo booth? This is obviously a more souped-up version of the same thing! "

"I'm neither a joke nor a ride—" I started with some dignity, but no one was listening. The menfolk of this ignorant tribe were combing the bushes while Rita hesitantly reached for her child, only to draw back her hand uncertainly.

"Clyde!" she called again, her voice rising in pitch.

Apparently, Sonny learned his manners from his dad. "Geez, Mom! It's all done by AI! Get a clue. It's like this thing."

He waved an arm at Gozon, who continued to pontificate: "…indeed, for the Mundanes will appreciate the poetic genius of it…"

Boy, not this crowd. Baby had started rocking on my back and kicking his heels enthusiastically. His right foot dug into one of the scales that got knocked out of place when I got smacked by a piece of the scaffolding I was "welding" to hold up the warehouse roof. I fought the urge to buck.

"Lady," I warned.

"Clyde, what if it's dangerous?"

"For the love of Pete, Rita!" the oh-so-concerned father called from near the pond where he was searching the rushes. "If you're so worried, get a picture of him and take him off. But if he starts screaming, it's your problem!"

"Whoa, Dad, look!"

Curious, the naiads had risen partway out of the water and were smiling suggestively. Dad went next to Junior to look. Neither seemed to realize they'd already walked far enough into the pond that water was soaking into their shoes. They even ignored the alligator glaring at them, it's mouth open in a predatory smile. One of the naiads, Lilly, rode on its back, keeping it calm. That was their new pet?

The naiads probably wouldn't hurt them, and Lilly would keep the gator docile. Nonetheless, given the common sense I'd seen so far—and the way the day had gone—I decided I'd better step in, so to speak. First, I had to get rid of the Baby Drag-onrider. "Ma'am, would you please..?"

But she was digging in her purse. Mr. Naiad-Talker and his sidekick were making weird chir-rupy sounds and giggling with the water spirits. Was the hotel trying to balance the IQ quotient by hosting a convention of the bottom two percent as well?

Gozon was still nattering: "...and by the incred-ible evidence I shall bring before the wondering eyes of these most worthy of Mundanes..."

Baby Dragonrider was bouncing in earnest. I swiveled my head to look at him. "Stop kicking the nice dragon, now, and climb down," I told him.

He stopped then, and frowned in concentra-tion. I heard a squelching and smelled something that made me glad dragons were never parents. Then he giggled and started rocking and kicking again.

"Lady, take your kid." I wrapped my tail around the kid's middle, plucked him off my back, and pointed him in her direction.

She, however, had decided to scold her son to get away from the naked swimmers.

Her son brushed away her command like an annoying insect. "They ain't real, Mom. These things are slap! Wait 'till I tell Cory they had naked cyber chicks in the hotel pond!"

Despite everything, I rolled my eyes. "They're not naked."

"Clyde, do something about your son!"

"In a minute, woman! I want to get a photo of these mermaids."

Mermaids.

He said *mermaids*!

Now the trouble began.

The naiads are pretty forgiving of human stupidity—after all, they depend on it for their prey at times—but one thing they won't stand for is the insult of being called mermaids. Their beguiling giggles turned to blood-chilling shrieks and—remembering my warning against doing any real harm to the Mundanes—they started to throw mud and pond scum at the Dufus Duo. Hastily, the two backed out of the water, laughing.

I called to the naiads in their own tongue to stop, then turned to the humans. "Listen. I'm trying to be as patient as I can. I'm going to say this slowly. We are real. *We Are Alive.* We are not animatronic, cybernetic, artificial, and definitely not amusement rides. Now please remove your child—"

I lost track of my tail and got Baby Dragonrider too close to my hide. His wild kick found its way under my scale, twisting it at an unnatural angle and digging into the sensitive half-healed skin beneath.

"Yeow!" I jerked, swinging Stinky away from his mom. Stinky squealed in delight. Stupid and Son almost fell over each other chortling. Momma, however, went from timid to tiger. With an all-too-human screech, she rushed me, swinging her purse at me. I held Diaper Dan back lest she hit him by accident.

"Give me my baby!" She whipped her purse at my head.

I ducked the wild swing. "I'm trying to! Calm down! Gozonvabosomofic, help me out, here!"

"...and in that sweet victory, my people will again realize the depth of my diplomatic prowess, my heroics, daring, and adaptability; lo, I shall be known as in the Mundane slang: hip, with it..."

Papa Laughsalot was leaning on the park bench, clutching his stomach and wheezing with mirth. I tried to set the baby down on the pavement, but he started screaming, which made Momma swing even more furiously. No way could I give him to her without risking his getting hit. I tried to pass Baby to his big brother, but the kid just raised his arms at him and said, "Whee!" which Baby echoed.

"Come on, kid. Grab your brother!" I snarled.

The naiads decided I needed backup and started hurling mud at the mother. Mom deflected it with her purse, which sent it splattering. Their pet alligator, agitated by the chaos, started to wiggle and snap.

"...cool cat, sly; lo, even foxy..." Gozon continued to list old slang.

From the corner of my eye, I saw a black guy in dreads and a pastry in one hand pull out a flip phone and start videoing. Great. Another one for the blooper reel. His T-shirt said, "That's on Florida." I couldn't have agreed more.

I started to lower Stinky to the bench beside me again when Momma's purse impacted against my chin. She must have just bought souvenirs—the cheap, heavy resin kind. This time instead of a human invective, I let loose with a dragon one.

Before things could get any worse—and believe me, with my luck, they would have—Grace came on the scene.

"Peace be with you."

The words, though sweetly crooned, were nonetheless a spell backed by the power of the Holy Spirit. A wave of calm, like cool water on smoldering coals, washed over us. Fun over, the naiads sighed and slid back into the water. Chortles and Chuckles stilled their hilarity. Momma stopped her screaming and lowered her bludgeon of a handbag. Baby's squeals became coos. Even the sting in my side subsided a bit. Thank heavens, the cavalry had finally arrived.

Grace flowed into the sea of calm. She held out her hands, and gratefully, I lowered the child into them. His diaper was now leaking and riper than an amusement park's garbage cans in August. She held him at arm's length as she handed him to his mother, who clutched him to her chest. Only after several moments did Momma grimace and withdraw her hand from where she'd been supporting his bottom.

"Everyone has a room now, including us," Grace told me with a weary sigh. "Shall we go get settled in before the evening's events?"

"Wait a minute!" Daddy LessSmarts exclaimed. "You mean this thing is for real?"

Grace's peace charm was still working, or I might have flamed him then and there. As it was, I clamped my teeth shut to keep from making a snarky reply. I let Grace explain; obviously, they were more likely to listen to a human than me. While she did, I used my hind leg to scratch at the spot where I'd been kicked until the scale slid back into place. Ah, relief!

While Momma changed the baby's diaper on the bench beside the pontificating elf, Grace introduced me to Tweedle Dee and Tweedle Dum— a.k.a. Clyde Irby and his son, Buddy. Clyde apologized while Buddy insisted that I was the most freaking amazing thing he'd ever seen—even better than the half-naked mermaids—

"They're naiads," I corrected. "And they are clothed. Don't call them mermaids. It's insulting."

"Naiads. Right."

Mrs. Irby returned with a freshly dressed Baby Irby, Grace snapped some photographs for them, and off they went at last.

I let out a long, cleansing breath. "Blessed are the peacemakers. Thanks."

"Do I even want to know what this was about?" she asked.

I knew that tone and took the prudent route. "Nope."

"Alright, then. Save it for a time when we can laugh about it. Is Gozonvabosomofic ready to respond?" She glanced at the elf, who had not moved during the entire exchange, and who had a clod of mud drying in his long brown hair. Carefully, Grace removed it.

"...Speaker for the Winds, Friend of Men, Ambassador of Eternal Winds—all of these shall continue to be mine." He blinked, smiled, and stood. "I trust that, having been audience to my brief tale, you better understand the urgency of my purpose and affirm your respect for me in this regard as indeed I, by sharing my story, do affirm my respect and regard for you, respect shown by all who encounter your dignified personage?"

"Oh, absolutely," I deadpanned.

Chapter Nine: Dis-Orientation

The cornerstone of the Citrus Stars proclaimed, "Est. 1957," but the hotel dwarfed the newer Broadmoor in Los Lagos: three six-story buildings, longer than they were tall, with alternating floors for guests and for conventions and entertainment, each angled to make a hexagon circling the large gardens. Ivy-covered walls divided the gardens into three sections—one with the pond, another with the pools, and a final with a playground and daycare facilities. It turned out that our building bordered the pond, and Grace had gotten us a room on the fifth floor facing it.

After my first encounter with Florida Man and Family, I was not interested in meeting more of their kind in the hallway. I launched myself to the roof of the neighboring building where I could see our room while Sister Grace escorted Gozon to his room and went to ours. When I saw her open the balcony doors, I flew to the balcony and wandered in.

If dragons could whistle, I would have. "Nice room."

And it was, for us. Wallpaper of striped greens over a matching green border covered well-insulated walls. It had an air conditioner and heater we could set to whatever temperature we liked without worrying about the bill. From the threshold of the balcony, I couldn't quite see into the bathroom, but I knew there'd be a bathtub rather than just a shower stall. And two double beds. It even had a little safe, and while I made myself comfortable on the bed, Grace finished putting the medallions and potions she'd brought into it, set the combination, and activated wards around it.

Natura likes to call Grace's wards the "Karma shield." It's fueled by that moment at death when you're suddenly aware of all the good and bad you've done and the consequences of your deeds, as well as the judgment of your worthiness. Anyone attempting to break into that safe would find themselves under an attack in proportion to the evilness of their intent. Their eyes are opened to their own damaged souls. For those who believe in the power of Confession, it can be a healthy thing. Even non-Catholic Christians usually recover well enough if they can find their faith in God. If Grace shows up while they're still curled in the fetal position and gibbering, she can help them. As for the rest...

I hoped we wouldn't need to call any psychiatrists on this trip.

Done, Grace tossed me an envelope with my registration information and fell back on the bed with a loud groan. "This may be the most annoying job we've not gotten paid for," she sighed.

"At least Kitty McGrue wasn't around to report on the 'pond incident.'"

She grunted agreement. "How are you feeling? It's odd that you got surprised by that family."

Embarrassing is what it was. Ambushed by a baby. "I am a little 'off,' but this is supposed to be a boondoggle, right? A working vacation? Yet, obviously, people were not prepared for our arrival."

I poked through the packet's contents: a program, some bookmarks and flyers, a lanyard with a wallet-like pouch, and a name tag with VERN in large letters and "Dragon Eye, PI" in smaller letters below. I also found a piece of paper with three stickers: red, yellow, and green. I held it up for Grace.

"Mensans are apparently a demonstrative lot," she explained. "You need to put one on your tag to tell folks your 'hug preference.' Green means you welcome hugs from anyone; red, 'Please do not hug me;' and yellow if you want to be asked first."

Days like this made me wish I had more expressive eyebrows. I chose a red sticker. I'm not the cuddly type.

Grace snorted, then turned on her side to face me. "I'm not sure this much trouble with the rooms could be accidental. Charlie had confirmed our reservations. He included the letter in the courier's package. Yet they lost *all* our reservations? Even more, we were assigned an entire floor; now, we have Faerie scattered all over the hotel complex—or would have. I managed to get them all into this building at least."

I looked at her more closely, and saw the circles under her eyes and her pallor. She'd obviously worked more than one spell since we'd gotten here, and even though the power was God's, she still shared in the strain. Looked like we could both use a nap.

"So who's splitting up the band?" I asked.

"'Band'? More like mob. Know what I found curious? The rooms that did have assignments: Gozon's original room was a suite on this floor, but the reservation they found placed him in a cheap single across the compound, where there's an electric guitar expo."

"For a 'hip cat' like him? That's not such a bad idea."

Having missed his speech by the pond, she didn't understand my comment but chose to let it slide. "How about this one: Brunhilde got their best penthouse suite while Siegfried was assigned the smallest room on the opposite side of the complex from her. Speaking of, we're going to need to watch out for Siegfried. He's insisting on wearing 'traditional dress.'"

I snorted. Related to the Siegfried of Viking legend, "our" Siegfried believed he had been born out of his time. Although a scholar by trade and temperament, he nonetheless liked role-playing his ancestor as much as he did talking about him. On the airship here, he'd kept a low profile, wearing modern Faerie clothes and trying to learn a few phrases of English. His only nod toward his obsession had been to make cow's eyes at Brunhilde. She, of course, hadn't wanted anything to do with him. Guess one Siegfried was enough. Now, however, he seemed to have decided to come out of the ancestral closet—wearing their clothes. I wondered if there was a Ren Fest in town we could ship him to.

"Well, he's got the muscles for it," I said.

"And the broadsword. I had to make him put it away before the desk clerk had apoplexy. Sped things up, though. But it's not that. I heard a couple of employees snickering and making comments about his helmet needing horns."

Great. If there's anything he loves more than Brunhilde, it's being historically accurate. He would not take the implied insult well, especially one based on inaccuracy and myth. "Let's be thankful he's not good at languages."

"And thankful for this room," she said, spreading her hands across the bed. Like I'd said, pretty ritzy by our standards. She sighed and pulled herself up. "So, since my vows do not include any proscriptions against luxury, I plan to enjoy it, starting with a long, hot bath. What're the chances everyone will stay quietly in their rooms tonight after the welcome dinner?"

"About the same as their all staying in the passenger areas on the flight over." I shrugged. "Enjoy your bath. I may snooze a bit, but this time, I'll keep an ear peeled." Dragons did have the ability, much like cats, to doze while still being aware of their surroundings. If there was trouble, I'd know it this time.

Speaking of... I checked my phone. Gapman had not texted back.

Grace paused at the doorway to watch. "Something wrong?"

"Cryptic text from our padawan earlier. Guess he handled whatever it was."

"He really is a capable young man," Grace said fondly. "We've done well training him."

I grunted agreement. What should I have warned him about? "Go get your bath. I want to be at the dining room early to check it out. Who knows what chaos someone might create with a bad seating arrangement."

Chapter Ten: Mensa and Mayhem

It was a good thing we left early for the banquet, even so. It took Grace and me half an hour to get to the dining room on the second floor because folks kept asking for a photo with me, but at least no one was looking for hidden cameras or trying to stick a quarter in my ear.

Of course, when we reached the banquet hall, I ran into my usual nemesis: tables and chairs. I've adopted a lot of anthropomorphic habits in my eight centuries of living with humans, but sitting at a table in a crowded room has never been easy. No one's yet built a chair suitable for my anatomy, and even sitting on my haunches made me too tall for the average table. Los Lagos restaurants had adapted, of course, but since we didn't have any centaurs or other large-scale Magicals, someone forgot to mention the dragon.

To add insult to injury, someone had assigned us a table in the middle of the room. What had I said about seating arrangements?

I glanced around. The tables were so crowded together that even humans would have to twist sideways to get through. They were already filling up with guests, Faerie and Mundane. Every Faerie had been assigned a Mundane chaperone who had met them when they'd registered at the conference table and was supposed to be helping them find their way. So far, it looked like it was working, despite the problems with rooms. Most of the Faerie were at their tables, speaking—comfortably, for the most part—with their Mundane hosts. Even Gozon's "handler" seemed to be enjoying himself; he had a tape recorder beside Gozon's plate and was taking notes at a furious pace.

It made sense. One Faerie on his own is a sideshow. Get a couple score of different Faerie, mortal and Magical, all eating at white-cloth-covered tables using the same cups and cutlery as any other convention-goer, and the sight becomes (pardon the expression) mundane. It helped, too, that the entire building had been reserved for the Mensans, who had all been warned about the unusual guests via convention packages, Internet chatter, and an article or two in their official magazine.

My eyes brushed over Brunhilde twice before I took in who she was. Rather than her breastplate and braids, the Valkyrie had pulled her hair into an elegant French knot and wore a turquoise halter dress that would have made Marilyn Monroe jealous. She was drawing a lot of looks, and she knew it. She'd always had a muscular physique—came from her job—but her arms, shoulders, and legs showed more definition than you get from just working. She must have subscribed to some bodybuilder magazines and, pardon the expression, been pumping iron.

At another table, Siegfried, in traditional furs, looked both uncomfortable and morose. From the way he kept casting glances Brunhilde's way, I don't think heat was the reason—at least not the kind that could be solved with more air conditioning.

That was a problem for later, and one I'd pass off to Grace if I could. Right now, I had about as much chance of getting to my seat as a minotaur navigating through a china shop: i.e., none, unless you didn't mind the broken plates. Tables. Toes...

"Obviously, the seating chart was not created by a Mensan," said a familiar voice behind us. An even more familiar laugh followed: nasal, forced, sounding something like Beavis and Butthead crossed with Sidney Greenstreet.

We turned. Cambridge Ramada looked just like he had when we'd parted ways years ago. Small but bright blue eyes twinkled in his large face, and his white suit covered his 350-pound blubbery bulk without looking loose or binding. Hope he paid his tailor well—he deserved it. His name tag had a green dot.

"You're a Mensan?" I exclaimed.

"Since the days we Mensans used to meet to do the dirty bookstore crawl—begging your pardon, Sister. I take it this is Sister Grace, for whom you were willing to risk so much? Cambridge Ramada." Despite their "hug me" stickers, he bent over her hand instead.

"I regret that you were hospitalized at the time...and any role I or my client may have played in that," he told her.

"On the contrary. Vern told me about you and how you helped him secure the Lance of Longinus," Grace said.

He laughed. "Generous words, considering I was one of his prime suspects. And of course, he did not so much 'secure' the Lance as melt it—"

"Wrong. I burned it, metal and all, and scattered what was left of the ashes." I corrected him with grim emphasis. The Faerie Lance of Longinus, the spear used to pierce the side of Christ, had been endowed with supernatural power. In the wrong hands, it had come close to destroying Faerie civilization. I'd destroyed that Lance, but the backlash damaged my body and soul. It had taken nearly a century for me to recover. That was back when I was working for the Inquisition.

I met Ramada when we were both after the Mundane version of the Lance—him for a collector who'd employed him, me to prevent another catastrophe. The Mundane Lance didn't have the power of Faerie magic, but it did have the power of faith. I destroyed it before some Nazi-wannabes used it to rally an army—and Grace nearly died because of it.

Cambridge nodded to acknowledge my correction. "Yes, my client was most disappointed, I'm afraid. Fortunately, I found something else to distract his interest. Well, I shall leave you to puzzle out your own journey to your seats. It was a pleasure to have met you, Sister Grace. Vern thinks quite highly of you, and I do see why." He bowed slightly to Grace and pushed himself through the crowd of tables, like a frost-covered tanker sailing through the icebergs. I followed him with narrowed eyes.

"Don't invite trouble," Grace warned.

"I never invite trouble. It breaks in through the window," I grumbled.

"Grace!" A lady in a long T-shirt and peasant's skirt skipped up to Grace and gave her a hug. When she pulled back, Grace introduced her as Eliza Smithing, one of the coordinators. Eliza looked me over, and her eyes widened with awe. She set a hand on her chest. "Oh, this is such an honor. You've no idea! So many of us—dozens, scores, maybe even hundreds—are completely thrilled that you could come. We're also deeply sorry you aren't a panelist, but perhaps you could just join some of us one evening and talk?"

You know, I could get to like Mensans, after all.

Eliza found us a more suitable spot in one of the corner tables and even asked if I would be more comfortable if I had a large platter on the floor. Of course, I would have, but I learned within a few weeks of living on the Mundane side of the Gap that if I wanted to get along with non-Faerie humans, I needed to act as human as dragonly possible, so I made do with the too-short table. Just call me a conformist.

Our tablemates proved polite conversationalists. I answered the usual questions—I'm omnivorous; I used to eat people; they were not my dish of choice.

"What about virgins?" one asked and was promptly kicked under the table by his wife.

"They taste the same as anyone else. Knights were different. Some tasted like chicken."

It didn't take long for them to get the joke. Yeah, I could get used to Mensans.

We settled down to a real meal of chicken served by a rather nervous waitress. Pretty soon, even she loosened up, and when someone ordered beers for the table and told her to surprise us with the brand, she brought back Kirin.

"Because the logo is half dragon," she explained as she set the bottles in front of us.

"This must go great with Knight a la King," said Lucy Cisneros, a petite Hispanic across from me. Before I could respond, her husband, Frank, cut in with "Spam in a Can." I raised my bottle to salute their puns and poured about half into my mouth. I noticed a guy a couple of tables over eying me with particular intensity. I didn't return his gaze but saw through my peripheral vision that he was taking notes.

Sid, who was an economist at Mary Washington, was asking about the strict prohibitions the Faerie had on the import of Mundane technology and the export of magic. "It's isolationist in design."

"It's not about isolationism," Grace countered, "so much as protecting both universes."

"Like ITAR laws," I said, referencing the federal regulations on the sharing of certain kinds of technology and information. "In your case, the United States doesn't want to share technologies that can be weaponized against them. For us, it's more about protecting the ignorant—and trust me, most sapients are ignorant."

"What he means," Grace said with affectionate exasperation, "is that magic is hard to learn and harder to control. Humans, like trolls, don't have the ability to wield magic on their own. They have to rely on trinkets."

"Like a wand?"

I snorted. Grace set a hand on my flank. "Wands are a Mundane construction. At best, they would hold magical energy, like a battery."

"For a human to use a wand would be the equivalent of holding a battery and thinking that made them a radio," I said. I pulled out one of Grace's medallions and passed it around. "But there are artifacts that can hold magic and a spell for a specific purpose. This one, for example, is for healing."

"Are you expecting to get hurt?" Lucy asked.

"I never expect to get hurt. Doesn't mean it won't happen, and being so far from the Gap and its supply of magical energy, I can't rely on my natural healing here." I felt a sudden vulnerability and suppressed a shiver. I resisted the urge to check the medallions Grace had filled with magic simply for me to "feed" off of. I resolved to eat more to help sustain myself. I would make liberal use of room service and charge it to Bishop Aiden.

Meanwhile, Grace was explaining the medallion. "I made this one with blessed magics. That means it will work as God wills not as Vern commands. Secular magics allow more mortal control, which means mortal misuse."

I told them about my first case, where a greedy, entitled young Mundane secured a "love" charm to manipulate a girl into falling for him. At the same time, his father had stolen a magical tree and ground it into fertilizer to increase crop yield. It had. It also turned the plants into murderous revenge seekers. Two people died before I'd figured out what had happened.

"Alright," Frank said, "but why not allow Mundane technology? I understand bombs, but can you go wrong with a microwave?"

"That requires electricity, which requires infrastructure. And we are working on some of that, just more slowly than entrepreneurs here would like," Grace said. "But we're taking care. You're talking about introducing twenty-first-century technology to a technologically underdeveloped world. A lot of it is disruptive, and not in the good sense. Cars, for example. Mundanes forget that when Ford first made the Model T popular, its top speed was forty-five miles per hour. It took generations to develop the cars you have now, and your infrastructure, rules, and reflexes developed with them. Imagine the havoc an uninitiated Faerie human can create with a Humvee going eighty on roads built like those of your seventeenth century."

"Then there's the iron in your steel, and the exhaust, which is far more dangerous to some Magicals than to humans," I added. "Trust me—those prohibitions are keeping both sides of the universe safer, and even then, some stuff gets through."

"Like Shogzallie," Eliza said.

"We're still cleaning up from that one, and it started as an 'innocent' song." I glanced an apology to Grace. She'd known something was off about "Mishmash," and I'd not believed her until it had summoned proto-empyrie monsters. So much for my incredible memory.

As if reading my thoughts, Eliza asked, "Your business card says, 'Wisdom of the Ages,

Knowledge of Eternity.' Are you that knowledgeable, or is it advertising?"

I shrugged. "I don't know as much as in my pre-George days, but more than Wikipedia, that's for certain." Whereupon we engaged in a friendly game of Stump the Dragon, which I won, naturally, and got myself banned from Trivia night in the process.

After dinner, we were invited to a mixer, but I'd been ignoring my padawan's texts for the last half hour. I figured I owed him a call. All in all, Grace and I left the banquet that night feeling a lot more optimistic.

At least about the convention.

It was just after eight when we returned to our room, which was after six, Colorado time. My phone had four texts and two phone calls, all from GapHQ. I ignored them. Why get everything second-hand from his mom? Instead, I called my padawan directly, putting it on speaker for Grace to listen in, too.

"'Bout time," Ron's irate voice answered. He sounded a bit muffled. In the background, I heard the scraping of stainless steel on porcelain. He must be home stuffing his face. One side effect of using his abilities was calorie superburn.

"Accent, Padawan," I warned.

I heard a faint swallowing sound. "I don't have an accent, friend dragon," he replied in his signature Gapman intonation—Mid-Atlantic with a touch of Leeds, England. "Nor did I have sufficient preparation for today."

Grace and I exchanged glances. "Did something happen in Los Lagos?"

"Something happened in Tokneo! You could have told me we were dealing with MOUSs."

"Moose?" Grace asks, but I could hear the acronym in his annoyed tone.

"Moles of Unusual Size?" I guessed.

"Yes, Moles of Unusual Size! That was not amusing, Vern! I went to a MOUS hunt with a butterfly net and a hamster cage."

Then Kenjo's words came back to me. "Right big" he'd called them. I'd assumed he meant big for moles, not big enough to be worthy of a hobgoblin hunt. That made them the size of boars. "Oh. Oops."

"Quite right, 'Oops.' I was expecting to scoop them into a basket or something, not go fist-to-claw with them. One of them swung at me and my supersuit clanged. How do you make magic and Spandex clang?"

As he went on with a graphic and detailed description of the hunt, Grace asked quietly, "We searched that area for proto-empyrie after Shogzallie. How did we miss them?"

I shrugged. "Hiding underground? Hibernating until Leesi's garden attracted them?"

Gapman had continued, "...then the ground opened up and, and accepted them!"

"Very poetic," I commented.

"Very creepy! Hitchcock/Stephen-King-level creepy! I couldn't move fast enough to stop them from tunneling away. Anyway, they've gone to ground now, so we're starting again tomorrow. I'm taking my Winchester, and I called the bishop for magical backup. He said he'd send us a Sister Eloise. She's supposed to be good with magical beasts and shield spells."

Sister Fangirl! The first time I'd met her, she couldn't stop staring starry-eyed at me. I hadn't experienced such adulation in ages, and I'd lapped it up. I wondered if the hunt would last long enough for us to see her when we returned. "Great idea. She can keep them from escaping. Tell her we said, 'hi.'"

Gapman snorted, exasperated. "Of course. And have you any useful advice to pass on?"

"Bring a shovel. That worked well against the wasps," I said, since he asked. "Hey, how come you insisted on calling the Wasps of Unusual Size 'Murder Hornets' instead of WOUSs, but the moles get to be MOUSs?"

"Because nothing with a foot-long stinger should be called a wuss."

We discussed a little longer. Kenjo was apparently satisfied with the day's hunt, but he thought they had at least another day or two of work, especially now that the moles were aware of their presence. Ron had introduced them to the idea of mole thumpers to drive them out of their holes.

"Maybe we can pour water into their tunnels and flood them out, but that's going to take a firehose—an actual firehose," he added.

Soon, he'd calmed down (I'm sure the food helped) and we ended the call with him suggesting that we check out the GapFan app. One of the hobgoblinettes had taken a video.

At first, it looked like Gapman was hugging a large, fluffy teddy bear, while the hobgoblins surrounded him calling out encouragement. It was almost cute. Then one of the obscenely wide paws reared back for a strike and you saw the claws were as big as Gapman's forearm. It backhanded the nearest hobgoblin and sent him flying into his buddy.

At that point, the others pounced, but they only succeeded in toppling Gapman onto his back, MOUS and hunters flattening him. A few moments of struggle as the hobgoblins stabbed and speared the beast, then with a roar of effort, Gapman flung them all off. The mole rolled, shook off its attackers, and ran. Gapman rushed toward it—he was a green-and-gold blur on the screen—but it caught him with a swipe. His suit did indeed clang.

Grace winced, but I thought he was doing pretty well, all things considered.

Gapman had commented on the video: As the day went on, our teamwork improved, and we were able to remove seven of these oversized pests. I've acquired a great respect for these hobgoblin hunters. *#KeepingLosLagosSafe*

#TeamworkMakesTheDreamWork #OurSuper-powerIsFriendship.

Now it was my turn to wince, but his comment had already earned over 3500 likes.

Grace and I did our nightly devotions, then she went to sleep while I wandered the hotel. I wanted to get the lay of the land and know exactly where everyone and everything was, all the possible routes into, out of, and around the building, including the ones accessible to flying creatures, and whatever might help me prevent or alleviate trouble. More than that, dragons are territorial creatures, and as far as I was concerned, Citrus Stars was now my territory.

The sun had set, and the nearly full moon played hide-and-seek in the scattered clouds, so I activated a stealth charm and took a flight around the building and the compound. Our section was pretty quiet, but the guitar convention predictably was in full swing; I had to shut my ears against the cacophony of twang, squeal, and static. I said a quiet prayer of thanks that Grace had managed to move Gozon and everyone else who got misassigned out of that building.

In the playground, a couple was making out on the bench; I toyed with the idea of popping up behind them and giving them the scare of their lives but quelled the urge. After all, they might buy into the "dragons eat virgins" mythos and decide to do something sinful (in the interest of saving her life, of course. Why is the cliché only for women?) And that would set me back as well.

Lead me not into temptation—even as a practical joke.

After taking note of the doors, windows, fire escapes, and any other openings a resourceful burglar or playful pixie might make use of, I toyed with the idea of ranging out further. The fireworks were starting over at Fanny Flamingo's Fantasyland, however, and Grace's stealth charm could only do so much. I returned to the balcony and without waking my nun, crept out into the hallway to make the rounds indoors.

The Citrus Stars followed a simple floor plan—two long arms of rooms joined at a 120-degree angle, with snack machines and elevators at the join and on each end. The heat and humidity left me thirsty after my flight, so I headed to the nearest ice machine. Out of consideration for human sensibilities and the fact that the door would snap shut on my nose, I used the scoop to get the ice and pour it into my mouth. I crunched the first scoop, then let the next melt in my mouth while I listened.

In the elevator, probably two floors below me, I heard the rustle of chiffon and some low giggling. Brunhilde. Guess she wasn't just interested in comfort after all. The elevator dinged, and she and her friend exited on the floor below me. Remembering what Grace had said, I turned my attention to the stairway and was not surprised to hear soft but heavy footsteps. Siegfried, I guessed. The stairwell door below me opened partway, paused, then creaked a little more, and I imagined the great hulk of a Norwegian gathering himself up for a confrontation. Great.

I headed to the stairs. I'm not really built for them, but a dragon's got to do what a dragon's got to do. Just as I'd put my paw on the door to rush down to stop him, however, I heard the footsteps retreating back down the stairs. Good boy, Sig.

Then I heard the sound of a pen on paper from my hallway, and as I turned, footsteps scuttling hastily away.

The pen may be mightier than the sword, but since my dragon version of Spidey senses weren't tingling, I decided not to pursue Scribbles and started my patrol instead. With most of the patrons asleep, I let my tail slide behind me and prowled the hall like a dragon, senses open not only to sights, sounds, and smells beyond human ability to pick up, but also for magic. At this point, I was more interested in identifying and making note of Faerie occupants and any wards or magical items they may have set up.

I traversed the fifth, fourth, and third floors without any more surprises. Unless you count that Cambridge snored a lot less than I'd have expected for someone of his bulk. I saw my note-taker on occasion, writing in his pad and ducking behind corners when he thought I might be looking his way.

He actually wasn't half bad, I thought to myself as I took the elevator to the second-floor conference rooms. Very calm, no sudden movements or anything furtive. He wasn't trying to be sneaky, as if he wanted to ambush me. Rather, he seemed to strive for unobtrusiveness, like he didn't want to interrupt but wanted to watch, though exactly what he was watching or why, I didn't know.

Natura's always telling me I need to be more tolerant of other people's idiosyncrasies. Didn't keep me from wondering, though.

I was entertaining myself with several amusing possibilities as the elevator doors opened, and didn't notice the security guard until he'd backed away with a yelp and drawn his gun. It was just a Taser, but I knew how uncomfortable those could be.

I sighed and sat in what was my most non-threatening posture, just outside the elevator, tail tucked close to keep it from getting caught in the door. "Let me guess. You didn't get the memo?"

"Don't hurt him! He's not dangerous!" Suddenly my shadow burst from the stairwell and threw himself between us, arms wide, a notebook flapping in one hand.

"What the heck?" demanded the guard. He lowered the gun but kept it ready. In a way, I had to admire him. At least he didn't assume I was some animatronic practical joke.

"He, officer, is *draco africano faerie*, having originated in Caraparavelenciana, in the

Rivaldebahn mountain range, a land in Faerie approximately where our Ethiopia lies today—"

Hey, he'd read my vitae. Wish he'd read my résumé. "More to the point, I'm Vern of the Dragon Eye Private Investigation Agency, hired by the Duchy of Peebles-on-Tweed to oversee the security of the Faerie." Slowly, I reached into my lanyard pouch and pulled out our card and bona fides. I don't know if my talking or my paperwork reassured him more, but he holstered his gun, finally, and took them from my claws cautiously.

"Why didn't we get told about this?" he grumbled as he squinted at the card. My shadow, assured of my safety, stepped to the side.

I answered, "For the same reason we never got introduced to hotel security? Someone didn't think about it."

"Are any of the Faerie dangerous, then?" he asked, suddenly all business. I liked that.

"About as dangerous as any human, I suppose. Meaning, you can never tell.

He grimaced, then introduced himself. "I'm Cory Delastrade. Listen, we should go to my office and I'll make a copy of this for the day shift. Get your picture, too, if you don't mind."

I grinned. "Sure. You know, you're taking this remarkably well."

"Ah, shoot. I've seen you on MeTube. I knew there were a bunch of Faerie guests. Been half expecting a centaur or a troll—"

"He didn't come. The Bridge group is about cards, not construction."

Cory snorted. "Thing is, when I first saw you, I thought some brainiac had set an animatronic animal loose."

"Don't start with me about animatronics!"

Wisely, he turned to my would-be protector. "So what's your story?"

"Bill Reed. I'm working on a master's degree in Faerie zoology, and well..." Suddenly he turned redder than me.

"This isn't my natural habitat and you're not *National Geographic*," I told him. "Tell you what, though; buy me lunch and I'll answer your questions."

"Deal!" He scribbled his room and phone numbers on a sheet of paper and handed it to me. "In that case, I think I'll turn in. A pleasure to meet both of you." He shook Cory's hand and gave me a little bow.

When the elevator doors had closed on his smiling countenance, Cory gave me a wry grin. "Get a lot of that?" he asked.

"Not as much as you would think, especially lately. The locals at home have gotten used to me."

"Yeah, right," Cory said, "though you'd think you'd blend right in here."

"I did get mistaken for a ride earlier," I said. "Come to think of it, where was the day shift when I was getting whacked in the face by an overprotective mother?"

"Probably at the GitPicCon. They had a disturbance in the exhibit hall. Never did figure out if it was over a guitar or a girl. Not sure they even knew."

Something pinged my audio radar and I lifted my head to listen. "Girl," I told him.

"How d'you figure?"

"'Cause they're fighting again. And it sounds like he brought friends."

Cory swore and got on his radio to his partner. "They don't pay me enough," he grumbled as he punched the elevator button. It opened immediately.

"Want some backup?" I offered as I slid into the elevator with him.

He looked at me, considered the effect of a dragon breaking up a bunch of marauding metalheads, and laughed. "This may not be such a bad night after all."

Chapter Eleven: Bedlam and Brownies

There's nothing like a bloodcurdling scream to wake you up in the morning.

The rest of my night had gone rather quickly. First I, Cory, and his partner Joe handled the fight in the playground. What I'd thought was a fight over a girl turned out to be a rivalry between two local gangs who thought an Irish folk metal concert would make a good backdrop to their posturing. While Cory called the local police, I broke up the violence with a strafing run over their heads. It was so satisfying to hear the screams.

Most of them scattered, but one guy decided he was going to catch the "flying lizard." He must have been related to the Irbys. He did share Mr. Irby's slack jaw and lack of common sense. All he needed was an ill-fitting T-shirt and an oversized camera. But the hoodlum was one of the instigators, and Bishop Aiden did say I was to have some fun. I landed, lured my prey into a false sense of security with a couple of feints and jinks, then when he charged, I leaped into the air over him and smacked him to the ground with one paw on the back of his neck.

I set my mouth close to his ear so he could feel my hot breath. "Stay still now, Meat."

"It talks!" he shrieked, then passed out.

I heard a gasp from the bushes and saw one of his buddies with his phone out.

"He'll be fine," I told him as I zip-tied his alpha. "Arrested, but unharmed. This time. Just like anyone else I catch. Go tell your buddies I don't want to see them misbehaving here again."

Cory and Joe had managed to tackle and restrain a couple of others. I found one from the rival gang heading toward a concert, probably hoping to blend in. I gave him the same message and let him go. I've found in Los Lagos that catch-and-release can be an effective means of keeping the peace as well.

By the time I'd gotten back, the local police had arrived and demanded I explain myself—not my participation in the bust, mind you, but my existence. It'd been a long time since I'd had to explain that I was indeed sapient, tame, and—this gets me every time—housebroken.

"I have better control over my bowels than you, officer. Want me to prove it?" I finally told the uniform after the third such question. I asked sweetly. I can be diplomatic.

After the cops had packed the last of the captured troublemakers into the squad car and had grudgingly admitted that I didn't need a license or rabies tags, the concert had ended and people were heading back to their rooms.

I was about to join Cory and Joe for some coffee when a familiar voice shouted my name.

I spun toward it. "Ray?"

"It is you!" Ray Rojas, known in our gaming circle as "Sir Balastar the Red," dashed up to me in surprise and joy. "Holy cow, Vern! I thought I was dreaming—or maybe you were animatronic."

"Don't get me started!" Quickly, I explained my assignment as an underpaid babysitter and introduced him to my new friends.

"You're Faerie, too?" Cory asked.

Ray looked at his costume—an upgrade from the bardic outfit he'd worn when we did adventure in Faerie, if by "upgrade" you meant louder colors. "Me? No. I was the opening act for Iluded."

"No!" When Titania, Queen of the Midsummer Court had granted him the ability to memorize any song he heard, she'd not made any promises as to the quality of his performance, and he'd been pretty bad back in the day.

"Yeah! It's amazing what practice and lessons can do."

I promised to meet Cory and Joe back at the security office for the six a.m. shift change so I could meet Gary Spade and Janey Taylor of the day shift, and I and Ray went to get some coffee and catch up. I returned to my room in time to join Grace for morning devotions and settled myself on my big bed for a luxurious sleep.

Naturally, that was not to be. Sometimes, I think God has proscriptions against my luxury.

The scream which had disturbed my well-earned sleep was coming from the other end of the wing, but by the time I'd thrown myself out of bed, the shrieks had morphed into vows of vengeance, so I relaxed. No one had been murdered.

Yet. We'd see what happened when the cranky and sleep-deprived dragon got to the scene.

Grace was already out of her bed and tossing on her habit. As she tucked her hair into her wimple, she said, "I've got this. Go back to sleep."

"Too late. I'll make up for it with a big breakfast." Dragons could trade sleep for food, and vice-versa. Even so, Grace gave me a concerned look before agreeing.

When we got to the room, Gary was shooing people from the scene. I nodded at him, and he let us pass.

"What's the problem?" I asked as I moseyed into the room. It was a smaller version of ours with a bathroom and closet flanking a narrow hall to the bedroom itself and done in the same tasteful but neutral color scheme. Soaps posed at forty-five-degree angles to the corners of the sinks, which almost sparkled in the fluorescent lights. Towels folded with five-star hotel precision... Either the maids had just cleaned or the occupant was a neat freak. Grace was already there, checking for magic, while a pajama-clad male Caucasian with thinning blond hair watched, his back to me.

"The problem? This is the problem!" he shouted and indicated the room with a theatrical sweep of his arm. The momentum from his gesture spun him until he was facing me. His rant died in his throat and became a small gurgle.

"Nick," Grace interceded cheerily, arms out for a hug, which he gratefully gave, though his gaze never left me. "We met last night? Sister Grace, and this is my partner, Vern."

I gave him my best tame dragon smile—me and Puff, we're like brothers, really—then looked around the immaculate room. "Something's missing?" I ventured.

"It's not that! Everything's... organized!" Losing his fear of me in his rage, he stormed to a freshly polished drawer and yanked it open. The shirts inside were folded more neatly than for a Nordstrom's Grand Opening. I glanced at the open closet, where the pants and Bermuda shorts were similarly perfect.

My imitation of human facial expressions must have gotten pretty good, because he glowered at my bemusement. "I'm color-blind! Before I left, my wife packed everything in coordinating outfits. Now I have to get someone to help me match everything. That's just embarrassing. And then there's this!" He shoved a puzzle magazine at me. *The Giant Travel Book of Magic Squares*.

He continued, "I know Sudoku is popular, but I happen to enjoy these. But someone's gone and filled them all in—wrong! In pen! Stupid, pranking..."

Grace offered to help Nick get his clothes coordinated while I perused his book. At first glance, it did look like random numbers, every number less than 19, some with halves, even some with letters. Nonsense.

If you were using the standard Mundane number system, that is. I didn't know whether to be amused or exasperated. What were Shoemaker Brownies doing on this side of the Gap? And in Florida? They weren't on the *Cloudskater*'s manifest.

I held the book under my nose, nostrils twitching, but I didn't smell anything other than paper and ink and all the stuff that gets on human hands that they never notice. I wasn't expecting anything, really. Brownies can cover their tracks very well when they don't want to be caught—and they never want to get caught.

Nick took one of the outfits Grace picked for him and ducked into the bathroom to change. Grace went to work on the rest. "Well, it's definitely brownies," she said.

"But why would they come to this room?" Janey asked, echoing my thoughts.

"And who brought them?" Brownies were essentially invisible. We never saw any on the airship, and none had been on the passenger list. But it did explain the cargo hold. That's one mystery solved.

"Who?" Nick asked as he came out of the bathroom in a pale blue polo and navy Dockers. He reached into the closet for his shoes, then sat on the bed to put them on. Suddenly, he stopped and looked at the sole of his clean and polished loafer.

"Broken before?" I asked.

"Just starting to tear. I noticed it at the airport. How did you know?"

"You, my friend, have had the privilege of living a fairy tale. While you slept, the wee folk snuck into your room and cleaned. They repaired your shoes—and probably anything else they found broken. They even finished what they thought was your work," I told him as I tossed the magic squares book on his bed.

"But it's all nonsense!"

"Actually, it's a legitimate numbering system—and one you're slightly familiar with, though it's far more complex than the one Mundanes use. You like a good mental challenge, right?"

Grace and I left him with a closet of neatly pressed coordinating outfits, a charm to keep out any future "assistance," and a grin on his face as he dove into his puzzle book, scribbling in the margins and trying to work out the number system. Crisis averted and no crime to report, Janey went back to her office.

"What are brownies doing here?" Grace wondered as we headed down the hall.

"Not selling cookies, that's for certain."

Neither of us was grinning. Faerie brownies would not be at this convention on their own. Someone brought them. That meant that someone coaxed them to "clean" that room.

Somehow, I couldn't believe it was a random act of kindness. At least it narrowed our suspects to those who could use magic.

I said as much to Grace, speaking in Faerie Gaelic against the curious ears of the Mundanes poking their heads out of rooms or passing in the hall. Once we got to our room, she checked the confirmation records against the computer assignments we found and the final room assignments.

She said, "That room was assigned to Gozonvabosomofic in the mix-up. I got Gozon upgraded. I checked; there's no trace of harmful magic or substances, and Nick didn't find anything missing. Seems to me that they were directed to the wrong room and, as long as they were there, did what comes naturally."

"Except Gozon doesn't like brownies," I protested. "In the centuries I've known him, he's never once allowed someone else to handle his stuff. Neurotic that way." Last night, I'd noticed that in addition to the "Do Not Disturb" sign on the doorknob, Gozon had put up security spells around his room.

"Breakfast?" I asked. Brownies didn't pose any danger, and my stomach was protesting. If I couldn't sleep, I could make up for it with a good meal.

Grace shook her head. "I don't think there's time. I need to tune my harp and get ready for my lecture. Remember how neat the luggage was in the airship? The purser only knew someone had tampered with it because everything was rearranged. No one's reported anything missing, either. So perhaps Nick's room wasn't just cleaned—it was searched?"

"Looks like it. So we're back to who and why." I twitched my tail in annoyance.

More work we weren't getting paid for.

Chapter Twelve: Food Fight in the Con Café

The room where Grace was giving her lecture was on the other side of the compound. As we cut across the green, we saw a bunch of Mundanes doing yoga on the grass near the lake. The naiads had decided to join them, including Lilly, who was doing her poses atop the alligator, which was floating on its back in contentment.

Just as we passed, the instructor called out the mermaid pose. I tensed, but the naiads gaily complied.

"I'm a mermaid!" one called out with mean girl sarcasm as she assumed the pose. "I'm so stretchy and I have a pretty tail!"

She waggled her feet.

"Oh, no!" cried another. "I broke a scale!" The ones around her squealed in mock concern.

We left them to their giggles and continued on our way.

Grace's lecture room had a very nice placard with her name and "Faerie or Mundane, Yet Still Divine: The Similarities and Differences of Liturgical Music Across Dimensions." We peeked inside to see forty or more people already settled into the tightly packed chairs, talking quietly or reading. I even saw a couple of GitPicCon T-shirts in the crowd.

I purred approval. "Nice turnout."

"Mmm-hmmm," Came Grace's tight reply. I felt tension and fear come off her in waves.

I turned to regard her. "You're nervous?"

"I haven't given a lecture in over a hundred and fifty years, not even to grade-schoolers." She looked across the crowd like she was looking into the maw of Hell itself.

"You lecture me all the time," I teased.

That broke her spell. She snorted, "Aye, but that would be a different kind of lecture, now, wouldn't it?"

I gave her my most reassuring grin, the one that warmed my gaze. "You've sung at papal ordinations. You've battled monsters. You've even fought demons."

"But that was music. That's my Calling."

"Well, you've been called to do this, and it's music-related. You'll be fine."

And after a couple of stutters and false starts, she was. It helped that she had an intelligent and interested audience who asked good questions. Afterward, people thronged her, wanting to share contact information, argue her premise, or find out when she planned to publish her work. When I sensed the attention-getting to be too much, I stepped in and rescued her. The dragon as a Knight in Shining Armor—there's a twist.

"You know, you really should publish," I said as we headed out, folks backing away to let me through.

"You know, maybe I will," she replied happily.

We put off breakfast to attend the lie detector seminar, which meant my stomach was growling when we finally entered the conference café, which everyone called the "con café," with the accompanying jokes about food being so bad it should be illegal.

But not this year. Rather than the usual snack foods and fruits, they had an elaborate spread thanks to the special guest, Jean Pierre Bargedecurie, a human chef from Faerie Southern France.

The serving tables were loaded down with food fit for kings—better than our Duke Galen got, that's for certain. Diners formed a line from the banquet table to the door.

People of all species packed the room; some had even braced themselves against the wall, eating while standing. The balcony doors stood closed, and no one was interested in heading out. The thermometer had already given 100 degrees a passing nod on its way up, and people preferred to crowd under the AC.

I saw a fair number of Faerie mixing among humans. Most seemed to have stuck with their hosts from the night before. Like last night, Brunhilde stood out. This time, the Valkyrie Vamp wore an off-the-shoulder peasant's blouse and styled her long blonde hair in sensuous curls that she flipped back with practiced ease as she leaned toward Cambridge Ramada and, with a corner of her napkin, dabbed something off his chin. He thanked her with his usual casual politeness, but his eyes sparkled. Several men watched on enviously.

I'd started to point the pair out to Grace when something far more pressing attracted my attention.

I actually smelled him even before I saw him, in human form and wearing tight leather pants and a black T-shirt, over which he'd tossed a dowdy tweed jacket. Guess that was his nod toward intellectualism. His overwhelming cologne might be enough to fool humans, but with my nose, there's no mistaking the smell of dog. Bacri Sauvage—could he get any more cliché? I groaned inwardly. Of all the cafeterias in all the hotels, why did he have to bring his fleas into mine?

"Let's spring for room service," I started to suggest, but it was already too late. Coyote's nose was as good as mine.

"Sister Grace! Vern!" Coyote shouted as he approached, smiling like a Labrador and trailing, as always, a couple of happy ladies. His membership button sported several green "hug me" stickers. His hair, dark and stylishly wild, went perfectly with his long nose and proud Native American features—or so it seemed, based on the number of ladies I'd seen fall to his charms.

Coyote, the trickster of Native American legend and North American Faerie reality. This assignment just got tougher.

"What are you doing here?" Grace tried not to sound accusatory. Despite the fact that she, too, wore a green sticker, she backed up a step.

I wasn't so polite. "Why aren't you in a Montana jail where we put you?"

Coyote had been a thorn in our side for years. The last we'd seen him, an irate judge had sentenced him to thirty years, plus ten more. He probably could have avoided the extra ten if he hadn't been flirting with the judge's teenage daughter who was there for "Take Your Child to Work Day."

Coyote gave us his best whipped-dog look. "I'm out on parole. Good behavior."

"Better lawyers," I snarled. I noticed Grace's face pinch, then smooth as she fought the urge to laugh.

"In fact," he said with some dignity, "my new lawyer got a retrial. That whole thing with Caitlyn—" he grinned a little as he said the name— "was just a cultural misunderstanding. Plus, the reservation adopted me, and I've dedicated myself to alleviating the plight of my people." One of his groupies sighed.

Plight of his people? He was a plight on his people. I noticed that he didn't mention which reservation. "That doesn't explain why you're here."

"I'm a Mensan—and a panelist. Hug me!" At his yell, several people around us jumped up for a group hug.

Yep. There went my appetite. Just as well. The line seemed to have stalled.

"What panel?" I asked. Behind him, I saw Jean Pierre approach a tall man in the line with a plate in his hands.

"'Thinking Outside the Box,' of course! But you're here, too! I'm sorry I missed your lecture, Grace. I saw you're also on the 'Magic in Music' panel, but what about you, Vern?"

"I'm not," I said, distracted. Jean Pierre had started arguing with the man.

"Oh, you're Grace's sidekick," he cooed. The ladies hanging on his arms giggled.

"I'm working," I replied, making sure my tone held just enough threat that he knew he'd better not cross the line.

Fortunately, a pack animal like Coyote was good at picking up signals. "Don't worry about me. I'm just here for some, uh...intellectual...stimulation and pursuits." He waggled his eyebrows at his friends who didn't so much giggle as titter.

At this rate, I was going to be off my feed for a week. Fortunately, Jean Pierre chose that moment to let loose a blistering torrent of top-volume French.

"I'd better see what's up," I said to the ladies. Without waiting for an answer, I pushed my way through the crowd.

Grace acquiesced to a quick hug from Coyote. After checking the pockets of her robes for anything missing—he might know better than to make a pass at her but was not above a little recreational pickpocketing—she followed me.

By the time we got to the banquet table, Jean Pierre was screaming about hot dogs and chips and the insults to his nation while a tall thin human sporting a tan cowboy hat, rodeo shirt, and jeans and holding a cooling steak on his plate stood there sputtering. Jean Pierre grabbed his chef's hat and was about to throw it—a traditional challenge in Faerie France. I snaked my tail around his arm and stopped him before he could slam it to the ground.

"So, what's going on?" I asked in as amiable a tone as I could.

Tex couldn't drop his mouth open any wider, so he paled at the sight of me instead. Thank heaven he didn't drop his plate. It would have taken the intercession of the Faerie Pope to stop an interdimensional incident if he had.

"This, this Mundane!" Jean Pierre spat the word. "He insults my art! He dares to dictate to me—me!—I, who have Cooked for Popes and Kings!"

"I just said that I'd like my steak cooked a little longer," the man muttered like a chagrined child.

"Do you hear?" Jean Pierre shrieked. The blood vessels were throbbing along his forehead, and his eyes were wider than could possibly be healthy. He sneered up at Tex, who, despite having six inches and seventy pounds on the chef, shrank back. Smart man. "What would you know, you leetle man, with your fast food, oversalted and overcooked and bound by ze rules of fear! I come to free—yes, free!—your palates, but no!"

He whirled on Grace, suddenly entreating, his accent thickening faster than cold gravy. "Zey test me, Sister! I, who live in ze tradition of ze de Bargedecuries; I, who learned at ze side of his own father, who Cooked for Popes and Kings—yes, they test me! Zey feed each other swill, yet zey test me on temperatures and hand-washings and fighting ze BAC! If zey want to fight, zey have come to ze right man! I am Faerie! I am *French*!"

In the silence (except for the muffled snickers of diners around us), Grace tried to soothe the fiery French Faerie. Meanwhile, I released him and placed my tail on Tex's shoulder to lead him away to the patio outside. He followed uncertainly; having a dragon's tail pressed against your back was not something to take lightly. Nonetheless, he kept his wits about him, and when we were on the baking balcony, he tried to explain again.

"Look, all I was saying is I like my steak well done. I know it ain't what most people expect from a Texan, but I just always have. I didn't mean any insult."

"Don't worry about it. It's just a cultural misunderstanding," I assured him, borrowing the phrase from Coyote. Meanwhile, chemical processes were going on somewhere behind my stomach. "While the Mundane French fought about religion and government, the Faerie French were fighting over how much pepper to put in the sauce. They had a whole war over desserts."

"You're kidding me."

"Cross my heart. Now, how do you like your steak?"

"Well done. Little crispy on the edges." He was looking at me funny now.

"Give me your plate and stand over there."

A minute later, I handed him back a flame-broiled steak, well, done, crispy on the edges. "Courtesy of Dragon Eye, PI," I said with a flourish. "But from now on, may I suggest you curb your tongue and stick to the chicken?"

Chapter Thirteen: Hobgoblin Havok

Curiosity got the better of me, so after we ate, I attended Coyote's panel. As usual—and I say this grudgingly, no respect intended—he was witty and charming and had everyone eating out of his hands. Didn't scratch himself once, either. Must have mixed a little flea repellent into that cologne of his. I had a vision of him as the spokes...thing?... for some major flea meds company. Or maybe just a new fragrance. *Bacri Frontline—for your truly savage man.*

I was glad I went, though; someone asked him about ancient Native American gods. I chose that moment to clean my claws conspicuously, and he took the hint and told the truth about the relationship of Faerie Native American spirits to the True Creator. He left with more groupies, but no cult followers.

With over two thousand attendees, the convention area was more crowded than I or my tail were comfortable with, so I decided to wander the upstairs halls and try to sniff out any clues about our hyper-hygienic interlopers. I wasn't sure what I was going to find, if I found anything. I still didn't know *if* there was something to find. All we had so far were some mysteriously cleaned-up suitcases and an organized room. Maybe it was just a mistake and a coincidence.

Yeah—and maybe I'd wake up tomorrow with my full size and prowess, the Spell of St. George lifted. Right.

Folks were getting used to my presence and had entered the "hesitantly polite" stage. Rather than flock to me for photos or duck fearfully into doorways as I approached, they now kept a cautious distance, perhaps giving a quick nod and smile, sort of like how you'd treat some incredibly famous celebrity with a reputation for biting off the heads of groupies who annoyed him.

I could work with that, especially today, since I didn't want to be bothered. Brownies could be, for all intents and purposes, soundless and invisible. In fact, it's part of their makeup not to be observed. The only way I would find them was to sniff them out while they were in the act of cleaning. I had enough competing smells without some tourist's body odor overwhelming me.

The problem with brownies who are told to clean is that they're, well, clean. Antiseptic, even. Ever tried to follow the scent of "clean" in a busy hotel? Good thing my sniffer is used to esoteric smells.

Unfortunately, none of them were brownie.

After an unsuccessful hour, I gave up and went to the security office on the off-chance that someone else had reported a random act of tidiness. Amazing smells of meat, roasted vegetables, and sauces wafted from the office and I found Janey at the little table, a book in one hand and a fork in the other, her back to the door.

I poked my head in and roared. "Feed me!"

Janey shrieked and her book flew from her hands

"You are not funny!" she said, her hand on her chest as if she could still her heart that way. Then she checked her uniform to make sure she hadn't spilled anything on it.

I moseyed in. "Sure I am. You should see me on stage. Janey, can you get me a list of everyone in the hotel?"

She rose and went to her computer. "Guests or employees?"

Huh—I hadn't thought of employees. "I wouldn't mind both, though I'm more interested in guests. Seems some Faerie didn't come through the officially sponsored route." When I told her about Coyote, she groaned.

I tilted my head, impressed. "That's one of the most intelligent responses I've heard."

She snorted. "My maiden name is Two-Feathers. My grandmother raised us on stories of the Trickster. If he's a guest, I'm glad I have the police on speed dial. Hey, that Faerie chef sent us some food—way too much food. Help yourself. I'll just be a minute."

As soon as she'd emailed me the lists, she rejoined me at the table. We talked a bit about Coyote, then she asked, "But what about you? Are you one of a kind, or are there others like you?"

"There are seventy Faerie dragons, all created from God's imagining on the Eighth Day, the day after He'd rested. We are unending in life and forever limited in number, but right now, I'm the only one in the world. The rest of my kin have gone into hibernation or hidden themselves. Even I don't know where they are."

I felt a lump in my throat—a ridiculous feeling when you have a throat as long and sinuous as mine. I stabbed a steak with my claw and ate it to force the lump back down.

"I'm so sorry! Why did they go?"

"I'm not sure," I hedged. "They'd held a conclave, but I wasn't there. I was in the middle of a fight with Saint George." I paused to wash down my steak with a bottle of water.

"Whoa! That legend's true?"

"Yep, except he didn't kill me. Dragons are immortal. But he did remove my powers, including my flight, and hurt me so bad that I sacrificed size for healing. I wasn't much bigger than a handbreadth when the fight ended. He wasn't in great shape himself, but somehow, he was alive. It wasn't all fighting, either. George was a pretty competent wizard and skilled statesman. In the end, he'd convinced me that God has some kind of plan for us. Twenty-twenty hindsight, I should have given in sooner, but I was more arrogant in those days. Anyway, once we were able to travel, he took me to the Vatican and presented me to Pope Pius."

"So God wanted a dragon to work for the Church?"

I nodded. Janey was quick. Maybe she could be a Mensan.

"What did the pope make you do?" Janey had finished her meal and reached for a can of soda.

"He stuck me with the moniker 'Vern d'Wyvern' and made me his pet."

She almost did a spit take and choked on her soda instead. "What?"

Just then her phone rang. Still coughing and gagging, she answered. "Security."

I heard the faint voice answer. "Hey, it's the front desk. We've got kids on the roof of the building tossing water balloons at patrons, including some of the Faerie." Even through the earpiece, I could hear Siegfried vowing revenge and complaining about his straw hat.

"I got it," Janey said. She shook her head as she hung up and grabbed her rain jacket. Smart cookie. I followed her to the elevator, which she commandeered for the two of us.

"The roof is locked. How'd they even get up there?" she complained. She'd had to turn a key to get access to that level.

"Mensan kids?"

"Why don't they go study for Harvard or something then?"

"Maybe it's an experiment on gravity and fluid dynamics?"

She snorted, but quickly turned stern as the elevator stopped at the roof. She strode to the outside door and shoved it open with a bang. The heat hit us like a furnace.

"Alright! Party's over!" she shouted before the door had bounced back.

Three middle schoolers in shorts, T-shirts, and—yep—Mensa lanyards were facing our direction, their hands in a bucket that held at least a dozen water balloons. Their heads jerked up at Janey's shout. Then, as one, they flung water balloons in our direction.

I stepped between them and my temporary partner. With outstretched wings, I caught the water balloons and deflected them back at our attackers. I'm good, but I must have had a little help from George at that moment. Every balloon was perfectly deflected to impact upon its owner.

For a moment, they simply stood there, shocked and soggy. Then they looked at each other and back at me.

"Awesome!" they chorused.

After that, it was apparent that no punishment was going to make up for the fact that they'd just had a water balloon fight with a dragon. However, that also meant no future shenanigans with water balloons would top a water balloon fight with a dragon. With their promise not to get into any more trouble—with a stern warning that more trouble would mean expulsion from the hotel and getting into hot water with their parents—we made them get rid of the rest of the balloons in the best way possible—at each other.

A few minutes later, they were laughing and dripping, and they willingly gathered the bits of rubber and followed Janey back down. They also told her how they picked the lock. To be honest, it wasn't hard. Isaac Monroe, the ringleader, had the makings of a competent felon—or a good PI.

I elected to stay and take in the heat. It was hotter than a demon's underbelly—trust me, I know—

but after having spent the last couple of centuries first in the chilly monasteries of the Faerie British Isles, then enduring the winters of Mundane Colorado, I found the cement-baking heat a welcome change. I used to sun myself at Vorago Diabolo—you call the area the Dallol Depression. I used to bathe in the Red Sea, too.

It hadn't been my territory, but I'd claimed the right since I was a red dragon. My childish logic drove my eldestkin nuts. I snickered at the memory.

I vowed later to fly to the Gulf of America and chase the local wildlife while I had a swim.

The heat and my conversation with Janey had left me feeling nostalgic. Mortals could be fun—I flicked a few drops of balloon water off my wing claw—but I missed my kind. I closed my eyes, tried to remember within my body a time when we had all flown together, darkening the daytime sky, our wing flaps rumbling the skies like the thunder we were.

I couldn't do it. Aside from the time when a genie wish artist sent me and my Mundane friends back into my past, I could not remember my time with my kin. God was protecting me, somehow, but I still didn't understand why.

There was a lot I didn't understand. I'd only told Janey half the truth when I said I wasn't sure why my kin had left. The future me had attended the Conclave, where Durrehkeh and Agarrabarresheh had proposed opening our own Gaps and entering other dimensions, other times, there to rule with the respect so many of us thought we'd lost in Faerie.

It was the Original Sin of dragons: to forsake our duty to Faerie and seek aggrandizement in other universes. We were never meant to cross the Gap.

Yet I had.

I snorted to myself. I had, indeed—because I was *told* to, ordered by the Church and a Calling I'd tried to ignore. And as for aggrandizement, I sure hadn't found that here.

As if to reaffirm that, my phone buzzed with a text from Gapman: *There's a bullet hole in the building on Pasu Street. Sorry about that.*

My padawan was supposed to be a good shot. I had a hard time imagining what chaos caused him to shoot an innocent building. No. Scratch that. I could easily imagine the chaos and decided I'd better have him describe its exact scope and shape before my imagination ran away with me.

Gapman answered on the first ring—odd, since he should have been in the middle of a MOUS hunt. "It was totally my fault, and I'll fix it or pay for damages," he said without preamble.

I liked that. High Elves aside, small talk was cheap. In the background, I heard laughing and singing and the sound of tiny teeth tearing into meat. A couple of hobgoblins yelled, "Hi, Vern!" and "He almost killed me, Vern!"

"I did not!" Gapman retorted, which only stirred the proverbial pot. Immediately, I heard him fighting to keep the phone from hobgoblins who were shouting about ducking for cover and bloodbaths. Gapman scolded them to stop exaggerating, that the gun had only gone off once. "And stop climbing up my leg!"

There was a whoosh and the hobgoblin voices faded. I guessed he'd taken to the air. At least Hobgoblins couldn't fly. I heard a soft crunch as Gapman landed on one of the nearby buildings.

"Sorry about that. It was one shot, Vern, I assure you, and the only thing I hit was the building. Hobgoblins are drama queens. Who knew?"

"Explain how Gapman is such a bad shot," I demanded.

Gapman sucked in a breath before answering. "I...was midair. I forgot about the kick."

"Rookie mistake, Padawan!"

"I know. Anyway, the hobgoblins went diving for cover and the moles went underground. We're waiting for Sister Eloise to arrive, and then we're going to try to coax them out."

"No more Tommy gun!" I heard Kenjo call from a distance. He must be climbing the side of the building.

"He's stuck in a genre, isn't he?" I commented wryly

"Indeed." Somehow, even with his Gapman Mid-Atlantic accent, he managed to pour a ton of frustration into that word. "And it's not like I can use that rifle right now, anyway. They bespelled it! When I shoot, it goes 'bang!' and a flag pops out— just like in the cartoons!"

I snickered.

"It's not that funny, Vern! They said if I try anything like that again, it will forever shoot blanks—and *so will I*. Can they do that?"

It took a minute to understand what he meant. In the background, I heard Kenjo chuckling.

"Vern!"

"I'd suggest you cooperate."

"Great," his response was strained and weak. He took a cleansing breath. "Anyway, while we're waiting for Sister Eloise, the ladies cooked up some breakfast. MOUS is actually rather good—kind of like bear, but sweet. By the way, yesterday after the hunt, I managed a quick patrol around town. Things seem to be—"

"Don't jinx it, Padawan!" I warned.

"Yes, Master," he said in his best Anakin Skywalker voice. I didn't think Ron was ever a surly teen, but he did manage the intonation well. In the background, scrabbling of nails on concrete told me Kenjo had made it to the top of the building.

"Do you need me to smooth things over with Kenjo?" I offered.

"Nah. We're copacetic. Aren't we, Kenjo?"

"Gun stupid," Kenjo said. His voice was muffled, but not from distance. He must have brought some MOUS meat with him on his climb and was talking with his mouth full. He swallowed. "Gapman get spear, fight like hobgoblin! Wrestle MOUS like hobgoblin. Besides, Kenjo get idea."

"What idea?" I started, but Kenjo merely said, "Later, later. Gapman come eat. MOUS meat good. Make strong tribe!"

"I think I see Herald Charlie's car," Gapman said. "I'll update you later. Sorry about the building. Have fun in Florida."

After he hung up, I flopped onto the roof concrete and spread my wings to the sun. Between hobgoblins in my home and mischief among the Mensans, I had better appreciate every chance to relax that I got.

Chapter Fourteen: Good Nun/Bad Dragon

Part of me kept trying to say that I was making a treasure hoard out of spare change. So someone brought some brownies to the convention? So they went a little rogue? Was there really any harm in that?

But the part of me that understood the workings of Faerie, Mundanes, and my own luck said there was more to this than hyperactive housekeeping. Instinct said Gozonvabosomofic was at the center of it all. Was there something in that diatribe I'd half-heard? But no, it had been all "the world doesn't understand me" and "my machinations lie undetected by the masses," which could mean anything from "I've made an inspiring speech" to "I will conquer the world!" He'd left no clues to make connections, despite all his hints about some grand purpose for his attending the convention.

I needed specifics. Guess I should implement a time-honored technique of private investigators: Ask obnoxious questions and make a menace of myself. I was going to need Grace to make it work.

I texted her, and she said she was in the Mensa Market. *I'm almost done. Want to meet me down here?*

The Mensa Market was the trade show portion of the conference, where people were selling their books or other wares, and where people who wanted to target the Top Two Percent with geeky T-shirts and ridiculously involved board games could connect with their perfect audience.

The convention center had set the market up in a hangar. At least that's how the convention floor felt. *Cloudskater* could have fit in it with all its air balloons inflated. The booths were arranged in neat rows but in sections dedicated to different themes: book signings, apparel, souvenirs, and yes, highly complex board games that take hours to complete. Booths were separated by tall curtains, but many people had their own setups with shelved walls and display screens. Despite the wide aisles, I'd be doing a lot of slinking around people to get to Grace, so I decided to take to the air.

The list of "authentic artifacts" requested by our Faerie friends and acquaintances included a lot of kitsch and clothes. The garment district was closest, so I checked there first. I didn't see Grace, but I did notice Brunhilde and Templegrass in deep conversation as the pixie examined something lacy Brunhilde was holding. A heavyset woman approached, curious, and Brunhilde gladly included her. I left them as they broke out in titters. Templegrass, sure. The Mundane, I can see, but there's something unnerving about a giggly Valkyrie.

Grace was in the souvenir section, at a booth selling magic and joke items. I landed beside her and scanned the shelves. Whoopie cushions, canned snakes, sneezing powder. Fake poop. I guess Mensans had puerile senses of humor? I knew who Grace had in mind.

"Don't get the duke a joy buzzer. He'll start an interdimensional incident just for a laugh."

Grace nodded. "Aye. They wouldn't make the duchess laugh, anyway, and that was his request. I considered a whoopie cushion, but it had the same problem. He'll want to be using it during a state dinner. We'll have to keep looking. However, I was thinking she might enjoy giving him this."

She showed me a package with a plastic hockey stick, a puck, and a small plastic mat with a field. The label read "Toilet Hockey—improve your putt while you poop!"

I snorted. "He'll never leave the bathroom."

I stretched my neck and perused the other items on display. "Hey—electroshock gum! Can I give it to him? That would make the duchess laugh."

In the end, we decided a rubber slingshot chicken had the appropriate amount of childish hilarity and innocence to amuse the duchess and the duke.

"So what did you want to talk about?" she asked as we left the market together.

I didn't want anyone to overhear, and I couldn't trust that Mensans wouldn't know Esperanto. Switching over to our own private creole— a mix of Tolkien Elvish, Klingon, Irish, and a few siren words outside most mortal's hearing, I summarized the misadventures of our resident superhero, then my thoughts about our own mystery. I concluded, "I think it's the time to stir some things up and see if anything reveals itself. Up for some Good Cop/Bad Cop?"

"Who's the suspect?" Grace asked as we headed back to the rooms.

"No suspect," I told Grace, "but I think Gozon has something to do with this. Those brownies were after his room, and he's established way too many protective spells, even for a pompous paranoiac like him. Plus, his talk keeps nigging at my mind. Maybe if we get him talking again, he'll spill something."

"Just remember I have a panel at ten tomorrow," Grace said.

We rounded the corner to Gozon's wing and saw an elf heading in the other direction. Not Gozon, but someone I knew from way back. "Galendor!" I called.

He stopped as if jerked, then turned and smiled. "Vern!" he called, and as he crossed the hall toward us, continued, "Oh Great Wyvern, Fellow Citizen of the Golden Land, Land of Magic and Beauty, Where the Eternal Winds blow gently on the softly blooming meadows of Caraparavelenciana..."

He managed to make the greeting end as we got within hand-shaking distance. I'd always admired how Galendor could weave Elvish courtesy and Mundane expediency. Class all around. "Galendor, I present to you Sister Grace Ann McCarthy of Our Lady of the Miracles, High Mage of the Faerie Catholic Church, Cantor of Little Flower Parish, She Whose Voice Graces Liturgy and Weaves Magic, and My Partner. Grace, I present the Husband of Princess Galinda Tavendor, Galendoropynphordaladys of the House Eternal Winds."

"Of the Forests," he added, bowing over Grace's hand.

Grace and I exchanged glances. Gozon was a member of the House Eternal Winds of the Shores. In normal circumstances, it was impolite to make the distinction to non-Elves; to do so was one step away from breaking off diplomatic relations. "Galendor, it's only been seventy-five years. Are things that bad already?" I asked.

He smiled, but it had an edge to it I didn't like. "We will resolve it soon. Let us speak of more pleasant topics. You are attending the conference, then? Of course, they would welcome one of your

vast knowledge, your phenomenal wisdom gar-
nered over ages of keen observations—"

"Actually, I'm here to babysit the Faerie," I
grumbled. This was starting to get embarrassing.

His laugh was sympathetic. "Well, you need
not worry about me, my ageless friend. My
Galinda keeps me well in hand."

"What are you two doing here, anyway?"

"Ah! An amusing tale I hope to pass on to our
children's children. Maurena, that copacetic, enthusiastic, distinguished beauty of the Mundane
feel-good television, asked us to be guests on her
show about 'cultural differences and the modern
couple.' They thought it would be enlightening to
have a human/High Elf pairing as guests. Galinda
was quite eager to accommodate so influential a
personality of Mundane society—and she is a big
fan of *The Maurena Show*. You know how it is
with humans; they develop attachments so
quickly.

"While there, we met a Mensan and her husband, and they invited us here after the taping. I
found it uncomfortably last-minute, of course; but
as we told that prodigious lady of the limelight,

such differences bring excitement into a relationship already burning strong in its passion."

That explained why they hadn't traveled with us. Galinda could afford her own personal jet, and she loved things Mundane. I remembered that. The first time I'd met her, she'd been wearing what was supposed to pass for an outfit like those I saw last night at the fight I broke up. Of course, she'd ruined the effect by purchasing designer clothes, when she should have just visited a thrift store. Despite her fascination, she was Faerie royalty, which her choice of mate attested to clearly.

I'd met Galendor about the same time. An unwitting accomplice to the theft of a necklace of hers, he'd been playing some kind of flirty love game with her at her coming-of-age party and had gotten her to take off the necklace and set it aside where his cousins could pick it up. He hadn't known they wanted the relics contained in that necklace—and her—for a ritual of dark magic. It turned out to be my first STUC (Save The Universes Case). Back then, I operated without a partner, but things worked out okay. I even got to be best dragon at their wedding. Interspecies love. So cliché.

"So you're attending the conference?" I asked. He wasn't on the schedule. There weren't a lot of Faerie Mensans yet, Coyote notwithstanding, so I'd be surprised to hear Galendor was a member. And Galinda? Sweet, and spunky when needed, but Galinda was not the sharpest sword in the armory.

"Peripherally. We are not Mensans, of course, but Galinda's father knows some of the guests of honor and has directed us to contact them on the kingdom's behalf."

I nodded neutrally, but I made a mental note to keep a careful watch over Galinda and her "contacts." The Tavendors were well known for their scheming—sorry, political maneuvering. We might pick up some important intelligence this trip as well—something that might even prevent another STUC. I knew too well what trouble the Tavendors could stir up.

I also knew that Galinda enjoyed her comforts and, nice as this hotel was, it was a little below the station of a Faerie princess, even one with a penchant for slumming. "You're not staying in this hotel?"

"The Penthouses in Building Two here have proven adequate. I was supposed to meet Kevin at his room, but I've gotten turned around somehow. In fact, I should probably be going. You know Mundanes and time..."

Before he could begin an Elvish version of goodbye, which takes about fifteen minutes, five when speaking Human, I interjected. "Listen, Galendor. I'm sure you know by now that Gozonvabosomofic of the House Eternal Winds of the Shores is a guest at this convention. I expect you to behave."

His jaw set, but he gave me a courtly bow. "Vern, Great Wyvern, Defender Against Evil, Conqueror of Mysteries, you who once saved my life, the life of my bride, and our very worlds! In gratitude for your selflessness, your valor, and your friendship, I shall exercise the utmost restraint in confronting this *representative* of the House Eternal Winds of the Shores."

Galendor only took three minutes to say, "goodbye." That barely qualifies as an Elvish "see ya," and I marveled at how well he'd picked up Human. It didn't even seem to be an effort to him.

In the back of my mind, however, I was adding things up.

And the sum of it was trouble.

Chapter Fifteen: Cowbell In A Gadda Da Vida

When Grace and I left Gozon's hotel room, the summer sun was setting and our stomachs were growling. We headed to dinner in silence until we were well away from Gozon's door. Once we'd turned the corner, Grace let out a sigh and rubbed her eyes.

"Am I misunderstanding, or did he tell us, 'You're not elves, so mind your own business?'"

I grunted. On the bright side, at least I hadn't missed anything in his earlier speech, despite my lapse of attention. Obviously, he was setting up a surprise—and grounds for justification, if I read his tone right.

I won't bore you with the full details of our interrogation; we were speaking in High Elvish, and it would take a week to read. Here's the Dragon's Digest Condensed Version:

Dragon: (Busting in and sniffing around, snarling, tail lashing.) "Okay, Gozon. What trouble are you hiding, and why did you have to bring it to a Mundane convention?"

Nun: (Placatingly) "Vern. Calm down. We still don't know—"

Dragon: "Yeah, right, we don't! We got brownies searching his old room, Galendor *of the Forests* poking his oh-so-statuesque nose around, and Gozon here was talking yesterday about a plot that will make him 'with it' and 'foxy,' and I'm sure it has nothing to do with posing for the cover of a trashy romance. Something's up, and I want to know what it is and how to contain the damage— and there will be damage, I'm sure—and I don't want to be here past dinner, or I may have to start snacking." (Looks at Gozon meaningfully.)

Nun: (Stepping in dragon's line of sight) "Easy. Gozonvabosomofic may be the victim here. If so, we have a duty to protect him. I'm sure if there's something going on, he'll tell us if we give him the chance—"

Dragon: (Circling past nun) "There will be a victim if I don't find out pretty fast why someone is messing up my 'cushy assignment' with a mystery. If this turns into a Save-the-Universes Case..."

And so on. The important thing to note is that we didn't let Gozon so much as sputter until we'd gotten the message across that 1) Something weird was going on, 2) We knew Gozon was involved, and 3) We wouldn't tolerate any Faerie trouble.

His response was 1) How dare you dictate to a "Grand-Muckety-Muck" of the High Elves? 2) He'd been setting up clues for the past decade, so I should already have context. If I didn't that was my problem, not his, and 3) You'd better keep trouble away or you'll be sorry.

Our part took about an hour. His took four.

Now I sighed. "Guess I should have known better; in his youth, he took on the Dark Elf Evalakkiduznogud and his tribe in single combat—"

"So he said. In great detail," Grace muttered. "Wait a minute—if it's single combat, why say 'and his tribe?'"

"Dark Elves cheat. Point is, he's not just a formidable politician, but a warrior. He wasn't going to be intimidated by an undersized dragon and a nun."

Grace smiled. "Yet we did get out of there before dinner."

"Yeah! We did." Grace always did know how to cheer me up.

Dinner, of course, cheered me even more. We debated room service, but how could a burger compete with Jen Pierre's *coq au vin*? I made myself comfortable in our room while Grace went to fetch some food. She came back with a huge platter of Bargedecurie's fantastic fare, and we settled ourselves to eat in peace.

"So what did we learn?" Grace asked around a mouthful of tuna steak. "I think you're right that Gozonvabosomofic's hiding something. Possibly literally. That place is warded tighter than the Faerie Vatican vaults—and you know what's in there."

I shuddered. I did know—I'd help put some of the artifacts in there and had the memories of the injuries and long recovery times to make sure I never forgot. "Whatever it is, it's good for his tribe or for him. Probably both, judging from his little speech at the pond yesterday. Don't smile at me like that. I was listening."

"Smile like what?" she said, lowering her eyes. She'd probably look like the Virgin Mary if she wasn't biting the sides of her mouth.

I decided not to answer. "Another bad thing: He's actually pleased Galendor is here, too."

Grace picked at her food. "Vern? How bad could a war between the Elves get?"

"Remember that pixie battle you zapped into Ancient Egypt?"

Now it was her turn to shiver. Two tribes of pixies decided to have a turf war over Los Lagos. I thought I'd been smart in getting them to have their war in the form of locusts, but turns out I was tricked by an Egyptian goddess who had engineered the whole thing and was feeding off their deaths. She'd arranged portals to bring them over from the Gap, so that when we arrived on the scene, the battlefield was ankle-deep in grasshoppers. Grace had managed to contain them, then sent the warring beasties to the most appropriate place possible—Ancient Egypt.

"Not I, but God. I was merely His instrument," Grace demurred. "Modesty aside, I do not want to take responsibility for one of the Ten Plagues."

"God does have a sense of humor," I said, then paused to scoop an entire chicken into my mouth. Felt good to eat like a dragon. Once I'd swallowed, I said, "Anyway, that was a minor turf battle. And High Elves don't transform into locusts."

"You don't think Gozonvabosomofic is looking for a technological edge?"

I thought about it, then shook my head. "Wards can't fool my nose. Other than that expensive briefcase of his, the Armani suit, and his Eddie-Bauer-to-DollarFaire casual wear, there's nothing Mundane-made in that room."

"Maybe he's meeting someone?"

"I don't think so, not someone like a weapons dealer. That would mean admitting weakness, and Gozon can't afford to do that—or to imply that the tribe is weak—without risking his position. Plus, think about Gozon's speech—unusually focused on himself. Even the semantics indicated a personal rather than tribal insult."

"Yet, he did mention a war and a weapon." She repeated back a five-minute phrase about the impending conflict and how his people would turn to him. Just hearing it again opened up a new level of meaning, especially when put against his story to me yesterday. That was the thing about Elvish: Even when you're trying to be circumspect and general, you can't help layering meaning within meaning. I'd have to parse the entire thing later to get the real message.

Still. "Yeah, but listen to the allegory—all very traditional, very ancient. 'In the manner of my forebears...' and such. I don't think he's got a new weapon."

"You're sure?"

"No," I said miserably. I was feeling stupid and slow. And we'd only been in Florida a day!

Grace seemed to pick up my thoughts. "You're still ten times the genius of anyone here, including the Mensans. Rest, eat. I'll pray."

We fell into a companionable silence. Faerie have an easier time with silence than Mundanes, I've found. Technology is simply noisier than magic, but that's not the only problem. Mundane humans make more noise than Faerie in general: small talk, singing to themselves, repeating one-liners from some TV show they saw...

I have my own theory for it. Machine sounds hit the ear differently than natural ones. As a dragon, I can tell the difference right away, and a few other Magicals can do the same. Some even migrated away from the Gap after it opened, and several species simply refuse to cross into the Mundane side because of the noise. It's under the radar, so to speak, for humans, but I think that subconsciously, it registers. That's why Mundanes feel the need to introduce even more noise, particularly that of the human voice.

Of course, Mundanes go about it using technology: radios, iPods, sound machines. Even Natura fills her restaurant with recordings of waterfalls and birdsong when she wants to create a relaxing atmosphere. Human ears know the difference, however, but rather than turn off the machines, you work all the harder to improve the technology and, in the meantime, fill the air with talk.

Personally, I think the cell phone craze has less to do with the need to communicate as it does with the need to hear your own voice. Of course, now everyone is texting, so that's been replaced by videos of people yammering about whatever's on their mind while emotional music plays overtop. More noise.

Our lair, built inside of a dwarf-designed artificial mountain, was naturally soundproofed. We've had clients and friends comment on the feeling of peace they get when they walk into our abode. Usually, they feel less need for idle chatter, too. But even then, there was still noise. The hum of the refrigerator, the whir of the fans on our space heater, even the mosquitoish buzz of electricity as it raced through the wires.

Dragons have extremely sensitive hearing. Back in the day, I could hear someone approaching my den from halfway down the mountain; make that a mile from the mountain base for a knight. Shining armor clanks. The smart knights learned how to blend into the sounds. Very few were that smart, but now and then you'd find one—like St. George, naturally.

As compensation for our sensitive ears, we dragons also have the ability to selectively ignore sounds. As Grace and I relaxed, I catalogued and blocked out distractions one by one: the air conditioner, the water rushing through the pipes on its way to a shower or toilet, the elevators (but not the "ding" as it reached our floor; that I focused on. I did not want anyone sneaking up on us, or worse yet—trying to "clean" our room.) Then the road noise, the boats, and airplanes. The human noise: footsteps, idle chatter, complaints about cell phone reception. Finally, the mosquitoes.

Bliss.

"What are you listening to?" Grace asked after about half an hour.

"The waves."

"So go tonight. I can hold the fort until you get back."

I grinned at her. "Has God given you a mind-reading spell?"

She smiled back. "No, but I think I can predict the chaos that will ensue if you go during the daylight hours. Soon as the sun's down, fly on over, enjoy yourself, then find me. There's a dance and a couple of room parties I've been invited to, anyway."

"You sure?"

"I can do without my sidekick for a while. However, I think I'll take a bath before you go. Eliza bought me some bubbles."

Grace celebrated the sunset by singing "Canticle to the Sun," and I headed off to the Gulf in a very good mood. Grace's singing always does that to me. There was nothing as beautiful in all of the universes or Time itself. The Costa kids used to tease that I had a crush on her.

Dragons don't "crush." Still, the world will be...less...when she is gone.

I brushed the thought away as I had the noises of the Mundane world. The song lifted my spirits, the weather was incredible, and the Gulf of America awaited me. I hadn't had a swim in warm, salty water since...well, there was the time when the genie Al'Beah sent me and my gaming friends back to Faerie's past. But that hardly counted. I was washing off the wounds Father Rich had given me when we were reenacting my battle with St. George, before we snapped out of the spell and realized what was going on. There was that little affair in Byzantium... Nah, it didn't count, either, since my attention had been putting out the brimstone some demon had set me aflame with. I hadn't known if genuine Fires of Hell could undo me, and I'm glad I didn't find out. That had been around 1938, I think.

Yeah, long overdue for a warm, relaxing bath.

As the last of the twilight haze gave itself to darkness, I went out to the balcony and launched myself off the railing. It was a clear, cloudless night, so I kept myself high enough to be mistaken for a plane or a drone while low enough to keep from colliding with one. Anyone catching me flapping my wings would mistake me for a bird or a bat. It happened all the time. I don't care how much Mundanes want to believe in magic and magical creatures; even now that they are confronted with the real thing, they'd rather come up with some implausible but comforting non-magical explanation. They'll pass me off as a plane, a hawk, or a Fanny Flamingo publicity stunt.

As I approached the Gulf, the moon shimmered on the small waves, looking more inviting than Grace's bubbles. In the distance, I could see a couple of boats, probably night fishing. Peaceful, calm. I steered away from them toward a large, uninhabited swath. My mouth fell open in a fierce grin.

I folded my wings and dove in like I had that day in the Caspian. Unlike that day in Byzantium, I could enjoy the speed of my descent, the quick sharp impact, the tickling of the bubbles generated by my dive. Momentum carried me down through a school of fish. I opened my mouth and wasted some air laughing. I caught a couple of slower fish in my mouth, forced out the water, chewed, and swallowed. Sushi, dragon-style. This was living.

Suddenly, the water around me lit up with a brief, brilliant flare. I spun around to see a human in a wetsuit swimming away from me as if his life depended on it, large rubber fins on his feet stirring the water. He looked misshapen until I realized he had a tank on his back. In the background, another diver paused long enough to look behind her and scream, bubbles seeping from either side of her mouthpiece and her voice warbling. Air exploded out of me as I laughed. I thought about chasing them. I thought about taking a pose for the camera.

Then I thought about taking another breath.

I broke the surface just as my lungs had started to burn and spread my wings to keep myself afloat. In the distance, I saw the boat that must have held the divers. It seemed to me they'd gone a little farther out than they should have, but scuba diving isn't something I am especially familiar with. As the waves broke and flowed over my wings, I debated swimming over to them and greeting them properly, maybe let them get a picture of my good side.

Then the warmth of the water called me to reconsider. It felt so nice sluicing over my outstretched wings, and I really didn't have much time. Grace would never forgive me if I started a panic; were these Mundanes more or less likely to panic if I approached the boat? There were sharks in the water, so would the crew have weapons?

Just when I'd convinced myself that I probably should head on over, I heard the roar of the boat's engines as it raced away from me. Guess that answered that question. I folded my wings and nosed back down, eager to see what other marine life I could scare up.

By the time I'd returned to the hotel, the breeze from my flight had dried and chilled me, but Grace had thoughtfully turned the temperature in our room up. I waited long enough to warm up, then headed down to check out the dance Grace had told me about.

The elevator doors opened, and I saw Brunhilde and some human I didn't recognize generating their own heat. They broke apart quickly, Brunhilde giving a titter more appropriate for one of Coyote's fangirls than a 175-pound Valkyrie as they exited the elevator. Her date hesitated at the threshold, apparently afraid of crossing me figuratively or literally. Scrawny. Bad skin. Didn't seem her type, but then what do I know?

After an awkward moment I let hang just for fun, she gave her date's arm a sharp jerk that would have toppled him if he hadn't collided with something soft—namely her bosom. He pushed away, sputtering apologies, but she just laughed as she linked her arm in his. They strolled away.

I shook my head. Humans. Or whatever. Dragons don't have an instinct to procreate. Even after millennia of observation, I didn't understand mating practices of sentient beings, and after my experience as a human and dealing with human hormones, I was glad not to. Just thinking about it made me shiver.

I pressed the button for the events floor.

When the doors opened and I heard the music, I felt yet another kind of heat.

In the main ballroom, an Elvish band was playing. The neon purple lettering on the sign near their speakers proclaimed them as F.A.E.: Faerie Acoustic Enchanters. True to their name, they were playing enchanted music. The kind that pulls in unsuspecting humans and keeps them dancing until they die with smiles on their faces and blood on their feet.

I hurried to the ballroom and ducked my head in. From the sweat on the faces and the slightly hysterical laughter of the dancers, I could tell they'd been at it awhile, but not long enough to be in any imminent danger.

I wove my way along the edge of the wall. The band was playing something Latino, and many of the couples were dancing an improvised tango with varying degrees of intimacy. On the other side of the room, a circle of dancers, hands on each other's shoulders, moved in a traditional Faerie Irish step. I lifted my head to get a better look at the dancers and saw Grace's ecstatic face as she sped by my line of vision.

Great. So much for magical backup.

The band was lost in the music as well. They segued flawlessly from Shakira's "Objection" to the Styx's "Come Sail Away." Now that took skill, especially when you take into account that they didn't have a guitar among them. I wondered if they'd heard about the convention in the other building. Part of me hoped not. After hundreds of years of practice, a truly talented band with a good singer could do a lot with a lyre, a pan pipe, and a hand drum. I shudder to think what they could do with Mundane instruments.

Galinda would have loved their outfits. "Faerie grunge": artistically ripped tunics over American military pants in forest camouflage. A couple of them even had combat boots. Their pointed ears glittered from earrings that went all the way to the point, but I knew these were clip-ons. No elf, self-respecting or otherwise, would pierce his ears. Their naturally smooth and flowing hair was kinked, dyed, and sticking out in unlikely directions. I wondered if they used enchanted mousse.

As I slunk around to them, I considered my battle plan. I couldn't just barge in and make them stop—the sudden cessation of magic could cause a shock to some beings' systems. From their glazed, focused looks and the way the lead elf was cradling his microphone, I didn't think they'd listen to a politely worded request, either. Got to take a subtler, yet menacing approach.

Menacing? Easy. Subtle?

Yeah, I can do subtle.

With the crowd all swaying and shuffling and half singing and getting in my way, it took me to the second verse to make it to the stage. The singer was whining about a lost pot of gold when I *subtly* climbed the stage from the back and *subtly* tapped the pipes-playing elf on the shoulder. He turned, looked at me, and took a hint. One down.

Beside him, the drummer looked up from his bells to see why his buddy had stopped. I subtly gave him The Grin. He tapped his cowbell a couple more times with decreasing energy then stopped. Two down.

I *subtly* wrapped my tail around the neck of the last player's lute and wagged the tip in a scolding manner. He blanched. Three down and one to go.

I set myself down between the band and the singer and started cleaning my front claws. After a few moments, the singer realized he was *a cappella* and turned to see what happened to his musical backup. His own voice faded into confusion as he beheld me. I met his eyes and cocked my head. His song ended in a weak, "Oh, ahem. Of course..."

Silence spread across the room as, in individuals and groups, the dancers stopped.

Then the room erupted with the cheers of more than three hundred tired dancers.

Humans. Or whatever.

The band took their bows. Once the ovation finished and folks had started flopping onto the floor to rub aching feet, the mesmerizing musicians turned back to me like chagrined kids.

"Did we get a little carried away?" I asked as if to preschoolers.

The lead singer shrugged. He spoke in Mundane English, with just a little bit of a singsong quality, as if he'd learned it from some tape with music in the background. "It's just that they're so appreciative. And their little jingles are deliciously complex, yet short."

"Except 'Inagaddadavida.' That's got some length," the harpist added. "Still, I felt it needed something. More edge, more...umph." He made a fist and twisted his hand to emphasize his feeling.

I'd never seen an elf at a loss for words. It took a minute to pick my jaw off the floor.

They hadn't noticed, however; they'd gathered into a huddle around the sheet music one of them had pulled out. One reached behind the speakers, grabbed a two-liter bottle of Ping, took a swig and passed it around.

"There's a sound that's missing...more bass in the harp?"

"I don't think that's it. A new sound: That's what it needs. Cowbell?"

"Cowbell!"

Natura and Bert were around when Bob Dylan, Jimmy Hendricks, and Cat Stevens first transitioned to electric guitar, and both said the sound had unique power to "soothe the mood" or enflame the passions. Faerie bands could already soothe or enflame humans enough as it was; I didn't want to think about them having even more power to do that, no matter how unique the sound. They could stick with cowbell.

I left them discussing the relative merits of different sizes and materials of cowbells and checked on Grace.

She circulated among the guests, healing blisters and checking to make sure none of the older members were having heart attacks. On the contrary, everyone was flush-faced and breathing heavily but positively jovial as they recounted moves they hadn't been able to do in years—or had never known they could do. One old codger who had to be at least seventy tried to demonstrate, but Grace slipped back before he could pull her into a deep dip. He turned to the closest lady with a green "hug me" button instead.

I stood by the door until Grace had finished.

She came to me still smiling and looking more relaxed than I'd seen her in a long time. "I'll sleep well tonight! I haven't danced like that since the time I visited the Summer Court as a novice," she said.

"I'm not surprised."

She took in my glower. "Oh, Vern, relax. I was protected." She held up a small charm of St. Cecilia, patron of music. It had just a little bit of magic left. "I was completely aware of what was going on and would have stopped the music at the first sign of trouble or before the ward dissolved."

"Yeah? How?"

She laughed. "They were taking requests. I would have asked them for 'Ride the Lightning.'"

I tried for a moment to envision Metallica played on a lyre, pan pipe, and hand drum. "They'll need that cowbell," I muttered.

Chapter Sixteen: An A-Musing Incident

"I'm going to have to talk with her, aren't I?" Grace sighed as we worked our way down the hall to Grace's "Magic in Music" panel. We were speaking in our creole, and even so, we weren't mentioning Brunhilde's name. We'd caught her sneaking out of Gozon's room this morning, wrapped in a long white dressing gown. Maybe it was comfortable, but I didn't think the clear plastic high heels with the fuzz across the toes were.

Neither, apparently, did Grace. "I know she's a Valkyrie and subject to a different set of morals than mortals, but there are certain rules they ought to follow around them, and she needs to understand that." She tsk'd with disgust. "The last thing I expected to do was to have to counsel a Valkyrie on controlling her...base urges."

"Better you than me," was all I could say. Some things a dragon did not need to get involved in.

"Here we are," Grace said as we stopped in front of the conference room door. She handed me her harp so she could double-check her program. "'A panel discussion on the magic in music, moderated by Mensan Shirley Starke of Valkyrie Publications.' Valkyrie. There's a coincidence."

"Who else is on the panel?" I asked. I set her harp against the wall with me between it and passersby.

"Grace McCarthy!" The voice was pure music, yet came off like a deodorant jingle.

Grace's face froze. Then she forced a tight smile and turned. "Euterpe, dear."

The Greek Muse Euterpe looked every bit as you'd expect her to. Her long, silvery-blonde hair didn't have a strand out of place, and when she flipped it—as she often did—it made a subtle sound like harp strings played at just above the level of human hearing. Her eyes were large and gray, her skin flawless, and her figure of—pardon the pun—Classic proportions. She smiled as tightly as Grace. Both ladies wore green dots on their buttons, yet neither moved.

Good thing. Judging from the tension between them, any embrace was going to be a wrestling move.

Grace said, "I didn't see your name on the panel."

The muse of music giggled a scale—yes, giggled. C Major. *Hahahahahahahaha.* "Isn't it the most amusing surprise? Kaliope told me about this darling convention and when I saw the panel, I just knew I had to come. It will so elevate the discussion."

"You mean, Kaliope mentioned it and you bullied your way in," Grace accused, but with a tone reserved for admiring baby rabbits or gamboling puppies.

I blinked in surprise.

But Euterpe just laughed—D Major, this time. "Tomato-tomahto! Isn't that what the Mundanes say?"

"Potato-Potahto. Tomato is the second verse."

"Not if I'd written it." Euterpe did her flip-thing—C resolving to A minor. "But, look at you! Here! Still a nun! I suppose that should be expected. Always the serious type, preferring an ethereal God to a real man. Just as well, I'm sure.

But why, oh, why did you choose an order with such obvious colors? And they make you hide your hair. I suppose that's for the best, but why?"

"My beauty is in the grace of God. But you, Terpie! Same as always." Grace's false sincerity was like nails on a chalkboard. She clutched her cross tightly. For a moment I imagined them as dragons, circling and hissing with wings half-unfurled. I didn't know whether to laugh or intervene. I decided to compromise by clearing my throat. Yeah, I know. How Mundane.

Terpie's eyes flew to me and her face assumed a pout usually reserved for looking at guinea pigs. "Oh, look! It's protecting your harp!"

Now, personally, I don't mind being called "it" by a Faerie, especially an immortal. Most species refer to me as "he," but as a sexless species, it's really a classification based on personality. No, it was more the implication that I was somehow a pet that rankled.

Rather than point this out, however, Grace just said, "And you brought your lyre. Still stringing it with your own hair, too." Then she added to me, "It helps her get a good tone."

The Greek Spirit of Music's face tightened a notch, and Grace pressed her advantage. "I haven't heard any of Sebastian's compositions lately."

Sebastian? I ran though composers in my mind, and remembered a Sebastian among some of Grace's music. Sebastian Baltazar. He had some early stuff that was rough but inspired. His later works—well, they had a technical perfection, but somewhere he'd lost his individuality, so that the last one, written almost a century and a half ago, had all the passion and charm of a toothpaste jingle. I never understood why Grace kept it.

Looking at her narrowed eyes, I thought I understood now, and what happened to his "individual voice." I guess he'd found a muse.

Again, Terpie's grin seemed just a bit more strained, but all she did was run her fingers through her hair—four octaves of C. "Yes, well. It will be such an interesting panel—for them, of course. And yourself. Coming?"

"I'll catch up."

"You always did. Toodles!" She waved her fingers in the air like a sorority wannabe and sauntered into the conference room.

Toodles? Somebody studied *The Faerie Book of Mundane Slang*. I turned to Grace, who was muttering a prayer for strength. I waited until she finished, then handed her the harp. "Sure you don't want me to go with you?"

"What? No. Go to the Real CSI panel. We could both do with knowing more about Mundane forensics." She smiled a genuine smile, though there was still a little strain in it. "I'll be fine. Terpie and I...have a history."

"Over Sebastian?"

"Over his music." Her eyes dimmed with sadness. "I tried to warn him. He had talent. He didn't need a Muse." Lost in her thoughts, she went into the room without saying goodbye.

Grace was right about the CSI lecture. Inspector Logeston knew his stuff. I picked up a lot of good information, enough for me to drive Captain Santry mad with suggestions when we got back. That alone made it worth the trip. As chief of the Los Lagos PD, Santry didn't care much for private investigators interfering in his business, and thanks to the Gap, Grace and I got to interfere more than the average PI. Nonetheless, I decided to corner Logeston at another time and left during the question-and-answer session to be at Grace's room before her panel ended.

Naturally, things conspired against me.

As I exited the elevator on the main floor, I caught a glimpse of a dwarf—Kent; no mistaking the beard and hair—heading out the door alone. Call it "Verney senses" or good old-fashioned paranoia, I hurried to stop him. I would just ask what he was up to—no harm in that, right? Alas, I was intercepted by my shadow, National Geographic Bill, carrying an expensive briefcase. I belatedly remembered we were supposed to meet for lunch. At least we hadn't said what day.

"Excuse me, Vern! You need to take a look at this."

I hissed between my teeth as my dwarvish quarry, still dressed like a Hollywood version of his own people, climbed into a taxi, and turned to the Mundane. "Something wrong?" I asked.

"I should say so! Look at this!" He strode to a part of the registration area away from the receptionists and set his briefcase on the counter. He opened it.

I peered at the contents. Papers, neatly stacked and clipped, pens and pencils in the little pockets, lined up by size, everything neat and proper and polished.

"Let me guess," I sighed. "Someone's completed your crossword puzzle book?"

"It's more serious than that. These are my slides for my presentation on Faerie zoology." He pulled out a box about two inches by two inches by ten. "I was looking for a particular picture to show someone, and I noticed it was not in the spot it should have been. In fact, most of them are no longer in the right spots. Someone has totally rearranged them. Fortunately, these are the backups in case my computer doesn't work."

"How do you know a human didn't do this?"

He showed me the money clip that was tucked into a smaller pocket. Not only were the bills still there, they had been arranged by denomination and serial number, and crisply ironed, too.

I thumbed through the slides, picking out a series of five to look at in the light. "How were they before?"

"Alphabetical within general type."

"Well, congratulations. Now they're in order by genus, species, and family. They must have a zoology buff."

"They?"

"Brownies. They're going around cleaning and organizing."

Reed beamed. "Extraordinary! Where can I find one?"

"You won't. They keep a low profile—as in functionally invisible. They don't like to be seen at work, stories of shoemakers peeking in on them in the middle of the night notwithstanding."

"There has to be a way. Perhaps we can trap one?"

I didn't bother to tell him that's what Grace and I had in mind. "If you manage to catch one, let me know. We've got a few questions for them. Is anything missing?"

"Just a couple of packets of Flavite. Berry. Probably mistook them for trash and tossed them."

"Probably." I handed him his slides and he put them away. We made some concrete plans for meeting up in my room to eat and talk, and I headed to Grace's panel.

I got there just as people were filing out. The Faerie were talking and chuckling, but the Mundanes were silent. Stunned, even. So stunned, they simply filed past my winged and scaled, gloriously dragon self without even a glance. I finally heard one guy say in a hush, "That was..." and his friend respond, "Yeah."

After the last person emerged, zombie-like, from the room, Grace came out. Her habit was rumpled and her wimple askew. Some of her red hair was singed. Wisps of smoke escaped from her harp case.

She was smiling with satisfaction.

She straightened out her habit and tucked in her hair. "How was the forensics lecture?" she asked as if nothing out of the ordinary had happened.

The doors opened again, and Euterpe came out, her saunter gone, clutching a section of her torn peplos with one hand and holding a lyre with two snapped strings in the other. Her hair looked as if she had been to a hairdresser on drugs. Her eyes were black and smudged—I hadn't realized she wore makeup. Her expression was somewhere between shocked and seething, but as soon as she saw Grace, she straightened and shook herself haughtily. Her hair, appropriately, played B-flat and became perfect, as did her makeup. Her dress repaired itself.

Again the two women smiled their insincere smiles.

"It was so good to see you," Grace volunteered first.

"Oh, we simply must do this again sometime," Terpie oozed. "But let's not wait so long. I'd just cry to see you with more wrinkles."

Grace held out her hands. Terpie took them, and they did a half-hug/air kiss.

"Please tell Poly I pray for her."

"I'm sure that'll mean as much to her as it does to me. Toodles!"

I peeked into the conference room. Sitting at a harp was, I assumed, Ms. Starke, her expression as dazed as those of her fellow Mundanes. She kept staring around her as if expecting to see something other than the usual disarray of a used conference room, but there was nothing out of the ordinary.

Unless you could sense magic. The arcane aftermath was enough to make my cheek crests flare and my lips curl back.

"Harp music," I heard Ms. Starke mutter. "I just wanted to talk about Faerie harp music."

I turned to my partner, my question obvious in my expression.

"I think Terpie had an interesting time," she said gaily.

Chapter Seventeen: Pucking Pixies

"Are you going to have to go to Confession?" I demanded severely.

She nodded, her smile going from giddy to rueful. "Aye, and again every time I remember how her hair sounded when it kinked—kind of like... Remember when Frankie first learned chords on the guitar?"

I grimaced. More than once we were submitted to a Costa concert of missed notes and squeaky feedback made up for with volume.

"D7 with half the strings not pressed quite hard enough. Ach, her poor hair didn't know how to respond so it just—" She made a little explosion gesture with her fingers and giggled.

"Sister Grace Ann McCarthy, you should be ashamed of yourself for doing something like that," I scolded, even though I was even more sorry I hadn't stayed.

"Oh, I'm quite repentant for finding it so funny—and I know I will be again." She stifled another giggle, then let out a breath. "But I didn't do it. She was so mad, her own spell misfired. I'm sure that hasn't happened in my lifetime."

The rest of the morning went by smoothly. We caught the Inspector and bent his ear for an enjoyable half hour, noticed a patron at the reception desk complimenting the housekeeping staff ("I've never been in a hotel where they even cleaned and organized the kids' toys!"), and caught a great panel discussion on the intelligence of humor. Of course, Yours Truly stole the show with his multilingual puns.

Afterwards, I left Grace to patrol and headed to our room to meet with Reed. I paused as I was passing a staircase because I heard some off-key singing... Looney Tunes does Wagner. I decided to take the elevator to the first floor.

Just to the left of the elevator doors stood a small, raised platform with a half-dozen chairs and tables around it. On the platform, a couple of guys with fake furs over their T-shirts and jeans and plastic horned helmets were holding an impromptu theater. I thought I recognized

SkinnyZits from the elevator and another of the hotel employees.

"Oh, Bwuuunhilda! You are so wuuuv-wee!"

Seated in a chair, elbows on knees, and hands up and making little clapping motions, was the object of their serenade: Brunhilde. Around her, a crowd of Faerie and Mundanes gathered, most snickering and clapping in appreciation. In a corner behind them, Siegfried loomed, cross-armed and scowling.

Siegfried made a fist, then turned and strode away to the gardens. I followed, wondering what to say or do and thinking that even if we were getting paid, I wouldn't be getting paid enough for this. I trailed behind as he stalked up to the pond and stood there, ignoring the naiads swimming about suggestively in front of him, his hands gripping the dagger the hotel staff had let him keep because he'd wired it to the sheath. They obviously didn't realize that that little plastic cord wouldn't even slow him down if he decided to draw it. Unlike his ancestor, he was reputed to be a gentle man, but I knew what a man in love and on the edge could do.

I hesitated. Wisdom of the Ages didn't prepare a dragon for affairs of the heart. I took some of Grace's advice and asked the Holy Spirit to send me the right words to say.

Wouldn't you know, all I got was, "Hey, Sig? You okay?" I must have had a faulty connection. Spiritual sunspots or something.

But apparently it was enough, for Siegfried huffed loudly and flung his arms wide. "Do you see her?" he cried in Norwegian. Even in his rage, he didn't yell. "Dressing in those provocative clothes, the makeup, the flirting. Making eyes at those men in their ridiculous costumes. Do you see her?"

"Uh, not socially," I said. That comment was all me; I'm sure the Holy Spirit was cringing.

He gaped at me for a moment, then deflated. "Then you and I are the only ones. Mundanes. Now that elf. She wants a patient man? I have been more than patient. No more, dragon. No more. The elf will regret. They all will."

He pushed past me, and I didn't have the heart to tell him to behave himself. Once upon a time, I would have pounced on him and eaten him just to spare myself future headaches. Now I watched his angry stride and felt a sympathy and an urge to help him.

I promptly squashed it. What did I think I would do, play matchmaker? Be his wingman? How ridiculous would that be?

Right now, I had other things to think about, like my stomach. Doctor Doolittle was supposed to be bringing lunch to my room so he could learn about Faerie dragons right from the source.

Reed met me in the elevator, and I was glad to see the size of the tray he was carrying. Dragons have unusual stomachs. We can gorge ourselves silly on something the size of a buffalo and be fine for weeks, or we can get by on frequent snacks of small animals and veggies. When I first moved to Los Lagos, I filled my belly on more than anyone's fair share of rats. I couldn't always afford a good meal and it counted as another good deed in the service of Man. Given the choice, though, I'm much happier with an overflowing platter of Faerie French cuisine. Besides, without access to magical energy, I was expending more physical energy. I needed calories.

"I hope I got enough," he said, sagging under the weight of the tray.

"It'll do," I replied. I'd enlighten him after I ate.

The doors opened on my floor, and I let Reed stagger out first with the tray. "We're sixth room on the right," I told him as I started to slink past, then stopped short as a piskie of pixies zipped toward us. I braced Reed with my tail to keep him from toppling over in surprise as they stopped short not six inches from our noses.

"Well, if it isn't the High Flyers," I said. "Staying out of mischief, I hope?"

There were some giggles, but the leader stopped them with a glare. "Vern, can you truly breathe fire again?"

"You know I can," I said suspiciously. "Why are you ask—"

Suddenly, every one of the pixies tossed a powder at us. Reed dropped the tray to cover his face, but it didn't help. He immediately started sneezing.

I snarled at the pixies, "What do you think you're do—a-choo!"

"Fire! Fire! Fire!" they started chanting.

"Are you out of your mi—" I sneezed three times in succession. They had no idea how tempted I was to oblige them, not that I could do anything about it at that moment, anyway. I tried to catch my breath, sneezed and coughed.

Then I saw Reed staring at me with panicked and watering eyes. Staggering and sneezing, he ran for the little red box on the wall.

The pixies' chants grew louder.

"Reed, wait! I—choo!" My sneeze blew a few pixies back several feet and nearly drowned out their catcalls.

Unfortunately, it didn't drown out the sound of the fire alarm, like a swarm of angry bees on steroids. Reed had broken the glass and pulled the handle. What few people were in their rooms at this hour started pouring out, confused, then terrified as they heard Reed calling over the din, "Get out before he starts flaming the floor!" and saw a horse-sized dragon wheezing and snorting.

Grace was gonna kill me. But I wasn't going down alone.

The pixies were taking that moment to make their giddy exit, but I was too fast. With a lunge and a snap that nearly made a lady faint, I'd caught one in my mouth.

"Lemme out! It was a joke!" He threw himself against my teeth.

"Nwow ftay ftill," I told it, "or I—schoo!"

"Ewww, gross!" he wailed.

I snagged a recovering Reed and, disregarding his protests about using the elevator during a fire, pushed him into the nearest car.

"There ish no fyer, you idgiot," I said as well as I could with a mouth full of pixie. I sneezed and rolled my eyes at Reed when he cringed.

We ran into Grace in the lounge on the main floor. She pushed her way through the fleeing crowds to us.

"What happened?" she asked me.

Outside, sirens were wailing. The fire department was fast.

I grinned. A sad, soggy pixie peered morosely from between my teeth. "It was a joke," he moaned.

Grace sighed and snagged a used but essentially clean cloth napkin as we were pushed past a side table. I deposited my prisoner into it, then tried to scrape the tickly pixie-dust feeling off my tongue by rubbing it against the roof of my mouth. Between that and the last vestiges of sneezes, I probably looked like a cat dislodging a hairball, but Grace wasn't laughing.

"This had better be good," was all she muttered. The pixie in her hand shivered theatrically and looked at her with overlarge eyes, like an anime character, but she just gave him a stern look and kept the napkin wrapped tightly around him to keep him from flying off. After a moment, he slumped and resigned himself to his fate.

"Come on, let's go explain to the fire marshal." She sighed.

I gave Reed a push. "And you stay right in front of me."

He staggered a little. "Why?"

"After your performance? There's bound to be someone out there raving about a 'fire-breathing dragon,' and if I'm going to get hosed down by the fire department, you're going to get the soaking first."

Fortunately, the presence of Grace and Reed blocking my snout from view gave the firefighters pause, and when she called out to be at peace and that there was no fire, they visibly relaxed. They still insisted on checking the hotel, and while they went floor by floor, calling in "clears," I, the pixie, and Reed explained what happened.

The fire marshal, who looked too young for the position, didn't seem to know if he should scowl or laugh. He decided to go for scowling at the pixie. "Setting off a false alarm is not a funny joke. It costs the county a lot of money for us to come out here, and what if there'd been a real fire we should have responded to? People could have died."

"Sorry, so very sorry. We didn't know about Mundane firemen, truly," the pixie lamented, once again giving his big, watery-eyed performance.

"You said you weren't alone. Who came up with this idea?"

"Puck."

A snort escaped his lips, but he quickly quelled it and turned to Grace. "Is he serious?"

"'Puck' is more of a title than a name. It just means the leader of that particular escapade. It's also a verb for pulling a practical joke," she said. "Be assured, officer, that we'll get the message to the appropriate parties."

Just then a news van pulled up.

"Channel Seven, right on time," he sighed. "Okay, listen. It was a misunderstanding. This is the first false alarm in this location in over a year, so we'll let it slide. No harm, no foul. However, now, I think we need to go and explain exactly why a dragon is not a fire hazard."

"I'll do it." Reed started toward the van where the reporter and her cameraman were unpacking.

I hooked a claw on his shoulder and pulled him back. The only thing I hate worse than talking to the press is being talked about to the press. "Why don't you let the real subject matter expert handle it?"

I went with the marshal to meet the eager reporter. Grace followed, then moved unobtrusively to the side, where she could see the reporter and the camera crew but still remain, as it says in your King James Bible, "unspotted from the world." As the reporter eagerly shoved her microphone into the marshal's face and demanded to know if I was indeed the dragon that had set fire to the sixth floor, Grace began praying silently.

I've never had luck with the press. The first television interview I had was when I'd just arrived in the Mundane dimension and was trying to get my citizenship. Instead of the impartial review of the facts, they made me look like a wild animal seeking new human prey. The veritable wolf in the henhouse. The fact that I'd just tackled a pick-pocket who screamed bloody murder probably didn't help, but did they even ask my side of the story? No. Needless to say, most days I'd rather eat an anchorman than talk to him. (But don't quote me on that.)

Grace, bless her sweetly scheming mind, came up with a way to fix that. She had adapted the Eighth Commandment spell. Instead of coercing criminals to tell the truth about their crimes, she can compel the media to report truthfully—live anyway, which is where it all comes apart with a newspaper reporter like McGrue. TV, though? The only misleading statements are the ones I give.

Totally, by accident, I assure you.

Really.

At any rate, as she murmured her prayer spell, I explained that for Faerie dragons, "breathing fire" was a conscious action that took some prep-aration. I didn't get into too many details, but by the time I was done, they were reassured.

"So what did happen?" the reporter asked.

I explained that some pixies decided to play a little joke that got out of control, literally. Then I told them about my job chaperoning the Faerie folk at the convention and a little about my work at home, playing up the humor and the things many may have already seen on MeTube. By the time I finished, people all around—guests, cops, even firemen—were rolling with laughter.

"I cannot believe I'm talking to a real dragon!" the reporter exclaimed. "How do we know you're not some Fanny Flamingo stunt?"

"Lady, can animatronics do this?" I launched myself into the sky. I paused for a moment, back arched, wings curled, hovering by magic. I'd pay for that later, but I couldn't help myself. Once I was sure the cameraman and photographers had gotten a good shot, I climbed toward the clouds, then folded my wings and dove, strafing across the crowd with my claws just inches above their heads. People shrieked, ducked, then laughed. I swooped back, hovered, and came down in a gentle landing.

As people applauded, the reporter turned to face the camera, "Well, there you have it. The alarm may have been false, but the dragon is real.

This is Roxanne Lewis for Channel Seven News. Have a mythical evening!"

After the light dimmed and the cameraman lowered his camera, she turned to thank the marshal, then smiled at me. "That was the most fun I've had in a long time. Is there any way we could do an in-depth interview?"

"Sorry." I shook my head. I knew I'd be pushing my luck. "Part of our instructions were to keep a low profile."

"Well, you've kind of blown that." She laughed.

"There's 'blown' and then there's 'hurricane.' I think any more would be a violation of at least tropical storm proportions."

"Well, if you change your mind. Floridians love a good tropical storm." She handed me her card. I gave her ours.

She took the card with one hand, rubbing the back of my paw with her other. "Your scales are so smooth," she said. "Is your skin very tough?"

"I can be hurt," I said. "But I get over it."

She laughed and blushed. "I'm sorry! I've just always loved dragons. I used to want a Komodo dragon as a pet. Had to settle with a bearded dragon—that's a lizard—but Gordo is a sweetheart. And now I'm babbling! Listen, thanks again. It was just...amazing!"

At that point, the cameraman laid on the horn of the van. She tossed her head, yelled, "All right, already!" over her shoulder, gave me one last grin, and hopped into the van. Grace came up to me as they drove away.

"Show off," she said fondly.

"Yeah. Too bad there wasn't a full moon—or would that have been too cliché?"

She shook her head. "Well, you've made a friend," she said.

I snorted. Too many years of experience with the Mundane press kept me skeptical despite her friendliness. "Maybe."

"No, I think this one's genuine."

"Think we can get her to move to Los Lagos?"

By the time we'd said our goodbyes to the marshal and made our way back to our room, it was mid-afternoon, and I was more than ready for a huge platter of food. So, true to the way this trip had gone, my meal was again delayed, this time by Gozon, who cornered us on the way to the elevator and spent the next half hour respectfully reporting the theft of his briefcase.

Grace and I braced ourselves and spent the next forty-five minutes questioning him, only to find out he'd left it in the meeting room where he'd been discussing Elvish syntax (which explained the two professor-types lurking just around the corner holding tape recorders). The Mensans had apparently lifted him bodily and politely frog-marched him from the hotel when the fire alarm had gone off. He returned to find the briefcase gone. Another fifteen minutes to assure him we'd get on it, and fifteen more for a just-this-side-of-rudeness "See ya," and Grace and I were free.

If you can call it "free," since we spent the next hour and a half casing the hotel for any trace of his briefcase. Just like our brownie friends, it had disappeared without leaving behind any evidence.

Back in our room, Grace started parsing out Gozon's speech, hoping to find a clue there. "Why do I get the impression he's not especially upset?"

"Because he isn't," I growled. My stomach growled with me. I was so hungry, I was actually disappointed to find that the housekeeping staff had already cleaned up the mess Reed had made when he dropped the platter. I'd told Reed to meet us in our room at seven and bring more food.

Fortunately, Reed came through, rolling in a cart with not one, but two platters. Grace joined us for dinner. We watched ourselves on the news—a positive story despite everything, what a novelty!—then settled down to some serious discussion on dragonology.

We'd gotten past eating and hunting, and I was dispelling the usual myths about virgins when Grace had to leave to listen to the workshop on comparative religions. (Or, more accurately, to attend the late-night workshop as a former Inquisitor of the Faerie Church and ensure none of the Faerie on the panel or audience decided to encourage Mundane freedom of religion by offering themselves as personal gods. We had a great cautionary tale now, too, thanks to Shogzallie.) By the time she'd returned, we'd covered territorialism and treasure, and Reed was ready to call it a night.

No sooner had he left than we got a phone call. Grace picked it up, but I could hear the conversation well enough. It was Cory from Security. "Listen, Grace, the police just called. They have a dwarf they arrested—he said you'd bail him out. Front desk didn't know anything about it, so they called us. Are we gonna have trouble with this guy if we let him in the hotel? Fanny Flamingo's Fantasyland said he was causing a disturbance."

Belatedly, I remembered Kent the Dwarf getting into a taxi. I should have known. Why else would he have done himself up like a Lord of the Rings extra? He'd come to the conference looking for an acting job!

Oh, yeah. Cushy assignment. If you don't count the hyper house elves, dwarves in detention, and an egotistical elf with some "genius" plan to get him back on top with his people.

And we're not even getting paid.

Chapter Eighteen: Dashed Hopes and "Loverly" Dreams

As we were about to go bail out Kent, I got a call from Ray. I could hear music in the background; he must be at the guitar convention still. "Vern, can we meet? I need a favor. I hate to ask, but..."

"I'll fetch our wayward dwarf," Grace said. "It'll probably be easier if we don't have to explain you to the authorities."

While she got a taxi, I made my way across the commons. The naiads were training the alligator to porpoise, grabbing it by the middle to help it rise out of the water on its tail, and squealing with delight whenever it seemed to hold its own weight. They had a small but appreciative audience, but I also caught sight of a very worried Barry Welles, Hotel Manager, peering out his office window.

Well, one problem at a time.

I found Ray sitting on a bench, his lute in his hand, strumming chords and looking very disconcerted.

"Forget a note?" I asked as I settled down in front of him.

"Forgot my lane!" he retorted. "Yesterday, I got approached by this Faerie princess—"

"Galinda?"

"That's the one! Anyway, she wanted me to write a love song for her husband. And I know—I know!—I should not have agreed, but she was so sweet and insistent and sad..."

"Sad?"

"I guess the romance is gone or they had a fight or something? She was kind of all over the place, but anyhow, I ended up agreeing to write her something by tomorrow. I'm a good mimic, but I'm not a songwriter! I can probably put something together, but she's a princess. It's got to be perfect, right? What do I do?"

"Write? Write like the wind and hope that your muse..." I trailed off. "Actually, I think I know someone who can help."

Minutes later, we were knocking on Euterpe's door.

The Faerie muse opened it just enough to lean out. She gave me a brilliant smile that made her eyes sparkle yet didn't reveal any true joy, unless you count the joy of a predator anticipating prey. "Vern! And..." She scanned the hall, looking for Grace, no doubt, then settled her gaze on Ray. Her smile slipped a fraction. "...friend."

"Not just a friend," I said, "a potential, *temporary protégé*. My dear bard here has gotten into a situation only a great muse like yourself can help him out of." Briefly I explained about Galinda's song.

Euterpe toyed with her braid, which responded with a series of triples in C Major. Her smile again made a subtle change and her voice grew icy. "Won't your dear nun protest that I'll destroy his *unique* voice?"

She gave "unique" an ugly, mean-girl twist, but Ray started laughing. "Lovely Euterpe. Lyrical Euterpe! Do not concern yourself on my behalf. I am a talented mimic and a fair musician. And I do have some ideas for this song. But I am not some genius songwriter whose gift must be protected. Nay, I desire only to write this one, perfect song for a lovely princess in emotional distress. I promise for this one song to be contented with your instruction. I'm even glad to share the credit."

"Many credit the muse," she scoffed.

"No, I mean like put your name on it as co-writer. It's only fair."

She blinked and released her hold on her braid. It plopped against her shoulder with a lyrical sproing. She turned to me. "Where, where did you find this enchanting man?"

I shrugged. "He's a friend. Can you help him?"

She backed up and beckoned him in. Ray made a fist and practically flounced after her.

I left them and headed to the roof to do my gar-goyle imitation on the balcony while I waited for Grace and our delinquent dwarf. I had just started feeling "one with the night" when my cell phone rang, destroying the mood.

It was Gapman—with good news for a change. "I've brought Sister Eloise to your place for the night. She arrived about the time a mole started to poke its head out again. She was a terrific help, absolutely brilliant."

I heard a giggle in the background. I supposed if I got complimented by a guy in green-and-yellow Spandex, I'd laugh, too.

Gapman continued, "We doubled what we managed yesterday in less time, even with my fiasco. Kenjo thinks we can finish by tomorrow afternoon if we can contain them all on the surface, and Sister Eloise thinks she may have a spell for that. She wants to say, 'hello.'"

He passed the phone over and Sister Eloise gushed her thanks for the opportunity and told me how cute the MOUSs were with their soft fur and that the meat was delicious and that she wasn't detecting any malignant magics in them. "I don't think they were part of the Mishmash spell at all. I'd like to try to capture one of the younger ones for study."

My Verney senses were tingling—literally, I got a feeling of dread all along my back spines—but all I said was, "Be careful."

"Of course," she promised and again reminded me that the best day of her life (aside from when she took vows) was meeting me and Grace.

No sooner did we hang up than I got a call from Kenjo. "You own mountain, right? You give us some. We feed you. Need right big piece—you no use. You got. You give. We feed. Good deal."

I did not like where this was going. "Let's talk when I return."

"No talk! Talk cheap! The loudest one in the room is the weakest one in the room. We show. You see. Make offer you can't refuse."

And he hung up.

I was about to call back when a Rhyde approached bearing my nun and our wayward dwarf. Setting aside the Kenjo problem for tomorrow, I glided down to the portico and met them at the door.

Grace stepped out first. "He's all yours," she said as she sailed past me without even glancing back. Kent the Celebrity-Wannabe waited until the hotel door closed behind her before climbing out of the car. I was certain he'd gotten an earful. Grace did a convincing Bad Cop when she wanted to.

"Come on," I said, and led him inside to the hotel bar.

The bartender gaped when we came in, but greeted me with a "Didn't I see you on the—"

"Not now," I interrupted him and ordered a beer for Kent and a Piña Colada for me, just to see the look on his face. When I'm feeling really mischievous, I order a Bloody Mary, but I didn't know the bartender well enough.

I glanced around the bar. Looked like the Faerie had pretty much taken it over. Pixies, elves of all shapes and sizes, a couple of empyrie, even an intoxicated dryad who was gazing at a particularly expensive and lush fake tree with a mixture of infatuation and confusion. About the only human I saw was Galinda, who was seated at a table near the door and delivering a blistering lecture to her husband. Galendor nodded mutely and sipped what appeared to be a cola. Great—trouble in paradise. Euterpe had better come through. I decided to avoid the tables at all costs, especially when I saw Brunhilde in a corner booth getting cozy with Coyote.

Maybe Bishop Aiden should have hired Dear Abby.

Kent didn't speak until after he'd had his first beer and was starting on his second.

"I was seventeen when the Gap first opened," he said. "Been working the mines since I was twelve, yet even then I knew I was destined for something...more. Then about a year ago, I was topside with some buddies...and I saw it."

I felt a sinking in my stomach. *Lord of the Rings* strikes again. Did he really think there was a great epic adventure awaiting him on the other side of the Gap?

"*They've Been Discovered*," he continued, his voice thick with emotion and drink. "That fateful episode, a bus driver in a local talent show got a recording contract. Mother Lode, Vern; do you know what that meant to me? People breaking free from their ordinary lives, becoming something else. It was the most beautiful thing I'd ever seen.

"I live for the stage, but let's face it: How much opportunity is there in Dwarvish theater? *The Day We Struck Gold, When the Diamond Mine Went Dry, Perriman's Pickax*. I was stifled! Then there was the fiasco at the Los Lagos Theater with *Captain Stupendous*. You've no idea what I did to get this far, the hours of research, the money I invested to perfect the look, but I'd seen my chance and, by Perriman's Pickax, I would take it."

"You were hoping Fanny Flamingo would discover you?"

"I did my research. Fanny Flamingo is smaller than Disney, of course, but more than thirty percent of the actors in the industry, movies and television, get their start with Fanny. I went there, intent on giving them my best performance—"

"And you didn't immediately get arrested for busking?"

He snarled and quaffed his beer. "Would that they had, but they just told me to leave. Vern, they treated me like a sideshow! Children pulling at my beard, people laughing and pointing. I tried to perform my soliloquy, and they asked me to sing 'Heigh-Ho!' People asking me if I was Dopey and when I finally lost my temper, they laughed and called me 'Grumpy.'"

"That's from—"

"I know what it's from!" He slammed his empty glass on the bar. "I have been typecast enough. I want roles of substance." He hollered for the bartender to bring him another and brooded, staring into it as if he could find his answers in the gold beneath the suds.

A pixie flew up to the bar, sat on it, and ordered a whiskey sour. The bartender must have been working the past couple of nights. He brought out a thimble without even blinking. The pixie sipped and spoke. "You're not alone. These Mundanes, they clap at us and say, 'I believe!' What's to not believe? We're staring them in the face, we are!"

"Peter Pan," I and Kent intoned.

"Peter started this? Which one's Peter Pan?"

Galendor appeared at my other side. "If I get called 'Legolas' one more time..." He sighed and ordered a Diet Chase.

"At least that's a character of some depth," Kent grumbled, "and much loved by the ladies."

Galendor took three long swallows, closed his eyes and blew through his lips. His whole body seemed to shudder slightly, then relax. Then he turned his attention to the dwarf. "Exactly my trouble, friend. What about you, Vern? You got used as a toy ride."

"I've had worse," I grumbled. "Today, in fact, and not even by the Mundanes. Pixie, you tell this afternoon's Puck he owes me a story."

Pixie raised his cup. It was a time-honored tradition among Faerie practical jokers that once the stunt was pulled, the victim could request a "story," an explanation of how they came up with the idea, the planning, the execution... A debrief, essentially. It gave the joker a chance to brag and the victim to learn. Sometimes, I wondered if Shakespeare had somehow tapped into our dimension when he wrote *A Midsummer Night's Dream.*

Of course, I wasn't looking for a lesson so much as an ulterior motive.

"But you know what the worst of it was?" Kent suddenly cried. He was on his fourth beer in less than half an hour and even with Corona, a dwarf was bound to feel its effects. "You know what the worst of it was? The manager, he said I wasn't convincing! I wasn't convincing as a dwarf!"

He banged his head against the bar and let it rest there.

He continued in Dwarvish. "Maybe I should take Garn up on his offer and go down to Astral-Austri- Aust-*ralia*. He's got the rights lined up on a faerimet mine. The way the market is, a dwarf could make a good living, retire er—er—early. Garn's not so bad, you know? A little obsessive about that pickax of his, keeps going on about his future and elves and bulls, but I mean, we all got faults. We all got faults. We're only, only— fae-rimet mining's good work. Money's good...I could start my own theater..."

I caught Coyote looking at us while Brunhilde was occupied with scratching behind his ears. I couldn't help but glance down and notice his foot tapping a happy rhythm. He grinned at me, then turned to lick her hand.

It was getting embarrassing in here. I pulled up my balmy dwarf with my tail while I paid for the drinks by charging them to my room. This was work, after all. "Come on, Kent. I think you've had enough. We'll talk more tomorrow. I might have a solution."

"'Not convincing.' Vern, dood—do you know how much I've studied my art? I even—even bought a TV/VCR and the complete collection of *Act Now! The They Were Discovered Complete Acting Course for the Hopeful Thespian*. You want convincing? Lish-listen to my Eliza Doolit-tle."

I dragged him out as he launched into "Henry Higgins."

"Pixie, don't forget to tell Puck I expect my story," I called back over the din.

"Pucking Peter Pan owes me a story," he snarled back.

Kent drew disapproving stares as he staggered to the elevator, still singing "Just You Wait," so I convinced him to show me his mime routine until we got to his room. He was surprisingly good, too; he just might have something with his "miming miner." I wondered if Galinda knew any agents. She seemed to know all the Hollywood types.

Garn opened the door, dressed in a nightshirt and carrying his pickax. What was it with him and that thing? Kent threw his arms around him, making them both stagger. Garn patted his back tolerantly with one hand, the other holding his pickax safely out of the way.

"Auditions didn't pan out, then?" he asked me in Dwarvish.

"Even humans don't get discovered off the streets very often," I said as Kent sobbed softly into his friend's shoulder. "Regardless of the television show."

"He said I wasn't a convincing dwarf!" Kent wailed.

"Of course ye weren't!" Garn responded with gruff empathy. "You were method-actin' someone else. Get to bed. We'll talk in the morning. Thank ye, Dragon."

"All part of the job. Yo!"

"Yo!"

As I left, I heard him saying to Kent, "Ye know, there are some actual actors in the convention. Ye should be asking them how the system really works. I heard there's even some teen star..."

It sounded like Kent was in good hands.

The night passed quickly. I met Cory at his office, and he gave me an extra walkie-talkie. This was the last night of GitPicCon. They were having an outdoor concert, but the hotel had hired some extra security after the fight the other night, so things had been quiet (relatively speaking) so far. I flew the circuit around the grounds. My wings protested the work, but it was one more day. I'd go hang out in the Duke's fields when this was all done and recharge.

Some drunken idiots decided to throw their empties into the pond and got the surprise of their lives when the naiads threw them back. The naiads, of course, sober and ticked off, had better aim, but fortunately, none of the humans needed much more than a bandage.

More worrying to me was the concert going on by the pool. I saw the harpist from the F.A.E. watching the guitarist with avid interest. So much for cowbell.

I circled the hotel complex a few times, drawing some stares and shouts . Just for grins, I did the silhouette-against-the-moon thing. The humans went ape. Never say I don't know how to play a crowd. After a while, though, the heavy static squeal that seemed to be the guest band's signature style got the better of my ears, and I decided I'd patrolled enough.

A different kind of sound caught my attention, and I wandered over to a fourth-floor ballroom where an all-nighter film festival was going on. The sign on the door said, "Tales of the Time Lord."

I played hooky for three hours. I liked *Dr. Who*. When you're immortal, novelty ranks high on your priority list. Besides, in between the episodes, we had short but intense discussions on how there could be a universe with magic and one without.

In my home dimension, physics didn't generate the same amount of study as magic. Mundane sociologists have been studying the phenomenon, and one of the most prolific, Dr. George Alistarre, claimed it was a combination of lack of environmental factors, economic necessity, a feudal system that in general works better in Faerie than it did in the Mundane dimension, and a "necessary but regrettable" religious oppression. Grace wasn't too pleased with that chapter of his book.

Of course, the discovery of an alternate universe—for us, the Mundane—has changed the face of physics, both for the Faerie and for the Mundane. The idea of intersecting multiverses has taken on new popularity, but of course, magic has thrown a monkey wrench into the works (or a newt's foot into the potion; choose your analogy.) Many Mundane scientists were trying to say Faerie simply had different rules, but that did not explain how those "rules" are managing to seep into the Mundane. (Otherwise, many of us Magicals would not be at this conference, after all.)

In Faerie, the laws of science were the same as those of the Mundane—except for magic. Both scholars and laborers were being introduced to "new" concepts that were always there. Just like your Catholic Church, ours started a new branch of its own Pontifical Academy, with Mundane scientists and wizards, both secular and religious, studying and contributing under our Vatican's sponsorship.

Interestingly, a lot of the non-Catholic Mundanes convert while researching under our "religious oppression." I understand Alistarre has refused several invitations to study there. He was also giving a lecture tomorrow—oops, today. It's on Grace's list to attend. I wondered if I'd need to hide her harp for that one.

The conversation moved to why humans could not manipulate magic.

"It seems a terrible disadvantage," a Mundane woman stood up to declare. "Other species can cast a spell, but the only way for a Faerie human to use magic is if they have a non-human in their ancestry. Yet no Mundane child has ever been able to manipulate magic, even those who now have Magical ancestry."

She glared as if it were somehow our fault. I wondered who she knew or if she'd simply heard some half-elf/half-mundane kid whining on Flôwer.

"I would not say that humans are at a disadvantage," answered another man from across the room, standing on his chair to make sure he was seen and heard. I smiled to see Frederico SanGermano, a true expert on Magicals. He'd nursed me back to health on more than one occasion, and I'd been hoping to catch up with him during the conference.

He continued, "It could be simply that humans take their advantages for granted, much the way dwarves take their ability to tunnel as simply a part of their natural design. Of all the sapients, humans, including Mundanes, have incredible adaptability. For example, our ability to ingest and process both natural and artificial chemicals exceeds that of any of the other species."

"Like iron?" someone called out. "I'm a doctor, and we studied the blood of different species of Faerie. Most are iron-based, yet too much exposure—even by proximity—is poisonous."

SanGermano nodded. "Exactly, but it's not limited to iron. It's one reason why we're so careful about what products cross the Gap. Humans also have a more adaptable perception of the passage of time. Nymphs, for example, have a less...sophisticated...time sense. They can perceive immediate events and understand the passage of the seasons, but phrases like 'see you next week' have little meaning. High Elves, of course, think at a different rate. We'd always assumed it was cultural, but lately, we're seeing evidence that there may be a biological basis as well."

The timer went off then, and we watched the Doctor battle the Daleks. I wondered, though, what could make Frederico believe that the Elves' perceptions of time were biologically based?

As the Doctor did something fantastic and unlikely with his sonic screwdriver, I felt a scrap of paper wriggle its way under my foot. I looked up and saw Frederico nod and turn his attention back to the screen. Figuring it was his room number, I, too, turned back to the screen.

I wondered if Grace could magic us a sonic screwdriver.

Chapter Nineteen: Creatures of Action, Ja?

The WhoFest was going on for another episode, but I made myself duck out. It was already past five in the morning, and I had some work to do before I met Grace for morning devotions. I dropped by the con café for a carafe of coffee, a half-dozen pastries, and some sausage. The sleepy-eyed attendant gladly carried them out to the balcony for me so I could settle down and eat more comfortably while I mulled over my next move.

Cory had sent me the guest list, and I pulled it up on my phone. I'd cased the whole building, and while I hadn't been able to scent out Gozon's briefcase exactly, I had located several that smelled similar. Now I checked them against the rooms where I'd caught the scent. Mundanes, one and all.

Who was I kidding? If the brownies had taken it, they would have cleaned it beyond nasal recognition.

I also noticed that Galendor's friend, Kevin, did not have a room in the Mensa block—and that his room was paid for by the Ping Cola Bottling Company. I needed to talk to Galendor about that. I put my phone away and turned my attention to the pastries. Then I remembered Frederico's note and pulled it out.

So good to see you, old friend. Too long has passed, but time flies, even for Elves, eh? Meet me after my zoology panel and we shall walk to my book signing. I will give one to you, courtesy of the Tavendors. Left hand pocket.

Great. More mystery. But possibly some valuable intelligence. "Time flies even for Elves"? Frederico never made idle chatter, so was he referring to his comment about the Elves' changing perception of time?

Frederico under the sponsorship of the Tavendors, hm? If what he knew threatened Galendor's tribe, they might have coerced him into keeping it under his hat.

"Left hand pocket" was written in the specific language of used for spells, but I think that was more than just a way to get the note to me unobtrusively. I don't have pockets. So his pocket, perhaps? If so, there would be something in that pocket he wanted me to get.

I'd have to check with Grace about when his panel was. In the meantime, I followed the old cliché and chewed up the note, washing it down with about half the carafe of coffee and a cheese Danish. Calories are calories. Then I went to question some suspects.

I found Brunhilde at a Nautilus machine in the hotel gym. At six a.m., the gym was already busy and smelling of sweat. Fans competed with the sound of grunts and TVs playing the morning show at a low volume. I saw Reporter Roxanne's smiling face as she talked about something in the Middle East.

Being extremely careful of my tail around all the weights and whirling bike spokes, I went to Brunhilde and waited until she'd finished her last rep. Her grimace turned into a pleased smile as she slowly allowed the padded handles to go back to their original position, then turned and wiped the seat for the next patron.

"You're up early," I said.

"Ja, it takes a lot of work to get all muscley feminine." She struck a bodybuilder's pose.

Around me, weights dropped and someone's foot slipped off the exercise bike.

She dropped the pose and giggled. "They like to look, ja?"

"It's not the looking that's causing problems. Where were you when the fire alarms went off yesterday?"

For a wonder, she actually ducked her eyes and rubbed one buff arm. "Do I have to tell? Ja, all right. I was in the bath-ing with Cambridge—"

"Ramada?" I choked out. Dragon or no, I did not need that image.

"Ja, but we were all sudsy and he said it was probably a false alarm and..." Then she switched to Faerie Norwegian. "Do you know what it's like in Valhalla? The men are all big and sweaty and they wear the armor and... Do you know what it's like to cuddle a man who died with sand in his boots and blood on his hands? Or kiss a man who's been drinking mead for a thousand years and never uses a toothbrush? Mundanes say, 'But they were so hygienic!'"

She rolled her eyes. I understood. Hygiene had changed a lot in a millennium, even more so between the Mundane and the Faerie.

"I don't want that anymore. I love my burly mens, ja, but I want to be a modern woman."

"So you want guys like Cambridge, or SkinnyZits in the elevator?" The words left my mouth before I realized I'd spoken them. Thank heaven I replied in Norwegian.

She dug her sneaker toe into the rubbery floor. "Ja, he was sweet. And minty. But I don't know. I am exploring new things."

"Is that what you were doing in Gozon's room two nights ago? 'Exploring?'" I could not believe I was having this conversation. Could I just block out the gross details?

She smiled. I didn't think a 175-pound bodybuilding Valkyrie could look coy, but she pulled it off. "A girl can't get what she wants if she doesn't do some searching."

Guess Grace hadn't had a talk with her. Great. A chastity lecture from a dragon—can you think of anything more ridiculous? I hoped God was giving me extra credit for trying. "You know, most intelligent species prefer to get to know someone by talking."

She burst out laughing. "Talking? With a High Elf?" While she buckled over in her mirth, I prayed, *Give me points for trying. Please give me points for trying.*

When she could finally control her laughter, she said, "The Mundanes, they tell me 'Talk is cheap,' ja? Besides, I am a woman of action. It is how I am made."

She thrust out her chest and beat it with her fist. Someone yelped as he fell off the treadmill. I gave her a standard warning about remembering the Ten Commandments and left before she could argue or worse, ask for clarification.

Brunhilde's story gave Cambridge an alibi, even if I hadn't suspected him of anything. Well, anything in particular—anything right now; I'd always suspect him on general principles after our last encounter. Cambridge was a different kind of PI, one who sought out and acquired unusual objects. He claimed to have a code of ethics, but near as I could tell, it had more to do with his personal assessment of a person and their money versus the risk. He'd been all too willing to give one of the multiverse's most dangerous artifacts to someone because he "believed he was not interested in it for its power." He'd seemed pretty nonchalant about my burning his client's prize to ash; I wondered how he'd made it up to him?

Perhaps I'd bother him later. For the moment, I headed to the end of the second floor. If Brunhilde was up and about, I figured this would probably be the best time to catch Coyote alone. I didn't have any real reason to suspect Coyote, except on general principles like Cambridge, but my instincts never failed me.

On my way, I passed the newsstand and did a double take. A full color underwater photo of my posterior was splashed across the front page. Literally. *The Citrus City Tribune* headline read, "Nessie on Vacation? Or Another Faerie Monster?"

Monster? Looks like Kitty McGrue has a cousin at the *Tribune.* I scanned the article and discovered the divers I'd inadvertently frightened were actually researchers for some environmental association collecting data on different subspecies of fish. It continued on page ten, but I didn't want to buy a paper right then. I wanted to get to Coyote while he was still alone.

Despite my haste, Coyote was not alone. Far from it, in fact.

A young Hispanic woman in a hotel uniform opened the door partway. Her eyes got bigger and bigger as her gaze traveled from my torso to my smiling face. "*Dios mio!*" she gasped.

Very politely and in Spanish, I asked if I could come in and talk to Coyote, please. She blinked at me but didn't move. Behind her, I heard the scurrying of several humans, then Coyote yipped a "come in!" and she let me pass.

Coyote's room had a double bed, but he'd taken the mattress off and set it in front of the couch. He half-sat/half-reclined on the mattress, his back against the seat of the couch, propped up by pillows. He wore silk pajamas. His ankle sported a metal-and-mesh police anklet. Stylish. A half-dozen ladies surrounded him, sitting, reclining, or even posing on the floor or couch. Somehow, it made me think of the gangster movies Kenjo and his tribe liked to watch.

They certainly made quite an assortment, from the little maid now sitting quietly on the arm of the couch to the dryad rubbing his feet. On the table and floor sat bowls with strawberries, whipped cream, and chocolate sauce. A copy of the *Tribune* lay on the floor, my photo up.

"Vern, join us! We were just reading about you. Too bad they didn't get your good side." Beside him, some of the ladies giggled.

"All my sides are good, Coyote." I let my smile curve into a stern frown. "Ladies, if you'll excuse us?"

With disappointed moans, they filed out. The maid stooped to pick up a couple of the bowls, then paused long enough to dip a strawberry in whipped cream, place it half into her mouth and, holding it between her teeth, share it with Coyote with a kiss.

It takes a lot to make a dragon retch. That little scene came close. I ground my teeth and filled my mind with thoughts of deserts instead of desserts as she sauntered past me with a grin on her face.

"I thought chocolate made dogs sick," I said as the door closed behind her.

"Only if I eat it. So, why are you ruining my fun?" He dipped another strawberry in cream, popped it into his mouth, and leaned back, his hands folded behind his head. He didn't seem too concerned about his spoiled fun. He could probably just howl and have another bunch of willing ladies flock to him.

"You were with Brunhilde last night."

"She got what she wanted and left. Said she's tired of crowds. So you've come to ask about my love life? Looking for tips in case you turn human again?"

Of course, he'd heard about that. The coffee and food in my stomach gave a sick twist. "Don't even joke about that. Where were you when the fire alarm went off?"

Coyote howled. Literally. "So you are looking for tips! Well, you should have asked before Marisol left. She could vouch for me."

Did I really want to know? I was beginning to wonder about these human conventions, or was it just the Faerie element? Next time, I'm telling Grace to make a libido alarm as well.

But Coyote said, "We met at the swimming pool. She was working the towels area."

"Practicing your dog paddle?" I quipped.

He laughed. "As a matter of fact, Brittany—the long-legged brunette—was teaching me to dive. I never have gotten the hang of diving. So, what's going on? That was a terrific joke they played on you, by the way!"

"And were you the puck that arranged it?"

"Oh, I wish I had! But, no. You may not believe me, but I was actually surprised to see you here."

Perhaps so, but I couldn't help believing that he was using that fact to make some fun for himself. "Coyote, just what are you doing here? You're supposed to be living in Montana—*Mundane* Montana."

"I told you. I'm a Mensan. Took the test and everything."

"Did you cheat?"

He shrugged unapologetically. "Only because I could. Look, Vern. I love my people, I do. They're my posse, my pack, my tribe. But they're Mundanes. And they're—I'm embarrassed to say it— poor. I'm living in a trailer."

"You used to live in a den in the ground."

He waved his hand dismissively, then grabbed the bowl of strawberries and held it out as if it were evidence. "That was before the Gap. Vern, there's so much...*much!*...here. The luxuries, the entertainments, the freedoms!"

I braced myself. If he told me he was stifled—

"I was stifled! There's so much to experience in this universe. Come on, Vern. You're an immortal. You know how it is."

I thought about my three hours of Who-hooky and the ShowStream subscription—the one bill I pay on time without fail. "I don't break the law for my novelties."

He tossed his head. "Of course not. You've got that whole Saint George thing to live up to. But Vern, I was made differently. And come on." He sat up and gave me his big happy-dog grin. "Don't I make the world a more interesting place just by being me?"

"Too interesting. It seems to me we've warned you more than once about making things 'interesting' with the ladies."

He whined. "Not all of them. Just the willing ones."

I had to concede that point. I'd sniffed at least three virgins in the group, Marisol among them. Chastity Speech Number Two. Grace would be proud. George was probably laughing his armor off. "Nonetheless, you're going to tone down the capers."

"But—"

I'd had enough of this discussion. I half-unfurled my wings and snarled. He fell onto his back, arms and legs up in a picture of classic submission.

"Okay! Okay! I'll keep my mojo on the low-jo." He stopped, grinned to himself, and sat back up. "'Mojo on the low-jo.' I crack myself up."

"No more groups." I said, and turned to leave. I'd intended to ask him about Gozon's briefcase, but I no longer thought he'd had anything to do with it, and I didn't want to give him any ideas. There's only so much temptation the Trickster can resist.

"Hey, Vern!" he called as I grasped the door handle. "You never told me about being human."

"Glad you noticed that." I turned the handle.

Either he had informants in Los Lagos or he knew me better than I wanted him to, because he asked, "How'd Grace take it?"

"Like a nun." That was all the answer he ever needed to know.

He made a pained noise. "Ouch. Yeah, she took it like a nun when I kissed her, too."

"You kissed Grace?" I spun around, chemical processes behind my stomach readying my fire. I clamped my teeth against the urge to roast him where he stood. *I will not set the hotel on fire. I will not set the hotel on fire.*

He looked at me as if I were an idiot. "Well, I tried. And I learned my lesson. What? You didn't even try? What kind of man were you?"

"The proper kind. She's a nun!"

"Well, okay. There is that. Still. You can't tell me there wasn't something between you two. I can sense it even when you're different species."

I didn't bother to answer him. In retrospect, that may have been all the answer he needed.

I left Coyote's room unsettled, my mind arguing against his last-minute implication. I'm a dragon and she's a nun. Anything else, any attraction (shudder) that we may have felt when I was in human form, was just part of the curse that had been designed to hurt her as much as to get at me. The curse was broken. I'm dragon again, and we're still best friends. That was all there was to it. Wasn't it?

God willing, I'd never be human again. For Grace's sake as much as for mine.

Chapter Twenty: Spirits and Stegosauruses

So lost was I in my thoughts, I didn't notice Reed until I practically bumped into him.

"Vern! I'm so glad to catch you. I have a present for you!"

He nudged forward a lovely Japanese lady holding a furry purse with a cat's face. She bowed low.

I returned the bow carefully, but was nonetheless confused. After Coyote and my own thoughts, my brain started down a totally bizarre path; fortunately, my nose and magic sense caught something unusual about her bag and brought me on target. "Hey, that thing's alive."

She wasn't holding a purse that resembled a cat; she was holding a cat that resembled a purse. The ginger's body formed the bag. The strap was the tail, curled around and attached to the neck just behind the bobble head. One hind foot, stretched to the back as if to scratch itself, formed the clasp for the flap.

"Thank you for noticing," the purse said wryly.

It was a kaminigi, a minor spirit that could animate an object. I'd seen them in Faerie—the Duchess has a wardrobe that gives her fashion advice. Not that it's especially good advice, mind you. A lot of weird trends were started on Peebles-on-Tweed thanks to that hunk of oak suggesting this blouse with that skirt or a new collar line. They thrived on attention. What was one doing with a Mundane?

"I'm not sure I understand," I said carefully.

"I got Nekosan from the InterdimNet," she said. "KamiKrafts. I thought it was cute, that they play on Shinto animism. They make you fill out an adoption certificate before purchase. I did not know it was a real adoption."

"And so you want to give me the bag?" I was definitely missing something here.

"Oh, no, honored dragon! I love Nekosan!" she said with an accent that told me English was not her first language. She rubbed the top of the purse affectionately. Nekosan purred.

"But we did think that this might be the answer to your brownie dilemma," Reed said. "Keiko has agreed to leave Nekosan in a mess in an out-of-the-way area, and..."

I grinned. Finally, something that showed some promise. I asked the purse, "You sure? You may end up spending a lot of time in a corner for nothing."

"Like I haven't done that before," the bag cat replied. "It'll be the most fun I've had in years. We'll have to do something to mask my true nature, though."

"Follow me, then," I said, "and we'll see if Grace has a spell that will make the brownies think we let the cat out of the bag."

Had to credit Keiko for her command of English. Even she groaned at that one.

I'd missed devotions with Grace, but we caught up with her at the con café, eating and laughing with Eliza and the moderator from the music panel. She waved us over and after we'd crowded around her table, and she made introductions. "We saw Shirley sitting here when we came in for breakfast, so I came over to apologize—"

"—which wasn't necessary," Shirley interrupted. "Once I got over the shock, I thought the panel, even the fight, was great. Everybody's talking about it, and it's going to make a terrific article for my newsletter."

"You are very gracious," Grace told her, then turned back to me. "Shirley plans to go out after breakfast to do some shopping, so I thought if you'd cover things here, I could take care of the last of Charlie's list. Several people want authentic Fanny Flamingo stuff, and there are some souvenir shops nearby."

"No problem."

"And Shirley is a test moderator," Grace said, "She's invited us to test for Mensa."

"I'm not a person according to U.S. law," I told Shirley.

"Well, the government doesn't tell us who we can or can't have as members," she said. "I already mentioned it to the Governing Committee, and we'd be honored to have you as a member—or at least to try."

She gave me a mischievous grin.

"Lady, I've got the Wisdom of the Ages. Bring it on. But first..." I explained about Reed's and

Keiko's idea to catch a brownie. Grace cleared her place on the table, and Keiko set Nekosan on it. She examined the purse carefully, while the other ladies cooed over it and murmured those silly inanities humans murmur to their pets. Made me glad that, even if I didn't qualify as a person I, at least, didn't rank as an animal. The bag seemed to like it, though.

Grace said, "I can do it easily enough. It'll take about twenty minutes. Have you thought about where you'll put him? We need someplace public enough to attract their attention and private enough that no one notices them."

Eliza asked why that was. "I realize that no one's actually seen the brownies in action, but why not just set up a messy room and keep watch? We can trap them when they come to clean it."

I tried to explain. "Brownies are interdimensional beings. They can only exist in our dimension when in motion, but they're only in motion when they're not seen by someone of our dimension. Even a surveillance camera observing them makes them cease moving—and thus cease to exist in our space-time."

"Kind of like electrons, then?" Eliza said. "Not literally, but in the fact that we can know where they are or we can know where they're going, but not both simultaneously?"

"It's a little more complex. There's also magic and uncertainty involved. If you know they're in a spot, they aren't. If you suspect their location and can suspend your certainty, they can remain there—or maybe not."

Shirley laughed. "Now we're talking about Schrödinger's cat. Except in this case, we're going to use the cat to catch the quantum elf."

Eliza spoke up, "What about the corner behind the convention registration table? No one will bother with it, and it certainly could do with a good cleaning. Plus, it's not an especially busy area now."

Reed wished us luck, then took his leave, saying he wanted to write up some notes while all this was fresh in his mind. Keiko and Grace took Nekosan to become a brownie catacombs. Keiko and Eliza would drop off the purse alone, so as to not arouse suspicion, and Shirley and Grace would head out on their shopping trip. "Pursey" would take a nice long nap, flap open, and hopefully, our do-gooder brownies would rise to the bait.

I hadn't really had a chance to look at the Mensa Marketplace, and I had some money Grace had gotten from the ATM for me. Most people were at some talk or the other, so the hallways were clear. I decided to go poke around awhile.

I checked the joke booth first and found the sneezing powder was wisely listed as "sold out." Then I spent a pleasant hour looking at the jewelry and art, woodcrafts and costumes. Many of the craftsmen were quite talented, and especially with modern Mundane tools, would give some of the finer artisans of Faerie a run for their money. In fact, many of them have, which has caused some trouble in Faerie.

Speaking of trouble. I noticed some of the fairies in Templegrass's booth gathered together, muttering to each other and casting dirty looks at the stall across from them. It sported, along with funny hand-sewn hats, those hard plaster knick-knacks like I was clobbered with by Maddog Mom on our first day at the convention. However, it wasn't the hats or the trinkets that caught their ire so much as the person visiting the booth.

Princess Galinda was holding a hat in her hands, but I could hear her talking with the owner about the bric-a-brac. As I approached, she cut her conversation short and left. Ignoring the booth, I went to greet the fairies.

"Princess Oh-So-Classy barely gave our booth a glance," Templegrass complained.

Starflower added, "Said, 'No offense, but I'm looking for the exotic.' Pah! She wants cheap and Mundane. No offense!" She called that last to the woman across the booth, but it didn't matter. They were speaking in a range outside human hearing, anyway.

I promised to have a talk with Galinda. I didn't save her life, not to mention her good standing with her family, so that she could help her family flood the Faerie markets with mass produced "hand painted" badly proportioned puppies.

Still, I had to admit the hats amused me. I wondered if I bought one for the Duke's wife, would she try to start a new trend? I lingered a moment, weighing the revenge value of the practical joke against what I might lose. Every good deed earns me back some of my former glory, but every bad deed means a loss. In this case, it all depended on God's sense of humor.

I decided the puck wasn't funny enough—not to mention the wrath I'd be facing from Temple-grass and her crew. I moved on.

I was perusing the games booth, thinking I might get something for the Costa family, when I felt a small but determined tug on one of the spikes along my spine. I twisted my head around to see a girl of about eight years regarding me thoughtfully. She took hold of the end of my tail.

"You don't have a thagomizer," she accused.

I'd thought about calling her "Snack" and telling her to let go of my tail, but she'd already released me and was regarding my tail with intent if befuddled interest. I don't mind kids much, really. I always manage to collect a gaggle of them around me after church, and my good friend Jerry Costa has ten of his own, so I'm used to getting tugged at now and again. Finding one with such good manners was a rare gift.

"So I've noticed," I said. "Not all of us do."

"I have a whole collection of dragons at home, and not all of them have spikes, either. Like dinosaurs. Stegosauruses have thagomizers," she announced. She continued to stare at my tail, my back, my wings, her brows knit in thought. I could imagine her trying to place me in whatever catalogue she'd made for her plastic models. I wondered if she might be related to Bill Reed.

"True," I replied.

Just then, her mother turned from where she'd been looking at jewelry, gasped, and pulled her daughter away. There was a reaction I was more used to. Holding her close, she stammered out an apology.

I gave her my best "Who-me?-I'm-harmless" smile. "It's okay. I'm Vern." I held out my paw to the girl, palm perpendicular to the ground like a human's. She grasped one claw in her tiny hand and shook it.

"Penelope Granger, and no. No relation to Hermione. She's fictional and I'm real."

"Glad to hear it. I'm real, too."

"I read dragons can change sizes. Chinese dragons can be as small as a raindrop or as large as a lake. Is that true?"

"Not in Faerie. We pretty much stay the same size all our lives unless we pull from our mass in order to heal. We do come in several sizes, though none as small as a raindrop or large as a lake."

"Is this your regular size?"

I grimaced. "My regular size is about ten times as big as I am now."

She thought for a moment. "So, like a stegosaurus"

"Yeah. But not as bulky." Smart kid. I noticed her mother relax and smile slightly. Around us, people paused to listen.

"Stegosaurus is my favorite dinosaur. They lived in the Late Jurassic-Albian period. Did your ancestors live in the Late Jurassic-Albian period?"

"Actually, *I* lived in the Late Jurassic-Albian period. Seventy dragons were created on the eighth day of creation, and we never die."

Among adults, that statement usually raised questions about immortality and religion, but Penelope had different priorities. "Did you eat stegosauruses?"

"Sometimes." I leaned a little closer and whispered, "They taste like chicken."

Don't know what it is about humans, but that joke never gets old. She giggled, and her mother took that opportunity to tell her that she needed to say goodbye so they could get to Kids' Camp. "You don't want to miss the concert."

Penelope tsked like any small child would do. "I'd rather talk to a dragon. I can see Rhoda Dakota on TV any ol' day."

Rhoda Dakota? A human would consider this a fortunate happenstance, but I knew better. I figured God wanted me to humble myself, again, and He has a real sense of humor about it. I tried to sound casual. "Rhoda Dakota? Is she doing a convention tour or something?"

"Do you like Rhoda? Do you want her autograph?" Her eyes widened with surprise and a little disappointment.

This was going to be worse than I thought. "I have a friend who's a big fan."

"Another dragon?"

"No, just a human, a Faerie human, to be exact. But he wants her autograph."

She turned to her mom. "Can he come watch? Then he can tell us about dragons while she signs autographs."

Oops! Did I just volunteer for an hour of getting climbed on and asked questions about my bathroom habits? "I don't want to be a disruption. And actually, I should go on patrol..."

"Please?" Now, she did get rude, boldly grabbing my nearest back spike with one hand and her mother's hand in the other.

Fortunately, Mom came to the rescue. "How about if we asked the staff if Mr. Dragon..."

"Vern."

"...Mr. Vern can come visit later, after the concert? We could get his friend's autograph for him and give it to him then, okay?"

Thank God for mothers.

Chapter Twenty-One: No One's Pathologically Anything

We headed to the Kids' Camp on the fourth floor, a large ballroom divided into stations. The activity level probably matched that of any busy Montessori school, but the lack of dividing walls made the noise quite a din. At the moment, the aides hustled about like human sheepdogs trying to get everyone rounded up and settled in front of the makeshift stage where a good-sized stereo system stood. I didn't actually go in. The aides were having enough trouble getting the kids to sit still as it was. Instead, I hung out by the doorway while Penelope's mom got her to her age group, then found the director. I could hear Penelope talking with another kid.

"I met the dragon today."

"You did?"

"Did not," said another child with a sneer. He sounded bigger but not necessarily older.

"Did so! He said he'd come visit us if I got Rhoda Dakota's autograph for him."

"That is so stupid. Why would a dragon want an autograph? You're lying. Stupid lying."

"Am not. He wants it for a Faerie friend."

I don't know whether the kid laughed at the "Faerie" part or at the cliché, but instead he said, "Are you a pathological liar? Or just pathologically stupid?"

"You're pathologically mean!"

Right about then an adult intervened with, "No one is pathologically anything," and Penelope's mom came to me with the "principal." He looked like a principal, too: short for a human male, with a square jaw softened by age and weight, neatly trimmed but not stylish brown hair, an equally neat beard, and glasses, but mostly he had that air of responsibility. Not harried, mind you, just very aware that he was molding young minds. I'd seen his type on both sides of the Gap.

When he saw me, however, his face broke into a grin that told me everything I needed to know about why he worked with kids.

"Amazing!" he said, though I knew his Inner Child was jumping up and down and squealing, "So Cool! So Cool!" I tried not to preen, but I do love it when I get that reaction.

Penelope's mom introduced us, and Principal Jerry Morton said, "Mrs. Granger said you'd be willing to come talk to the kids this afternoon? That would be just wonderful! Wonderful! We'd been hoping to have a few Faerie citizens come talk. We managed to get Princess Galinda and her husband because one of their friends has a child here, but well..."

"Did Galendor talk them to sleep?"

Morton looked uncomfortable. "Actually, quite the opposite. He was...impatient...with the children."

A High Elf, impatient? Galendor loved children, too. I filed that one away for future investigation. "Glad to help. I've done some school programs in Los Lagos, and I think I can round up a few other volunteers." Kent would probably love having an appreciative audience. Coyote? I could tell Coyote it was community service. That could work. He might stir up some mischief among the kids, but I'd know where he was for a while, and even Coyote had some limits.

Morton beamed with delight and suggested some available times, and I agreed to come back in an hour to talk.

At the elevator, my radio went off. "Vern? It's Gary Spade from the day shift. Can you come down to the security office? I've got something for you."

"On my way."

I walked into an immaculately clean office and made a guess. "Briefcase?"

Spade raised his eyebrows and wordlessly set Gozon's freshly buffed leather briefcase on the desk. "Gonna share how you came to that conclusion?"

I liked Spade. Even the first time he met me, he didn't get awed or freaked; he just treated me like another colleague. He'd said after ten years with the NYC PD and another fifteen as a detective in Miami, nothing surprised him. I settled myself in a corner. "Office looks too clean for you—or the maids, for that matter—to have cleaned it up. I figure the brownies dropped it off here and decided to do what comes naturally while they were at it."

"Yeah, well, you got that right. They even scoured the coffee maker. I'd forgotten coffee could taste like that."

"Don't clean the pot at home either?"

Spade said something rude that few people would ever say to a dragon. Like I said, one of the guys. "Briefcase is locked, not that I think it made any difference to them. Any idea what's so special about it? We've been getting calls from guests, complaining that someone came into their rooms when they were gone or asleep, but nothing is ever missing, just cleaned, repaired, and organized. We went ahead and told them it was brownies. Some think we're freaking nuts; others want to know where they can get some to take home."

"Hope you told them they can't. Brownies are free spirits. Coerce them, and they're likely to turn on you—and they can be as destructive as they are neat."

"Yeah, Sister Grace told us. Where is she, anyway? Thought she had the day shift."

"Picking up some stuff for friends."

"You got sent with a list?" Spade laughed and tilted back in his chair. "Haven't they heard of the Internet?"

"That's what I said!" You know, I was beginning to like Florida. I wondered if there was a place for a dragon to make his lair? I heard that Florida had problems with invasive species—pythons and such. I could help with that and kept fed. How long could I be away from the Gap? Maybe I could be a, what do they call it? Snowbird. A snowbird dragon.

Gozon was at a luncheon with the governor and some local bigwigs. His attendance had been arranged by the House Eternal Winds and did not involve me, thankfully. He wouldn't be back until five, so Spade locked the briefcase in the security office safe, and I headed back upstairs to entertain the kiddies. Belatedly, I realized I hadn't mentioned that I don't give rides.

Amazingly, it didn't come up. When I got there, the kids had gotten their autographs, had had some time for running around, and were settling back in front of the stage. The stage itself had been cleared, so I settled myself up there, told them a little about my life as a dragon, St. George, and what I did now. A couple of them were almost as interested in my detective work as they were in my being a dragon.

Penelope raised her hand. "Do Stegosauruses really taste like chicken?"

I laughed. "It's actually kind of hard to describe in human terms. It's more of a cross between beef and lizard."

"Lizards taste like chicken!" someone hollered.

"Actually, to a dragon, nothing tastes like chicken except chicken. My taste buds are much more discerning than a human's. And I didn't eat a lot of Stegosauruses. Too chewy."

That led to what kind of food I liked, and what my favorite foods are now. They were disappointed to discover I didn't like chocolate or soda, and I didn't mention beer. Then someone asked how I ate—like a lizard or a person.

"I can eat like a human. I have opposable thumbs, see? But most silverware is too small for me and my teeth and jaws make knives redundant, so I usually use my fingers. Don't let me hear that any of you went home, ate with your fingers, and then told your parents, 'but that dragon does it.' You're not dragons. I also catch my own food, and I don't think anyone wants to join me on a rat hunt...unless you want raw rat meat?"

There was a chorus of "ew!" until someone called out, "Do they taste like chicken?"

"No, wise guy. They're vile, but there have been times living here when I couldn't afford to buy my food."

"Do you have to eat a lot?" Penelope asked.

"Depends on what I'm doing. In general, about as much as two humans in a day. And you're making me hungry. Anybody else got other questions?"

A boy about nine wearing a shirt that read *Don't Be Scared To Be A Saint* asked if St. George had converted any more dragons, and I told him no, that St. George died not long after he'd converted me. He'd been protecting the Pope's niece when it happened—a hero to the end. I felt a little pang when I remembered; I had been the Pope's pet at that point, and had sensed the demon around the child and told George about it. George was a pain in the tail, but there was never anyone braver or more caring...except maybe Grace.

A little girl with round brown eyes like Catarina's raised her hand and asked shyly, "May we pet you?"

I could have said, "No." I'm sure the adults expected me to, but the kids had impressed me with their behavior. Besides, I did like small humans. I told them, "Six at a time, and no climbing on my back." I thought about adding that when I get cranky I tend to snack on naughty children, but wasn't sure the joke would fly with some of the younger ones.

I don't often admit it, but I actually like getting petted and fawned over by sapients. Dragons spend a lot of time getting groomed, a luxury I don't get to indulge any longer. Besides, there's something different about human touch: an understood admiration if not affection. Or maybe St. George's spell had attuned me to the touch of humans. I didn't know, and I didn't care to investigate. After all, I deserved some perks in this life.

Starting with the preschoolers, they came up and gently stroked my scales and touched my spikes. I unfurled my wings so they could feel the soft leathery membrane. A teenage girl who came up with the ten-year-olds found the spot behind my cheek crest and I leaned into it and purred while she scratched.

"You're hired," I told her.

"No fair," a boy on my other side whined. "You get everything."

"Do not," she groaned, rolling her eyes.

"Do, too, *Rhoda Dakota*!" His sneer told me he was her brother.

I turned my head toward him, still keeping my cheek firmly against Rhoda's fingers. "What's your name, kid?"

"Jason."

"Well, Jason, see that scale right under there?" With my tail I pointed to the spot where Junior Dragonrider had kicked me two days ago. "It's out of alignment, can you see that? You'd make me one happy dragon if you could rub it back in place. That's right. There. Good! Now press down real hard."

While Jason took to his task with gusto, I said to his sister, "So you're Rhoda Dakota? I heard you made a lot of kids happy today."

"Thanks. And my real name's Heather. Heather Haskell. I try to keep a low profile when I'm not on stage, you know?"

"I don't do 'low profile' well," I said, and she laughed. "Say, did a girl named Penelope ask you—"

"For an autograph? Yeah. I thought she was totally kidding that her dragon friend wanted an autograph. That's why I stuck around. This is too cool."

"Not me. A friend of mine. He's got quite a crush on you."

"Is he some pretty-boy slacker like most of her boyfriends?" Jason asked from where he still worked under my wing.

"Shut up!" she shrieked.

"Actually," I said before the fight could ensue, "he's a herald for the Duke. He delivers messages and important announcements."

Jason asked, "Like a mailman?" Having decided his work met his satisfaction—mine, too, for that matter—he went back to examining my wings.

"Jeez, Jace—do you have to be such a total dweeb? Bet he's more like an *ambassador*."

"Well, a courier, but that means more in Faerie than here." I did my best to explain Charlie and his job. I did it up right, painting Herald Charlie as the Duke's most trusted courier, first-line diplomat, and intelligence gatherer.

"That's so cool," Heather said, and of course Jason then took the opportunity to tease her that she had a crush on a mailman. Fortunately, it was time for the next group, and I didn't have to have children bickering overtop me. I got enough of that at the Costa's.

After everyone had had a chance to pet the dragon, Heather brought me a manila envelope. I peeked at the autographed picture inside.

She'd dotted the "i" in "Charlie" with a heart and included her private Xinga contact information.

Little brothers. Sometimes they know you better than you think.

I tried to go to Brunhilde's lecture, but the room was so over-packed with people—mostly men, big surprise—that the doors stood open and latecomers jammed the threshold just to get a glimpse and listen. I rolled my eyes and went by without slowing down. As I passed, I heard her say, "Oh, ja, they're really mine," but didn't care to back up to find out if she was referring to her adventures or something more personal. Some things a dragon does not need to know.

All the talk about food had made me hungry; coffee and Danishes were too long ago. I dropped by the con café, grabbed myself a big platter and settled down on the balcony. With the temperature already well into the upper nineties and the air humid as well, I ate in privacy. On the grounds below, I heard someone complain about the humidity. Turks, by the language. I saw a man and a woman in long robes heading down to the naiad pond and wondered how Grace was faring in the heat.

Grace had said she'd be back in time for the naiads' event, so I decided to go to our room and see what goodies she'd picked up.

I found her with Shirley in the hallway just outside the elevator. She was flushed, but with happiness rather than heat. It was good to see her that way.

"Hi. We just got back. I got almost everything. I even found an autographed poster of Rhoda Dakota. It's not the real thing, but—"

"No need," I said, and handed her the envelope I'd been holding with my tail. While she opened it,

I shook out the kinks; tails really aren't made for holding thin paper like that.

Her eyes grew wide when she saw the autograph and took in the Xinga address. She sniffed at the fresh marker smell. "How?"

I struck a proud pose. "I am a dragon, wise and cunning—"

"—and your ways are beautiful and mysterious," she concluded. "Ach, Shirley, don't be stepping in any of that. Vern, we're off to see the naiads. Why don't you put this with the rest of the stuff? Or maybe you should put it in the safe. I'd hate for the brownies to find it and 'clean up' the scribbles."

"That would be bad." I took back the envelope. Grace's spells would keep them out.

On my way back to the convention, I passed Gozon's room. I heard motion inside. I paused at his door, extending my senses: Gozon, and he was alone. He shouldn't have been back for another hour and a half at least.

This was going to be a long story—what else could I expect from Gozon?—so I ducked into my room and put away the photo, then rapped on his door.

For 87 minutes, Gozon told me, in excruciating detail, what had happened at the governor's luncheon. At times like these, I could almost pity Kitty McGrue, who had to report on the city council and PTA meetings at Los Lagos. Gozon's story sounded much the same, just with food. The only thing more torturous was hearing it with commentary in Elvish. Not even the poetic language of the High Elves can make highway easements interesting. Then some environmental group did a presentation about some sub-sub-species of fish from the Jollie Trench they were monitoring—

Gozon's voice trailed off, and I took the opportunity to interrupt. "But why did you return so early? What happened?" (Keep in mind we're speaking in High Elvish, which meant I had to summarize what he'd said, compliment his storytelling, comment on his attendance and grooming, then note the time and weather, traveling conditions, etc. In all, another fifteen minutes.)

This led to a much heated but nonetheless long tirade about Galendoropynphordaladys and the Princess Galinda getting themselves invited to the luncheon and schmoozing with the Mundanes there. In the end, Galendor had folks laughing at his oh-so-Mundane jokes and completely ignoring Gozon. He'd finally made a quiet exit in disgust.

I got a sinking feeling in my gut that had nothing to do with digestion. Galendor had always spoken Human well, and had improved greatly since his marriage to Princess Galinda. In fact, he was probably there as Galinda's husband rather than in any official Elvish role. However, neither Gozon nor his people would see it that way.

For all his faults and difficulties fitting in with the new world, Gozonvabosomofic of the House Eternal Winds of the Shores of the High Elves was Speaker for the Winds for the entire House. There's no equivalent in modern Mundane society; in some ways, he's like a king's right hand and a standard for the House and for his tribe. Galendor, by his actions, had effectively put himself in competition for Gozon's job, and the people at the meeting had just as effectively endorsed him.

I prayed that I was mistaken. If so, I might be able to do some spin control.

"There have been three in the Forest tribe who would displace me," Gozon replied to my question. "Galendor is a recent rival—spurred on, no doubt, by his wife's family. He has adapted to their ways too well, speaking their tongues and drinking their technologically made beverages. He laughed at me—laughed!—when I chose their fine wines over that 'cola' draught the Mundanes so prefer. Viler, however, is how he has disregarded the patient, flowing cadence of our ways—ways, I can see, that the Floridians cannot respect."

So, to summarize: Galendor recently re-emerged as a rival for Gozon's job. Gozon's and Galendor's tribes stand on the brink of a war. Galendor just wedged his way into an important ambassadorial function (in Elvish eyes) and displaced Gozon. And the people who represented the state of Florida let him do it.

Conclusion: If the elves go to war, Florida had just declared itself on the side of the Forest tribe.

Chapter Twenty-Two:
Danger, Danger, Danger!

I spent the better part of another hour counseling Gozon against making hasty decisions, trying hard not to comment on the irony. (If I had, that would have added an hour to my lecture.) In the end, he agreed to hold off judgment on Florida until "after."

But after what? "After he'd talked with them again" didn't seem plausible. I'd have to consult the bishop on this one. Dragons don't do politics unless it starts interfering with our treasure or our food supply. Or when we were playing with the mortals, but that was usually me and my twinkin, Gris. I wished she was here.

At any rate, we had a couple of decades to figure things out. By then, there'd be new governors, new presidents. Who knows? Twenty years was enough for some Mundane countries to change their entire political structure.

With the "immediate" crisis averted, I told Gozon his briefcase had turned up, and we headed back to the security office. I was starting to feel a sentimental attachment to the elevator.

Janey now occupied the security desk, and she insisted he open the briefcase in her presence and verify that nothing had been stolen.

Gozon unlocked it, peered inside, and declared that everything was as it should be.

Still, I didn't like the sly grin he had on his face as we left the office. "Gozon..."

"There you are!" Grace called out, short-circuiting what probably would have been yet another long and fruitless conversation. We paused until she caught up to us. She and Gozon shared a standard greeting. Folks flowed past us in the hallway, although one Mensan lingered, hand on a tape recorder in his pocket. He tried to be discreet, but I heard the gears whirling and guessed Gozon did, too, because he preened just a bit, though he resisted the urge to add extra flourishes to his salutation. Good thing, too, because once they'd said their hellos and he'd gone with the lingering Mensan, Grace placed a hand on my flank and pushed me down the hall.

"We're going to be late for the testing. Do my eyes deceive me, or has Gozon returned a wee bit early?"

Her accent was coming back, as it often did when she felt very relaxed or very stressed. In this case, she was smiling and her eyes had a little sparkle of merriment. I hated to snuff that out. However, I also knew from experience what bad things happened when I didn't tell my partner everything that affected us or our clients. Switching to our creole, I explained about the meeting and diffusing a potential war between the elves and the Sunshine State. "I'll tell you the details later. It's a long story," I concluded.

"Is it ever anything else with Elves?" She rolled her eyes. "I don't like this, Vern. I can understand strife within the House Eternal Winds, but doesn't this seem a bit out of hand?"

"We won't solve it today," I reassured/not reassured her. "Put it aside. We've got a test to take."

Of course, just then, the Berry Welles intercepted us.

"Could you please talk some sense into your naiad friends?" he begged.

Outside, we saw them arguing with a couple of uniformed men. Not police—animal control. Three of the naiads had their arms around the alligator, who was giving the men a dangerous stare. Although he didn't snap, his tail lashed in agitation.

Grace sighed. "That thing is not getting on the dirigible with us."

The naiads caught sight of us and started waving and calling for us to save their "sweet Sprout."

Meanwhile the animal control folks caught sight of me and glanced at the equipment in their hands, as if wondering if it was enough. Guess they hadn't seen the news today.

"It's not a pet," I called out, "and neither am I."

After much protesting about how much they loved their "sweet scaly stumper-nums" and Grace and I protesting how he belonged in his natural habitat with his other gatory friends, they made the animal control men promise to treat him gently.

"We're taking him to the De Leon National Everglades," one of the catchers reassured them as if they were children. "He'll have lots of room to swim and other gators to hang with. He's still young; he'll probably find a girlfriend this mating season."

"See?" Grace added. "You wouldn't deny him love, would you?"

I fought not to roll my eyes as the naiads all threw themselves on their Stumer-nums and begged his forgiveness for their selfish impulse.

"Vurnerrah!" Lilly cried, "You'll make sure he's alright? That he'll have a nice home?"

If that's what it took. "Yes, fine. I promise."

Finally they acquiesced, and Grace and I left them crying in each other's arms.

Shirley had set up the testing area in one of the fourth floor rooms. Three others sat at their own small table, already taking the test. She sat at another table facing them, with a watch, pencils, and our tests in front of her.

Shirley, bless her, had set up a corner of the room for me, with enough clear space that I could settle comfortably and a large smooth board on the floor so I didn't have to take my test at a table. Having to take it in pencil raised some problems, however. They don't make pencils in my size, and I never learned to write the way humans do. Instead, I have one claw specially sharpened to take ink and I write with it; but even though I insisted I could take the test in ink, it was against the rules. I had to hold the pencil pressed between two fingers. Fortunately, it was all fill-in-the-dots, so I managed, even if I did have a cramp afterward.

Naturally, the test itself didn't prove much of a challenge. I may not have all the knowledge of your world, but one thing I can do is reason. I made short work of it and dropped the finished exam on the desk in front of Shirley in about half the time allotted.

Shirley didn't even blink. "Not the fastest time we've had," she commented with a grin.

Ouch. Yeah, she and Grace were birds of a feather, all right. "The pencil slowed me down," I protested, shaking my cramped paw for emphasis.

"Of course it did." Behind me, I heard Grace snort and try to disguise it as a cough. I'd protest that she wasn't acting nun-like, but she'd just reply that it was within her Calling to keep me humble.

I tried to think of some similarly snide reply, but gave up. I was too tired and that's saying something. In fact, I hadn't done much more than catnap all week. But now I had a promise to keep.

"I'm going out for a bit. Stretch my wings. Do you think the de Leon National Everglades is a good place to keep a low profile?"

"Should be," Shirley said. "It's a protected habitat; they only let in a couple of tours a day."

I turned to Grace. "I'll be back in a couple of hours?" I didn't have any illusions about finding Sprout, but I'd check out the place, and maybe catch a nap while soaking my scales.

Grace didn't look up, but made shooing motions with her free hand, so I decided to let the Faerie fend for themselves and go take a nap in the swamp.

First, however, I took a little time finding some Faerie to talk to the kids. I never ran across Coyote, but Templegrass offered to do an art demo. Kent and Brunhilde also agreed. Eagerly and together. I didn't want to ask. I didn't want to think about it. Some things a dragon does not need to know.

Janey showed me a map of the everglades, and I found it with no trouble. Although too damp for my usual tastes, in the heat of the afternoon, the tepid water refreshed my scales. I could confidently tell the naiads that Sprout would find a happy home here. After scaring off anything stupid enough to get in my way, I settled down among the reeds for a snooze, keeping alert just enough to note any creatures coming my way. Mundane fauna didn't recognize dragons as a natural predator. My size might deter most of them, but I didn't want to take a chance on some alligator or puma with delusions of grandeur thinking I'd make a nice lunch.

I also dozed with my canines sticking out. Usually, they stay nicely concealed under my lip, but I can expose them for threat or showing off. Very few sapients got treated to that version of The Grin, but it might make some would-be attacker think twice.

Of course that also meant that half an hour into a nice nap, I became aware of humans talking. Two of them had mouths so foul that if they'd been on television, the conversation would have sounded like this:

"Whoa! What the (bleep) is that?"

"(Bleep) if I know. (bleep) (bleep). Let's (bleeping) stay the (bleep) away from the (bleeping) thing. (bleep!)"

"Like (bleep). I want a closer look."

"(Bleep) that. It looks (bleeping) dangerous. I'm staying (bleeping) far away, (bleep/personal insult)."

"You (bleeping) coward. I'm the one who's gonna get (bleeping) close to the (bleeping) thing. You just keep the (bleeping) camera rolling."

Obviously not a tourist group; maybe some natives out for thrills. I stayed still and feigned sleep. I was going to give them the thrill of their lives.

I almost blew it, though, when someone said, "Action!" and PottyMouth screeched out, "Sheeeew-dang! Can you see that big red snout hidin' in them thar bushes? I'm tellin' you, chile, I ain't nevah seen no gator that size or color a'fore."

Big snout? Me? Now he was asking for it.

"Look at them teeth! I sweah, they's the size of my bowie, they is! Jes look." I heard something snap and a friction sound as the blade slid against a plastic case. I waited for him to try to lay his knife near my canines, but surprisingly, he didn't approach. I guessed the camera was doing a close-up. At least this time they'd get my better side. I wondered who these jokers were.

I heard him put the knife back in its sheath and say, "Yessir! This here critter ain't like nuthin' I ever seen! We may've jes found us a new species. You know the Everglades is home to twenty threatened species and fifteen endangered species, including the Day-Lee-Own sable sparrow and the South Florida American speckle-headed turtle. She-oot, we ain't got no turtle here, do we? Let's see if'n we can get ourselves a closer look."

Humans. The one species that sees a dangerous creature and thinks, "I should get closer."

I waited while he snuck up close, muttering reassurances and facts to me and the camera audience. Then as I heard the tendons in his knees creak as he knelt, I opened my eyes and said, "Shee-ooot! That thar accent is thicker than cold pea soup!"

Some days, it's gratifying to hear the screams.

Chapter Twenty-Three: Siegfried Snaps

I walked into the hotel in a better mood. Naturally, the first thing I heard was something that sounded something like "ghkkkrrkhk!" along with yelling. Norwegian yelling no less. Then Janey calling for him to "put Garret down."

Somebody'd finally pushed Siegfried over the edge.

Siegfried wore civilian clothes for a change, his muscles under his T-shirt bulging from the effort of holding a hotel employee six inches off the ground by his throat. Garret, I presumed. Completely ignoring Janey and Welles, Siegfried kept his victim pinned to the wall while he shouted in Norwegian about ignorance and historical inaccuracy.

From the struggling and wheezing, I could tell the guy was breathing, but Janey didn't seem so sure. She'd given up tugging on Siegfried's arm and yelling for him to let go and was pulling out her Taser when I barreled in. I heard a poink and felt something bounce off my scales.

I stuck my nose between Siegfried and his victim. Victim screamed and even Siegfried jumped back, releasing Garroted from his grasp. Garret tried to dash away, but I pinned him in place with my tail.

"Hang on. I have some questions for you," I said. Then I turned to Siegfried and said in Faerie Norwegian and using my best imitation of Grace's sympathetic patience: "Siegfried, why are you doing this? It's not like you at all."

Siegfried looked down for a moment, then brought his chin up defiantly and said in halting English, "For days, he and friend follow me. They laugh and make fun of my furs. I ignore them. I think, 'They are wrong in the head,' ja?"

"Ja, ja," I said, with a glare at the hotel employee, who was coughing and rubbing his neck. What a baby; he wasn't even bruised.

Siegfried continued, "I see them with Brunhilde. I know they flirt. This, too, I ignore. She deserves better, but I ignore! But today, they come—and tell me *my* costume is *wrong*. I cannot ignore. Horned hats? Have they no shame?"

"It was a joke," Garett tried to say, a weak defense that only made his case worse.

Welles had initially shooed away everyone the moment I'd arrived and broken up the fight, but people had again gathered, and he was too busy scowling at his employee to notice. Again, we had a crowd, including one blond woman I now remembered. She'd been talking to Garret earlier. She watched the proceedings with big, horrified eyes.

I'd worry about her later. I replied to Siegfried in Norwegian. "Siegfried, take it easy. I don't think he was calling you out on professional integrity as much as making a stupid joke. Now calm down and listen to a Master Puck."

I turned my attention to Jokers Mild. "So, this is what happens when you harass other people in the name of fun. Worth it?"

He shook his head violently.

"Learned your lesson?"

He nodded with equal enthusiasm.

"Good. Since you're so interested in history, let's try a traditional Norse apology, shall we?

Repeat after me—and don't mess it up. On your knees, hand on your cheeks...the other cheeks, smart guy."

Once he'd complied, I told him to repeat after me and began in Siegfried's native dialect. "O Great Siegfried the Benevolent."

"O-o-o Great Siegfried the B-B-Benevolent."

"You're stuttering. You just told him eggs poop in the sun. Try again," I told him. He hadn't actually said that, of course, but it was so incomprehensible he might as well have.

Chiding him against stutters and keeping the phrases short, I had him say, "Please forgive me. I am an idiot. I am very sorry. I am a puny girly-man. You are smarter, stronger, and better looking than I can ever hope to be. Thank you for not killing me. If I ever saw a real Viking, I would wet my pants—"

By now Siegfried was trying hard not to chortle. "Ja. You're forgiven. Good apology."

Had to hand it to Siegfried, he let him off a lot sooner than I would have.

"Now," I said to my much chagrined but no-longer-a-target-for-Viking-stomping charge, "You should go apologize to your manager and

Officer Janey for causing so much trouble. Professor Siegfried—"

"Professor?" This from Barry.

"Yes, one of the leading Faerie scholars on Vikings and Scandinavian history. He's here at the invitation of your universe specifically for this conference. This could have been an Interdimensional Incident, you know." Anything was possible. After all, I already had Gozon ready to include Florida in a war because of a perceived slight.

"But he almost killed me!" Apparently, now that Siegfried the Viking was Professor Siegfried, Girly-Man was getting brave.

"And you've been harassing him since he got here, haven't you?"

He looked ready to protest, but I bared my teeth and he crumpled. There we go—an intelligent reaction.

"Yes," he mumbled.

"Let me tell you something. You got lucky. Done that with another Faerie, and you might have found yourself with a slow debilitating curse that you might never have connected to your little shenanigan. Keep that in mind the next time you're tempted to take a joke too far."

Then I turned to Siegfried. "Apologize."

He heaved a sigh. "I lost my temper. I am sorry." He held out his hand and they shook. Girly Man grimaced as his hand was enveloped and crushed.

Everyone dispersed, the bellhop dragging along behind Manager Welles. The blonde lady was looking at Siegfried and making unsure motions toward him, so I decided to back out of the scene. I went over to Janey. "Thanks for not shooting anybody," I said wryly.

"I didn't expect you to get between them like that. You're lucky you've got scales," she said.

"I've had worse." I was glad that she'd missed my wings, however. I'd been tasered before and it was no fun.

Janey looked past me to Siegfried, who conversed quietly with the blonde. I could hear her apologizing in Norwegian. "He won't go postal again, will he?" she asked.

"I'm surprised he did this time. Professor Siegfried, unlike his namesake, is actually very mild-tempered."

"Huh. Like the Hulk," Janey muttered.

I snorted. "Seriously. He's been on the edge lately because..." What was I going to tell her? He had a crush on a Valkyrie who'd decided to play Venus?

Guess I'd said enough or she'd been aware of the issue, because she smiled and jerked her chin toward him. "That may not be such a problem anymore."

I turned just enough to see Siegfried and his new friend head to the restaurant arm in arm. Good for him. Good for me, too. I had enough worries.

One more day of this conference to go, and I still hadn't figured out what to do about Gozon's speech. No doubt Galinda'd schmoozed a seat of honor at the ceremony for herself and Galendor. Whatever happened to that shy little girl who'd nearly been sacrificed to the Powers of Darkness? With Gozon already feeling ill will toward Florida, I needed to figure out something before he convinced the Shores tribe to declare war on the Mensans, too.

Grace and I could discuss that over dinner, preferably in our room, so I said goodbye to Janey and headed back to the testing room. If she was done with her test, we could grab a bite before Frederico's lecture.

Unfortunately, as I passed the lounge, I heard a familiar sniffle. I suppressed a sigh and the urge to walk away. I was best dragon at their wedding, after all.

I walked into the bar to comfort Princess Galinda.

She was seated in a far booth, her back to the door, tears dripping off her nose and into her Chardonnay. I reached into my pouch and pulled out a hankie. I heard a little gasp from the table beside me and an awed whisper: "Like a sea otter!"

Galinda, however, did not care that dragons had special pouches or what we carried in them. She accepted my handkerchief and thanked me absently. Her eyes met mine, and she gave me a watery smile.

I settled myself at the end of the table. No way could I squeeze into a booth, but who was going to disturb a dragon? I gave a warning glance behind me at the lady who'd gasped, and she quickly turned her attention to her wrap. We may have been conspicuous, but we had privacy.

I didn't know what to say, so I didn't say anything. Sometimes, people say more to their dogs than to their psychiatrists. Dogs don't analyze.

I'm not a dog, but I can play one when I need to.

After a few protests of "I'm okay," to which I just gave her the puppy eyes, she finally pressed her fist against her mouth, heaved a sigh, then let it all spill. "Oh, Vern. I'm just being silly. I—I love Galendor with all of my heart and I know he loves me. I mean, he flew in an airplane with me, didn't he? And he's so smart and handsome and—but he's just not the man I married anymore."

I could have said something banal like "people change," but that's even more stupid when applied to a High Elf. Besides, I'm sure she'd heard it already.

She blew into the hankie with a honk like the mating call of a Canadian goose. "Once upon a time, he would spend hours talking to me, describing my beauty, the way my hair shone in the sunlight like the golden-tinged sands of—oh, someplace I couldn't pronounce. Now...now, I can dress in my finest and all he says is, 'You look terrific, babe.' I mean, I know he loves me, and Betanna says I'm lucky he notices and compliments me at all, but...'babe'? It's—I don't know. It's not like him, if that makes any sense..."

It did, and it didn't. It certainly fit in with the Galendor I'd seen at the conference: short sentences, speaking Human like a native. Not very Elvish. I could see him making himself do that in public to communicate better with humans—but at home?

"And Elsie says I should talk with him. I've tried, really I have, but he cuts me off! He tells me, 'I love you. Isn't that enough?' It should be, shouldn't it? But I can't help feeling there's something wrong."

Me, too. Elves interrupting? That wasn't just unusual; it was abnormal.

"Then today, I, I commissioned a song for him, and it was so perfect. I thought he'd sweep me in his arms. I thought he'd be late to his next appointment because he'd take so long thanking me..."

"But..?"

"But all he said was, 'Aw, thanks, babe,' and then he went back to watching MeTube Quips!"

"Quips?" Quips were snatches of video 15 seconds or less. Any self-respecting High Elf thought they were like nails on a chalkboard. "Where is he now?"

"He and Kevin went to look at some bottling plant. Then he was flying back to Los Lagos to meet with his cousins. He said it couldn't wait until next week, and that he'd be back tomorrow. Father's trying to start a soda industry. Not that he's had much luck getting past the trade barriers. You'd think that'd be pretty innocuous, wouldn't you? Stupid laws. I mean, how much harm can soda be? Mundanes drink it like water. Anyway, please don't talk to him. It's really not as bad as it sounds. I'm just stressed and letting things get to me, and... He does love me, doesn't he?" Her voice got high and quiet at the end, and she reminded me more of Penelope than a Princess.

I set my knuckle on the back of her hand. "When an Elf gives his heart to a human, he does it for her entire life. It's a cliché."

She gave a dainty laugh and blew her nose once more. "Thank you, Vern. You're such a good listener. It'll be all right. I know it will. I should go freshen up now." She left some money on the table. I told her to keep the hankie.

Galinda might be feeling better, but I wasn't.

A High Elf, impatient?

Chapter Twenty-Four: The Seductiveness of Modesty

"An impatient elf?" Grace muttered as we made our way to Frederico's lecture. I'd promised to meet our mage friend after he finished. Grace joined me. I'd told her about the note from this morning, and she wanted to learn what mystery required such a covert invitation.

We were speaking Faerie Aramaic because of the crowds and because I'd seen someone with a tape recorder lurking. We didn't want anyone learning our code. By the time a Mundane figured out this language, which was rare in both universes, the problem would be here or solved.

"I know. Sounds like one of the signs of Armageddon. My little princess wasn't the only one to mention this to me." Briefly I told her what Morton had told me about Galendor being snappy with the kids, and about his reaction to the song Galinda commissioned for him.

Grace whistled through her teeth, then turned thoughtful. "This song. Is that why Euterpe came to thank me for the 'peace offering'?"

"Just run with it," I teased. "Humility is good for the soul, remember?"

She shook her head at me, at once annoyed and amused, then returned to the subject of Galendor's behavior. "Could he be sick? Maybe some kind of Mundane illness that affects elves differently? That would be catastrophic."

"Slow, down," I said, thought, I'd had the same thought. "So far, it's only Galendor."

"True. Still... Do you think Frederico will have some answers in his presentation?" she asked.

"I wouldn't count on it," I told her.

I was right. His lecture on the biological differences between Mundane and Faerie humans and how this might correlate to magic was interesting, but inconclusive. Still, he drew a nice crowd and had to push his way through to us afterward. He greeted me warmly, slipped Grace's arm through his own, and invited us to his signing. We walked together, me on the right and Grace on the left, chatting amiably, and it was an easy thing for me to use my tail to slip the folded paper from his left pocket to Grace's right. I doubted even he noticed.

I wondered why he hadn't thought to slip us a note in his book, but I got my answer when we entered the signing area and I saw the two heralds waiting beside a box of books. Unlike our Duke, Galinda's family, the Tavendors, preferred brawny, stupid heralds who followed orders with minimal independent thought. While they managed to glare and look impassive at the same time, Frederico released Grace and gave her a courtly bow. I noticed his hand surreptitiously press against his pocket to check if the note was gone. Then he took his seat and, acting as if he always had armed goons at his book signings, accepted a pen from one and a book from the other as people lined up behind us for autographs. Under the guise of helpfulness, they pulled books out of the box one at a time, opened them as if to test the spines, then set them in front of him to sign.

Grace accepted the book for us and murmured a blessing of protection. The guards thought nothing of it—she was a nun, after all—but Frederico recognized the spell hidden in the blessing and relaxed visibly. If things got too hairy in the

Tavendor Kingdom, the spell should protect him long enough to reach a church and claim sanctuary.

We grabbed a large bag of food—hot dogs and hamburgers this time, as some of the Mensans working the con café had taken Jean Pierre out for dinner—and headed to our room in silence. Grace flipped through Frederico's book in the elevator. The dedication read, "To Grace and Vern, who have done more to keep peace in our worlds than any other two beings. Keep up the good work." I wasn't sure if it was a genuine thank you or a plea for help. Probably the former; he would have found a clearer way of asking if he'd been in any real danger. At most, a call to vigilance, then.

Just chaperone the Faerie, eh? I was beginning to wonder just how much Bishop Aiden knew about what was going on.

I told Grace my suspicion once we were in our room.

"Bishop Aiden has always been up-front with us. Why be circumspect now?" she said as she sat on one of the chairs and set the book on the table beside her.

"Maybe he's not sure what, if anything, is going on," I said. "Maybe he just suspected something was up at this conference and wanted us here just in case, but didn't want to admit to anything. Maybe because if I'd known we were going to get caught in a mystery, I'd have charged him by the hour."

"Well, should we call him?" she asked. She reached in her pocket for the note.

Just then, her phone rang. Raising her eyebrows, she pulled it out instead and spoke into the receiver. Her eyebrows climbed further. "It's the reporter, Roxanne Lewis, for you." She put it on speaker.

"This is Vern."

"Vern. Roxanne Lewis from WCWG. Enjoying the conference?"

"It's been interesting." I shared a look with Grace.

"No more fires?"

"Not that I've started."

She laughed as if that were very clever. "I hope you got a chance to see the piece we did on the false alarm yesterday. Millions of people did; it got picked up by the nationals. And Gator Louie's already posted reels about his encounter with you this morning. I'm surprised you haven't been swamped with requests for interviews today."

"Most of the national networks know better by now. I don't give interviews." Belatedly, though, I noticed the blinking message light on the hotel phone. Guess some didn't know better.

"Oh." She went quiet for a moment. "No exceptions?"

"Roxanne, you seem honest, but I've been burned by the Mundane media before—and that's saying something when you're a dragon."

"Okay. I understand. The business is vicious sometimes, like sharks. But let me ask you one thing: What if I could guarantee you've got an ally? Let's talk about why you're at the conference, or what it's like to be a dragon in the Mundane world. I can arrange to do the interview live, unedited, if you want. Tell me what I can do to reassure you."

"Why are you so keen to do this?"

"Because you're magnificent. Because all my life I've dreamed of dragons, and suddenly, here you are."

She fell silent, waiting for my answer. I felt my resolve weakening. I believed her. I looked at Grace, who shrugged.

"All right. Tomorrow, after lunch. Say two o'clock?" We made arrangements and she hung up.

Grace put the receiver back in the cradle. "What is it with you and reporters?"

"At least this one likes me," I said. I had to admit, wary as I was, Roxanne did not set off any alarm bells.

"And you're not even human this time," she said, shaking her head and grinning slightly.

I flopped down next to her and set my head on her lap. "And I'm eternally thankful for that," I said.

As long as we'd started down on the subject of cross-species affections, I decided to ask, "When did Coyote try to kiss you?"

She made a disgusted face. "Did he tell you about that? It wasn't much of an attempt. My defense spell knocked him across the room."

"Ouch!" That was my nun!

She shrugged. "I think he exaggerated the effect to play for pity points. At any rate, I placed a nice little spell on him: Should he ever again attempt to kiss a woman who has given herself to God, he's going to get a case of the mange like he's never had before."

I thought about how vain he was about his hair. "What about if he's in human form?"

"Male pattern baldness—and you won't believe the pattern."

I laughed. "Now that's my kind of justice."

"You're rubbing off on me, 'tis a fact."

"Speaking of..." I tilted my profile to her beseechingly. She chuckled and rubbed behind my cheek crests.

We stayed like that awhile, content in each other's presence, then Grace pulled Frederico's note out of her pocket.

"Is he prone to paranoia?" she asked.

"Doesn't mean someone isn't after him," I replied as I pulled my head up and around to read over her shoulder.

It was a report to the Tavendor Minister of the Economy asserting that they needed more studies on the metabolism of certain chemicals found in recreational drinks of Mundanes.

"Recreational drinks?" Grace asked.

"Soda, I'd guess, and I'd also guess that Tavendor didn't take this memo too seriously." I told her about Galendor's tour of a bottling facility.

"We need to check out the Mundane/Faerie Trade Proscriptions list."

"Why us?" I groused. "We're not being paid for this. I say, we pass it on and let Duke Galen's people handle it." I yawned and stretched. "In the meantime, I think I'll catch a nap—"

A loud, persistent pounding on our door nixed that thought.

"Coming!" Grace called as she folded the note back into her pocket, but the pounding continued unabated. With an annoyed toss of her head, she murmured a cantrip and the door swung open. The man was hammering so heavily on it that he nearly toppled when it did.

"Can we help you?" Grace asked in her sweetest, most sisterly voice.

"I'm so hoping!" our knocker cried.

Our entreatant was a tall, lanky guy wearing a bright yellow silk shirt with sleeves too billowy for Mundane styles and not billowy enough for Faerie. He'd pulled the top half of his over-moussed black hair into a manbun, and shaved the lower half. With his thin mustache and goatee, he looked like the kind of guy who'd get a grant from the National Endowment for the Arts for painting a picture of the Virgin Mary doing bizarre things with a cross.

Wait a minute....

I looked at the name tag. Melchior Rawlings. He was the guy who got an NEA grant for "Naked Mary at the Cross."

Oh, this guy came to the wrong place.

"Please! My seminar comes up in half an hour!" He brushed past us to the table, dumped his portfolio bag on the bed, and slammed his briefcase on the table hurriedly. It looked like Gozon's. The store must have been having a sale.

"I've been attacked," he said as he pulled out a file and shoved it at us.

Grace took it, and together we looked over the photos it contained: men and women in suggestive poses, wearing traditional Faerie dress. The clothes were skillfully but obviously painted on after the fact with enchanted paint.

"Templegrass's crew?" Grace wondered, but I shook my head.

"I think the brownies found the Erotic Photography lecture."

Wouldn't you know it? Grace could not generate any sympathy. "Interesting medium."

"Medium, smedium! Those..." He floundered for words.

"Brownies," I supplied.

"—brownies have painted clothing on all my nudes! I tried everything to remove it, but I just ruined the photo beneath. Oh, my beautiful art! It's just too much to process! Deep breaths! Deep breaths! Please, please, tell me you can remove this, this violation!"

Grace sighed—insincerely, I knew—and handed him back the file. "I can't," she told him. I noticed she didn't say she was sorry about it nor that she hoped he had other copies.

He pressed his fingers to his temples theatrically. "I'll have to make do with what's stored on the computer. Oh, tragic day!"

High strung, this one. Back in the day, I would have let him go rather than eat him—too much adrenalin for my taste. But since I'm a changed dragon, I said, "Mel, babe. Deep breaths. Maybe you're looking at this wrong. Work with me: What if you don't think of them as ruined art? Think of them as trendsetting expressions of social repression using an unexplored combination of medium, flaunting the modern Mundane's rebellion against morality and enticing viewers to experience the seductiveness of modesty."

Grace's jaw dropped, and Rawling glared at me from beneath his hand. I tilted my head compellingly. "You'll be a pioneer. 'Daring juxtaposition of primitive, yet radical gestures.'"

We watched as his face moved through expressions of anger, doubt, uncertainty, and then the joy of discovery. "You're right! What a commentary on the base impulse of the masses incapable of appreciating a culturally promiscuous environment where the body is art! You're genius!"

"That's what it says on my website." Or words to that effect.

"This could be the start of a whole new movement—and I'd be its founder! I must have more! Do you think I could convince these...brownies...to join me in my studio?"

"Probably not, and it would be dangerous to try," I answered. "But we know some people in the magical art world. We can connect you."

"Yes, yes, of course! This could be big—I mean, big!" He spoke rapidly now as he put the file lovingly back into his briefcase. Then he turned, pumped Grace's hand and my, er, claw. "I have a new lease on life! A new direction! I am reborn! How, oh, how can I ever thank you?"

"Burn 'Mary Naked at the Cross,'" Grace said immediately. "If you were ever Catholic, go to Confession. If you aren't, convert."

"Yes, yes, of course," he repeated, not really hearing what she was asking. Still, I'd heard the undertone in her voice, a kind of siren call on behalf of the Holy Spirit. If he had any inclination toward conversion, her words would haunt him until he followed it.

Grace led him to the door, and we listened to his flittery, retreating footsteps. When I nodded that he was well out of earshot, we hooted with laughter. "'The seductiveness of modesty'?" Grace laughed. "Some days, you still amaze me."

"Some days, I amaze even myself!"

Chapter Twenty-Five: Do Quantum Brownies Go with Diet Cola?

By the time Melchior had flounced out of our room, it was time for Grace and me to do evening devotions, after which she had opted to get some sleep. Her magical duel with Terpie yesterday and the spellwork today had tired her out more than she'd wanted to admit and, she laughed, she and Sheila had gotten a workout from all their shopping. She'd nearly nodded off during the rosary.

I, of course, had the night shift.

For once, we had an uneventful evening. I poked my snout into a couple of parties and late-night events, but everyone was behaving. I had a moment of concern when I saw Brunhilde with a now-neatly-trimmed Kent sitting in her lap, but Siegfried only had eyes for his Nordic lady. I didn't see Coyote, Ramada, or Galinda. GitPicCon had ended, so even though I flew a circuit around the hotel, it wasn't the same without the appreciative audience. I decided that right before we left, I'd buzz Fanny Flamingo and give folks a one-in-a-million thrill they didn't have to pay for.

That, however, was for daytime tomorrow. I had to get through the night. I wandered over to the security office and met up with Cory and Gary. We took turns prowling the halls and in the meantime, drank too much caffeine. Just for kicks, we had started looking up the ingredients listed on the side of Cory's can of Diet Chase.

Hours later, I could only conclude that Mundanes are the luckiest, or maybe the most protected, species in the multiverse. If the Faerie played with magic the way Mundanes did technology, humans would be just a memory to me by now.

Or maybe Mundanes were just too contrary to die.

As we looked at "studies" blaming the artificial flavor scanatine with everything from migraines to lupus to baldness, Cory started giving his Diet Chase suspicious looks. Unfortunately, many of those "studies" were not listed in their original form—so it was someone drawing conclusions from data we couldn't find.

Then there were the conspiracy theorists. One even accused Kevin Olson of the Ping Cola Bottling Company of purposefully overdosing the President and the FDA commissioner through "free samples" in order to impair their judgment and approve the product.

When we did find the original study, even I had a hard time determining if anything significant was uncovered. I needed to chat with Athena, or maybe a Mensan with a doctorate in biochemistry.

"'The aspartic acid moiety was transformed in large part to CO_2 through its entry into the tricarboxylic acid cycle.' What does that even mean?" Cory asked.

I shrugged. In the Mundane world, dragons are liberal arts majors. To make things worse, everything we read applied to humans, not elves, which didn't answer the questions topmost in my mind.

What we were managing to decipher was that, in humans at any rate, scanatine broke down in the intestines into three components, one actually known to be helpful in that it bonds to other toxins in the body—though there was some argument that because it was artificially produced and not natural, it actually increased the toxicity or mutated the toxins or something. Another caused problems for people with a specific genetic disorder; Cory checked and saw the warning label on the side. The final one was methanol, and that seemed to be where the real controversy lay.

"Here's something: the 'Unbiased Story Behind Scanatine,'" Cory read. I snorted—like they'd be truthful about their bias.

Why is methanol a problem? Methanol is a well-known toxin absorbed through air and by ingestion that converts in the small intestine into formic acid and...

"Formaldehyde?" Cory shrieked, pushing back into his chair and bumping into me. "That's what we pickled frogs in, back in high school biology!" He picked up the soda as if it were one of those science experiment frogs and poured it down the bathroom sink.

"What are you doing?" Gary Spade asked as he walked in from his turn on patrol; Joe had called in sick and he'd volunteered to pull a double shift.

"Did you know that this stuff becomes embalming fluid?" Cory asked as he tossed the can away.

Spade shrugged. "What? Scanatine? Beer and juice have methanol, too—even the stuff without artificial flavoring. I've read studies that say there's not a significant difference in absorption between them and sodas."

"Forget it. I'm not taking any chances," Cory said. He took the radio from Spade and left.

Spade rolled his eyes. "Scanatine's been around for decades. Millions of people ingest the stuff. I think by now we'd know if it posed a serious health threat."

I grunted. Millions of Mundanes over decades, but only a handful of elves over a few years.

The clock read four-thirty. I yawned and stepped out into the hallway to stretch and shake out my wings. Gary followed. "You're really *draggin'* tonight."

"Ha, ha. I haven't done more than doze since I got here. Some cushy assignment." I yawned. I considered taking a quick flight around the grounds, but the muggy heat would probably put me to sleep midflight.

Spade leaned against the doorframe. "How long can you go without sleep?"

"Depends on the need, diet, activity… I've been awake for weeks at a time, but that was with a gorged belly and in a high-threat situation where I was operating mostly on instinct." That was pre-George, and I was surprised I remembered it. Pleased, though, I told Spade the story once we got to the office. He told me about an all-nighter he'd pulled tracking down a murderer in Long Island. Exciting as the story was, I nonetheless found my head drooping, and I dozed.

It couldn't have been a couple of hours later when Spade woke me by nudging my shoulder. "Vern? Get up. We've got trouble."

Chanting broke through my fog of sleep: "We want the dragon! We want the dragon!" They didn't sound like they were interested in autographs.

I took a long, catlike stretch. "Are they carrying pitchforks? 'Cause if so, I'm going to need a moment to get my flame on," I said, then added, "That was a joke."

Spade grimaced. "Doesn't have to be. We've got some rabid environmentalists out there protesting about fish. Welles is ready to blow a gasket. It's too early in the morning for this nonsense."

"See? Flaming liberals. It'd be redundant." I followed him out. My phone rang: Gapman. I ignored it. A moment later, it rang again, followed by a text from Kenjo. *We need land now. You make happen!*

Dealing with something here. Handle it, Padawan. Call as soon as I can, I texted Gapman. Hopefully, he could keep our homesteading hobgoblin in hand. Meanwhile, I asked Spade, "So what do fish have to do with me?" When we got to the lobby and I could read their signs, I got my answer.

Protect Our Gulf!

No Faerie Contamination!

Earth for Earthlings!

Our Gulf is Not a Dragon's Pool!

Gators, not Drakes!

And the like. A couple boasted a silhouette of a dragon with a red slash through it.

Figured. Get a little free-range sushi in this world, and the humans go ape. Or is that redundant?

Among the crowd, I saw Roxanne with her cameraman interviewing one of the protestors. I wondered whose side she'd be on—or more to the point, whose side her network would favor. Guess I'd find out. I adjusted my wings nicely, put on my dignified "Mostly Harmless" expression, and headed into the fray. Spade stopped at the door so it wouldn't look like I was coerced.

Stepping out onto the portico, where the police were holding back a group of thirty protesters, I paused, then flapped my wings once. They stretch twelve feet and when I snap them, they make an impressive sound as well as an impressive display.

The chants fell to awed silence. Better.

I folded my wings, settled myself into a regal position, and waited. This wasn't my argument; let them make the first move.

After a moment of confused, subdued muttering, the guy Roxanne had been interviewing squared his shoulders and strode up to me. "It was you, wasn't it, prowling around the Gulf and disturbing the rightful inhabitants."

"I did take a brief swim two nights ago, though I disturbed the tourists more than the fish."

"Those 'tourists' were marine biologists counting the mahi-mahi," he sneered.

"Oh, well, subtract two."

I heard a muffled snicker from one of the policemen beside me, but my accuser was not so amused.

"So you admit it! Not only were you traumatizing the fish with your unnatural invasion—"

"—actually, it was very natural. Washing them down with a Diet Chase—that would have been unnatural."

That drew even more snickers, but FishLover was working himself into form. "—but you admit to diminishing their numbers!"

I fought the urge to toss my head in the dragon equivalent of the sarcastic eye roll. "I'm sure the sharks do more."

"That's not the point! They are part of the natural habitat!" He turned his back on me to address his little throng and continued his speech, interrobangs almost visible in his voice. "Is it not bad enough that humankind has encroached upon the natural habitats of our world?! Is it not enough that species after species on this earth fades into extinction at a rate of one per minute?!"

I did some math. "That means every species on your planet would be extinct in ninety-six years. When did you start counting?"

But he wasn't listening. "No, my friends, no, it apparently is not, for our government has seen fit to bring in new predators, new threats, new dangers!" He gestured theatrically at me.

So much for my snowbirding plan.

I gave them my best "Who me? I'm an overgrown puppy" smile, tongue lolling and wagging my tail, Labrador-like, for emphasis.

His back to me, EnviroGuy continued. "Is this what we want for our world?" He paused, confused by the weak response. "I said, do we want the Faerie bringing their contagion, their unbridled killers into our fragile Mother Earth?"

Unbridled? Fine, as long as we were going over the top... I struck my most comical, playful kitty pose, wagging my butt and pawing at the ground like I was getting ready to leap onto a refrigerator. Unbridled killer of dust mites and moths, that's me. What I really wanted to do was pin him beneath my claws, crush his sign with my tail and let him know just how many times I've saved this stupid fragile world and that only the grace of God was keeping me from eating him just for being an annoying git. I knew where that would lead, however, so I played the audience and prayed he would lose heart before I lost my temper.

The crowd started snickering.

He refused to turn around. Clueless to my satire, he continued, "My friends! This is no laughing matter! The fate of our world hangs in the balance! Already, this creature has done visible harm to a threatened species—"

"So it is threatened?" Roxanne interrupted. "The International Union for the Conservation of Nature has determined this is a separate species of mahi-mahi, and that the evidence meets its guidelines for red listing?"

EnviroGuy hesitated, caught between the need to keep credibility and the desire to keep momentum. Had to hand it to him, he chose credibility.

"Not yet," he said. He turned his attention to her and started talking about his first inclination that there was something different between this fish and some other fish in the same species.

If I sub-classified humans that minutely, much less fish, I'd need an even bigger memory than I'd had in my pre-George days—and trust me, that's saying a lot.

I was about to make a snide comment to that effect when I heard the earth-rumbling roar of an enraged dwarf. Normally, I would have been exasperated, but for once, I welcomed trouble.

"Been fun, but I've got to work now. Good luck with the fish!" I called and launched myself at the balcony of Garn's room.

Chapter Twenty-Six: Pickaxes and MOUS Ranches

Through their sliding door, I saw Garn pull the mattress off his bed, yelling at Kent while the other dwarf held out a pickax to him. Garn grabbed the pickax and flung it toward the glass.

I ducked, but the crashing of glass never came. Grace had entered the room and magically stopped it midair before it hit the door. The pickax settled to the ground, then she strode over and unlocked the balcony door to let me in while giving Garn a tongue lashing for carelessness.

"...property damage aside, there's a crowd of people out there! What if your pickax had hit one of them?" I heard her say as I slid open the door and let myself in.

"That is not my pickax!"

"It is your pickax," Kent asserted cautiously and gently, as if reassuring a child—if that child were armed with an AK-47 and had skipped his Ritalin dose that day. He picked up the pickax and held the bottom of the handle where Garn could see it. "See? Look here—your teeth marks from when you gnawed on it during the flight here. And look." He turned it around to show him where the handle met the ax head. "Here's that scratch you polished so well. It's yours, Garn."

Garn snatched the pickax from his hands. "It's not the same! It's been...tampered with. I—oh, I can't explain. It's gone. I'm ruined." He sat down on the bare box spring and moaned.

Grace knelt down beside him and said in halting Dwarvish. "Yo, Garn. Start at the beginning, please? What's different about the pickax?"

"I can speak English, Sister," he said with a sad smile. "Still, ye wouldn't understand. It's been tampered with. I—" Suddenly, he glared at Kent. "She did it! I'll kill that Valkyrie wench!"

"Now, Garn, she didn't even touch your pickax," Kent said placatingly. "You know that—"

"What about when we were asleep? She could have then, she could have—"

I interrupted. "Wait a minute! Brunhilde was here? Last night? All night?"

The two dwarves shared a look that answered my question. Grace opened her mouth to speak. Closed it. Tried a second time, then threw her hands in the air. "Vern, let's go talk to Brunhilde."

"No!" Both dwarves shouted at once, and I had the feeling they shared at least one reason in common. And I thought humans were bad.

Still, I didn't believe Brunhilde was guilty—not of messing with Garn's pickax, anyway. I'd been looking around the room and, with the exception of where Garn had trashed it in his temper, it looked and smelled unusually clean. "Was this place cleaner when you woke up than when you went to sleep?"

Kent considered. "Things were a bit...blurry after last night. Mundane tequila... Yeah, it was. I thought Brunhilde had straightened up before she left."

"I'm betting you were the next stop on the Brownie Clean Sweep Tour. Maybe their 'tampering' was just an attempt to fix something they thought was wrong on your pickax?"

"Whose brownies are these?" Garn demanded in a dangerous voice.

"We think they're pretty much free agents now, and don't get any ideas about avenging yourself. You let us figure this out."

Garn didn't look too agreeable to that, but all he did was hunch over his pickax and grumble. "Elves and bulls and now brownies? What's a dwarf gotta do to get by in this world?"

We reassured Garn we were on the trail of the "maids errant," and helped him and Kent put the room back together. That was Grace's idea, not mine. Me, I figure anyone who makes a mess should clean it up themselves. I was tired and grumbling as we headed back to our room.

Grace said, "Chalk it up as a corporal act of mercy." She shook her head, her mind back to our newest mystery. "'Elves and bulls and brownies'?"

"Oh, my," I quipped, then stayed silent until we'd gone in our room. "I want to know what's so special about that pickax? I don't buy the 'dwarf and his pickax' story. Nor do I believe the brownies somehow tampered with the balance. If that was the case, why not say it right off? Why all the 'You won't understand' stuff? Even if I didn't, Kent would. Besides, he could fix that easily enough when they get back to Faerie. There's no reason to get that angry."

"Different people have different triggers," Grace sighed. "Speaking of, how'd the thing with the demonstrators go? I was heading down there when I heard Garn's roar—or should I say felt? It was like being next to some Mundane car with the stereo too loud and the bass too high. The floor rumbled."

I told her what had happened and how I had clowned it up. "I got the feeling? Some of those demonstrators were paid participants. They joined in the chanting eagerly enough, but when I gave them a show, they forgot what they were demonstrating against. Still, I'm glad I got out of there before the Fisher King accused me of peeing in the water. No one ever asks a dwarf if he's housebroken."

"Dwarves wear pants," Grace pointed out.

"So I'm wardrobe challenged, is that what you're saying?"

She laughed. "Do you want to take a nap? I've already messaged the Faerie to be ready to board the buses at six."

"The farewell ceremony is at three. There's no way Gozonvabosomofic will be done by then."

"Actually," she said, "last night while you were on patrol, he came by the room and told me he'd cut his commentary to an hour and a half."

"He changed his speech?" God was giving us a break at last!

"No, he said he had an epiphany and changed the phrases. Even more bizarre: He only took half an hour to tell me about it."

"Will miracles ever cease?"

"Apparently, that little incident with the governor convinced him he needed to be more adaptable. In fact, he even had a can of Ping in his hand."

I thought about Frederico's memo as I settled onto my bed. "Is that a good thing?"

"Normally, I'd say no, but I looked over Frederico's notes—what I can make of them—and they seem inconclusive, which makes sense considering he's asking for more time and money for further experiments. Of course, the Tavendors won't be too keen on either."

"Of course." The Tavendors loved to acquire wealth, hoard wealth, even flaunt wealth, but spend it? Kind of like dragons that way, except dragons don't flaunt. Not worth our time. Damsels and Knights, if I didn't wish I had some treasure to flaunt, though.

"I'm surprised they're putting so much pressure on Frederico that he feels the need to play cloak and dagger with us."

"I think we can thank Mundane business for that." I briefly told her about what I and Cory had learned about scanatine the night before.

"Saints preserve us," Grace prayed. "Well, Bishop Aiden is going to get more than he bargained for this trip."

"The Duke, too—and I intend to make him pay us for it," I said.

"Well, the important thing is we're aware of the situation now. The Church can put pressure on the Tavendors. In the meantime, I don't think Gozon will have access to Ping once he's back home, and I don't think short-term exposure will harm him. Galendor seems fine, and I've hardly seen him without a soda in his hands the whole conference."

I thought about Galinda crying that he'd "changed," but didn't say anything. Right now, all

I wanted to do was get through the next twelve hours and see our charges safely back in Faerie. I'd worry about artificial additives, industrialists, and troubled marriages after that.

What had I just said?

This is your fault, George, I snarked at the saint. I could almost feel his smugness.

Of course, there was something else to worry about even before I worried about the conference. I called Gapman.

When he answered, I could hear squealing, shouting and laughter in the background.

"Not to worry," Gapman answered without preamble. "I handled it, like instructed."

"Yeah? Why is Kenjo texting me about land?" I demanded.

"They want to ranch the MOUSs," he said. When he didn't hear the sound of Grace slapping her forehead, he continued. "Sister Eloise's containment spell worked, and she set up a kind of pen where they can't get out or go into the ground. And after the barbecue was such a hit, Kenjo thinks they could raise them for the meat."

I wondered briefly what the environmental protestors would think about introducing a new species to the Mundane solely for culinary purposes.

Meanwhile, Gapman was saying how they got an early start, found a hole, and retrieved some while they slept. "We already have a half-dozen in the temporary pen."

Suddenly a cheer rose among the hobgoblins.

"What's going on?" Grace asked.

"They're tickling the MOUSs." Gapman said. He didn't seem exasperated at all. Had Kenjo and his tribe already broken my padawan?

"They...what?" she asked.

"Well, it started out as mole-tipping..."

"Mole..."

"...tipping. Like cow tipping? The moles sleep standing up, and Pinjal thought it'd be funny to knock them over, and then one of the girls cooed about its fuzzy belly and... Well, the MOUSs don't like it much."

Gapman texted us a video: Pinjal atop a prone MOUS twice its size, scratching at its ample belly for all he was worth while kicking at the mole's snapping jaws.

"They were head-to-head first, until one almost took off Higgenbo's scalp. Don't worry. He's fine;

more than fine. Plinsina won't stop gushing about his courage. Anyway, now, they're taking bets on who loses a boot—"

"What happened to keeping control of the situation, Padawan?" I demanded.

He replied with a derisive snort. Yes—my padawan snarking to his master! Leave a superhero alone for three days...

He said, "You never taught me how, Master! You assigned me to help with a mole hunt without telling me they were enchanted and huge, and as for the hobgoblins? I don't even know how to tell Kenjo not to do anything stupid."

"'*Plin kiccha tai*, Kenjo,'" I heard Leesi offer helpfully. "Two minutes!"

Gapman cheered. "Yes! Bravo, Pinjal!"

"Padawan!" I snapped.

"Oh, come on! I just won a bet with Kenjo. He's going to fix my Winchester so it never misses."

"You're making bets, now?" Damsels and Knights! They'd struck him in his greatest weakness—his need to make friends!

There was an awkward silence, then he rallied. "Anyway, it's not that bad an idea, really. We're setting up the amusement park—"

"The park? On top of my mountain?"

"I'd offer some land, but the problem is containment. It needs to be in direct line-of-sight of the Gap to keep the spell powered, and if it's on flat land, there's a chance they could escape. If we use the top of your mountain, Sister Eloise said she could make a barrier spell all around and about six feet into the ground—"

"You've already discussed this with her?" Grace asked, aghast. "And she's okay with this?"

"My mountain?" I repeated atop of my partner.

"You said to handle it. Besides, it'll give them room to burrow and still be fully self-contained. That would help limit the numbers. I'll clean it up of anything too dangerous, and some of the rides would make good enrichment toys for the MOUSs. Kenjo said in return, he'd give us each a MOUS every Spring plus a share of the culls."

"*You'll* get a MOUS...for offering *my* mountain?" I didn't think my jaw could get any lower. I'd left my padawan with the hobgoblins for less than a week and he'd already gone native. Next thing, they'd be inducting him into the tribe and setting him up with one of Leesi's daughters.

Finally, my ire pierced his super-thick skull. "Look. Nothing has to be decided right now. You're coming home tonight, right? Let us finish containing the MOUSs, and if we can't come to an agreement, we can always slaughter them...although that'd really be a shame at this point."

"Oh, would it?"

My sarcasm went past him. "I'd better go. Kenjo looks like he wants to try to ride one bareback. *Plin kiccha tai*, Kenjo!"

There was a distant yelp and then nothing.

Chapter Twenty-Seven:
Steak and Brownies

Grace and I discussed the scheme our enthusiastic super-apprentice had dreamed up. Grudgingly, I conceded that it wasn't that bad an idea. Groceries were expensive, especially for a dragon, and on the days he was superheroing, Ronnie needed somewhere around 6,000 calories. A steady supply of meat was always welcome.

"We can let the hobgoblins have the abandoned restaurant level below the amusement park," Grace said. "It'll take some work to make it livable, but they are hard workers. Plus, it spares us a lot of negotiating with the movie company for living space. And it keeps them from getting underfoot. There'll be hundreds of feet of dwarf-packed dirt between us. Besides, if the hobgoblins are between us and the MOUSs, they'll be the first to know if one manages to break the barrier. You did tell your padawan to problem solve."

"Not with my—our—stuff!"

In the end, Grace declared I was just "cranky" and insisted I get a good nap. As soon as she left, I curled up on the bed with my tail encircling me and shut my eyes. A nap wouldn't get me my mountain back, but maybe I'd feel better about it.

I slept blissfully until I woke up from a dream of eating a moose—or maybe a MOUS; the details were unclear. It didn't matter. I woke up hungry. A large meal would stand me better than another half hour of snoozing. Besides, this would be my last chance at Jean Pierre's cooking. So I moseyed on down to the con café.

The week, fun as it was for most, had worn everyone down, giving the room a slightly melancholy feel. Even Jean Pierre's fussing and abuse as he chewed out some tolerant Mensan about putting ketchup on his steak was subdued, and when the guy had walked away, I saw Jean Pierre grin sadly. The line wasn't long, but everyone moved a little slower and lingered just a bit more over a dish or a conversation. Tired, but not ready to let go. A couple of folks were already talking about next year. I wondered if I could convince them to hold it in Los Lagos and make my life easier.

Brunhilde, I noticed, sat at Coyote's table, but passed wistful glances toward Kent. Kent was speaking in low tones to a still-distraught Garn, but now and again, I caught him glancing back her way. Interspecies love. Not only was it cliché, but it could get awfully weird. I suppose I should have expected Cupid's arrows, but he didn't come to the convention.

As I got to the table, Jean Pierre saw me and pushed away the lady who had grabbed a tray for me. "I will tend the dragon. Go! Tend to these mere...diners." He spat over his shoulder away from the food, but he didn't fool me.

I spoke to him in Faerie French. "You're going to miss this, aren't you?"

He pulled himself up haughtily, then deflated and shrugged. "Never, Vern, never have I seen mouths in such need, such...poverty among the riches! I have come not only to educate but to learn, and so I have been to many of their restaurants and perused their cookbooks! It is not my France, to be sure, but they can create much beautiful, succulent fare. Yet they return again and again to swill! You live among them, Vern, tell me: Why?. Why do they do this?"

"You're asking a creature who's eaten rats."

"Ah, but that is only because you must." As he spoke, he piled my platter full of steaks, enough to make a mountain. Next, with quick strokes and flourished fork, he added vegetables as foliage, then drizzled a light sauce, making a stream down the mountains, and finished by surrounding it with a circle of little pastries. It was so beautiful, I almost hated to eat it. It smelled so good, I wanted to snap it right out of his hands. My mouth watered.

"You see?" he said in triumph at my greedy gaze. "You recognize fine cuisine. Tell me honestly: If you could eat this way every day, would you not?"

I hadn't realized how hungry I was. I didn't want to take my eyes off the plate. I wondered what he would do with MOUS meat. "Anytime," I answered.

"*Mais ouí,* no? But these Mundanes—they leave the hotel, get into their cars, and drive for miles to purchase cheap cuts of greasy meat oversalted to hide its poor quality. Ah, but the blood of the Bargedecuries flows in my veins. I was breaking through, Vern. A few more days and I could have retrained their tastes. I, who have cooked for Popes and Kings, had met my greatest challenge among the palates of the rabble, but I would have won."

Jean Pierre was about to carry his culinary Hanging Gardens of Babylon to the balcony for me, when Bill and Keiko came rushing into the con café, the catbag in Keiko's arms, purring like the cat that ate the, er, brownie.

"Did you catch one?" I asked excitedly.

"I can't be sure—isn't that the point?" the bag answered. Schrödinger the Cat Bag. "Something cleaned me up real nice, though. Outside and in, and whatever's inside decided to take a nap."

Well, this day was looking up. I asked Jean Pierre to set my dish aside and left him grumbling about how the French would eat first, then work. Made me wish I were French. But I wasn't, and I had a job to do. Besides, I was curious.

However, to be able to talk to it without "observing" it was going to take magic. "We need Sister Grace," I said.

"She's on her way," Bill said. He heard Jean Pierre huff over by the crêpes, and went to rescue my lunch. Keiko exclaimed over its artful display.

We set it on a corner table and just admired it. Finally, I couldn't stand the anticipation. I excused my manners, arched my head over my meal and took about a third of it in one bite. Heaven. I made appreciative dragony sounds. Jean Pierre allowed himself to be appeased.

"So what is Sister Grace going to do?" Keiko asked.

"She'll be able to set up a spell so we can communicate with whatever's in the bag."

"So if talking to the brownie means 'observing it,' and we can't observe it while it's talking, how will we talk to it?" Bill asked.

"First of all, we don't know that there's a brownie in there. Don't forget that. We must remain uncertain. As for communicating with the thing in the bag, if there's anything in the bag, we'll use magic." When Bill rolled his eyes, I said, "It's simpler than it sounds, really. Grace will set up an intermediary. We ask it questions, and it relays them to the alleged brownie. Same goes for the answers. Because there's a time delay, we won't be directly observing it. Like communicating through e-mail."

"But if the intermediary records and plays back its messages, won't it be observing?"

"Lower-tech intermediary. We'll be seeing the effects of its actions—kind of like when they clean a room, repair a shoe, or finish your crossword. As long as we don't see him doing anything, we're all fine," I said.

Bill thought a moment, then frowned with concern. "Wait a minute. This sounds like a *Dr. Who* episode. 'The Weeping Angels.' They couldn't observe each other either, or they turned to stone."

"Well, this isn't a show. Brownies don't turn into stone, and they can interact with each other."

"But won't Sister Grace have to observe the brownie to put a spell on it?"

Grace stepped in and saved me from answering. I turned my attention back to my meal and did some demolition work on Jean Pierre's Steak Mountain while Grace explained that she would set the spell in the area of the alleged brownie and invite it to participate.

"Kind of like your legend of setting out a bowl of milk to draw them—" she started.

"—except Grace's spell actually works," I said around a mouthful.

Grace shrugged in agreement. "Are you almost done with that?"

"I want seconds."

I heard Jean Pierre give a happy cry.

"All right. Bill, would you get me a tray and a couple of salt shakers? This shouldn't take long, then you can eat to your heart's content." While Bill went to get the stuff, she and Keiko cleared the table of everything except my tray and Nekosan the Schrödinger Cat Purse. When Bill returned, they emptied the salt shakers into the clean tray until the salt formed a neat white layer. Taking a seat next to me with the tray in front of her, Grace crossed herself and began to pray.

She didn't say anything, and she sang her spell below human hearing. Nonetheless, people sensed something was happening at our table. Folks turned our way and a few came over. One person started to ask what was going on and was immediately shushed by his friend. I didn't worry about it; only a few people had any beef with the brownies, and none of them were at the table.

Grace finished her song, laid her hands over the tray and Schrödinger, and then breathed out.

The salt shimmered for a moment, drawing an "oooo" from our onlookers.

"Ready," she said. "You eat; I'll write."

Before I could suggest a question, lines started to draw themselves in the salt, in English, of course, in accordance to the spell.

Thirsty. Got any Ping?

"Ping? This some kind of joke?" murmured the guy who had spoken before. Again he was shushed, by a couple of people this time.

I wished it were a joke. Brownies on Ping didn't sound like a good thing—if it was a brownie asking for Ping, of course. "Tell him he can get a drink when we're done."

Grace nodded, smoothed the salt with a sweep of her hand and wrote in our reply.

I'm Done. All Clean. Ate the Yummies.

Yummies? "Keiko, what was in your purse?"

She shrugged. "Cough drops. A flavor package to put in my water."

"This flavor package have scanatine?"

She shrugged. Meanwhile, Grace had written another question.

Great fun! Much Cleaning. Some Fixing. Put Things where they Belonged. Drink Ping. Like Ping. More Ping?

Great. A veritable commercial, this one. Already I could see it: A bunch of brownies rushing around the house, probably in some stupid little aprons, cleaning everything, then stopping for the slogan: *We do it for Ping!* They'd never be able to film a real brownie, but I didn't think that would stop a smart ad executive. I told Grace to ask it about the briefcase.

...All assuming this were actually a brownie, which we couldn't know for sure or the whole spell would fall apart.

Fun game. It hides but we find! All Clean. Things where they Belong. Boss Happy. Lots of Ping. Chase, too. I like Ping.

Behind us, our commentator was sounding out the words quietly. He didn't say anything about the word "Chase." I'd expected to see it, though. Things were coming together, and I wasn't happy with the result.

The question had to be asked, so Grace traced in the salt, "Who is Boss?"

"'Gallant-or-a-pimp-for-da-ladies?'" Our guy pronounced the word in a whisper, then repeated it louder. "What does that mean?"

Grace and I exchanged a look. The word was obvious: Galendor. But what did his involvement mean?

Chapter Twenty-Eight: Best Laid Plans of Elves and Dwarves

Keiko took her purse to an unused room to release the alleged brownie contained therein. Meanwhile Grace and I went to Galendor and Galinda's room.

The door bore a temporary plaque that read "Galinda and Galendor" with lots of swirls and frills.

"That's adorable, if a bit excessive," Grace said.

"You should have seen the wedding invitations," I replied.

One of Galinda's servants opened the door, but refused to let us in. "I'm quite sorry, Sister, and er, sir dragon, but Princess Galinda is indisposed," he said in a stereotype of a Mundane British servant. In fact, he was Mundane. I wondered if Galinda had decided to import some help or if she was just renting him for the stay.

I was about to insist when Galinda called from the other room, her voice muffled. "Dragon? Let them in."

With some reluctance, Jeeves stepped back and allowed us to enter, then led us to the other room. Good thing Galinda had someone to open doors for her, though; if she'd opened the door in her current state, I would have jumped back hissing.

Galinda was reclining on a dentist's-type chair, her face smothered in green clay. I caught a scent: Not clay, but avocado. Cucumbers covered her eyes. She held a mouth guard between her teeth; gel leaked out. Her hair—where strips of foil didn't cover it—hung stringy and greasy from some kind of treatment. Her legs were slathered in heavy cream. Foam inserts made her toes stick out at unnatural angles while a lady in pink painted her toenails lavender. Another lady worked on her fingernails. A third lady paused in polishing Galinda's elbows with a loofah, checked her watch, pulled out the royal mouth guard, and wiped Galinda's teeth with a linen towel.

Galinda spoke while trying to move her mouth as little as possible. "Come in, dear Vern, and don't mind me. I'm just getting beautiful for this afternoon."

Obviously, I was missing something about beauty. I glanced at Grace, but she seemed equally dumbfounded. "Galinda, where's Galendor?" I asked.

"Oh, not back yet," she said airily—or as airily as a person can with her face cemented in place. The lady finished with her hands and Galinda started flapping them enthusiastically.

"When's he coming back?"

"Before the farewell ceremony. He said he was very anxious to hear Gozonvabosomofic's speech. Isn't that sweet? I think he feels a little sorry for what happened at the governor's luncheon. Poor Gozon; he's just no match for my Galendor. I'm sure Galendor will take care of him when—oh, but here I am nattering on. Did you need to see him for something specific?"

Nattering, huh? Sounded like she nearly nattered out some kind of secret. "Galendor's moving up in the world, isn't he?" I pressed, but she didn't fall for it.

"Of course! He married me, after all." She turned her head to give me her coquettish smile, but one of the ladies jumped in shrieking about causing wrinkles and forced her to turn her head back and relax. Meanwhile, the other lady had finished with her toes and started wiping her legs with a steaming washcloth.

"Do you want me to tell him you're looking for him?" Galinda asked.

"Yeah. We want to see him before the ceremony if possible," I said.

She stopped flapping long enough to wave, and Jeeves let us out.

On the way back to our building, we stopped by the pond to check on the naiads. One complained that the algae content was bad for her hair, and they all seemed ready to head home, but otherwise they were fine. I caught a familiar scent, so I left Grace to give the naiads our departure details and moseyed across the lawn to where Roxanne, Gator Louie, and two camera crews were unpacking their gear.

As I got near, I hollered out, "Well, shew-dang! Tan my hide and call me a gator! Y'all come back fer a rematch?"

"(Bleeping) funny. Very (bleeping) funny." Gator Louie droned, but I caught a trace of a grin.

Good thing, too; back in my pre-George days, a sense of humor could save a knight's life. While I don't eat humans (anymore), I have been known to give the humorless ones a tougher-than-normal time. At least they weren't being digested.

"Watch your mouth around the ladies," I told him. It was a reflex from hanging around Grace and our friend Rita, who never let her kids swear.

Louie gave me a funny look, which I returned with The Grin. Then I turned to Roxanne. "Our interview's not until this afternoon."

"I know, but with the demonstration this morning, I was wondering if we could move it up so we could have something to show for the lunch hour?"

Grace walked over just then, and I made introductions. Louie took in her habit. "Sister? Are you actually a nun, then?"

She nodded. "I am a sister in the order of Our Lady of the Miracles of the Faerie Catholic Church."

"That like Roman Catholic?" he asked.

"We're in communion with the Mundane Catholic Church, yes."

"Yeah? Well, shi—shoot. I did not know that. I don't really know much about the Faerie."

As he spoke, I realized he sounded different, with a mix of Southern and Northeastern tones that I'd heard from most of the Floridians. "So what's with the accent?"

He grinned, unabashed. "Gotta have a trademark, you know. Lots of nature shows out there, but everyone recognizes 'Shee-oot! That thar's sum gator!' At any rate, I saw the news this morning, put two and two together and decided to come over and, as you said, seek a rematch. That was some fu—er, freaking scare you gave us."

"'Scare'?" Grace asked, a dangerous, sisterly edge in her voice. She cocked a brow my way.

"He disturbed my nap," I said. "I get cranky when my sleep's disturbed."

"Cranky, were it?" Louie said with mock anger and in a growing mock accent. "That why we could hear yew laughing half a mile away?"

"How could you hear anything what with the way yew-all were screamin'?" I asked.

He rolled his eyes, "Shee-oot! Ferget them big-ol' gators. I's gonna wrastle me a fer-real dragon!"

"Sher as shootin' yew ain't," I said, then continued in my normal voice. I can speak two dozen languages fluently, but fake Deep South accents make my jaw ache. "If I wrestle, I fight to win; and if I win, I get to eat the loser." This time, I gave him a tamer version of The Grin to show I was kidding—about the eating part, at least. "I'm not sanguine about you making a show out of me anyway. I'm not a dumb animal by either sense of the word. Besides, my natural habitat is mountainous desert, not swampy bayou, and I haven't lived like a dragon should since St. George bespelled me over eight hundred years ago."

"But you're a dragon!"

"*Draco africano faerie*, but more importantly, I'm an Eighth Day Creation, born of God's great imaginings to remind the world of His glory. Unfortunately, in the Mundane, walking on four legs and having a tail seems to blind people to that."

Roxanne stepped in. "That's the kind of stuff I want to talk about, Vern. The opening of the Gap should have caused an opening of our eyes. We have a new standard against which to judge our perceptions, yet we fall back time and again to familiar stereotypes."

Grace and I gaped at her. It was disconcerting to hear Natura's words come out of the mouth of someone in a conservative business suit.

She continued. "You're not a monster. You're not an animal. But you're not a human, either. You are something new under the Mundane sun."

"Please don't feed the dragon's ego," Grace said.

"Yes," Louie snarled. "Don't (bleeping) feed the dragon's ego. I'm trying to negotiate for my show. You're getting your turn."

Oh, great, just what I needed: angry press. This required some quick thinking; fortunately, I'm good at that. "Look, Louie—"

"Sinclair."

"Really? Look, Sinclair, you host a wildlife show and I'm not part of the wildlife. However, the multitude of Faerie creatures would fill years' worth of shows. I may even have your first episode. "Briefly, I told him about the MOUSs.

"Shee-oot! I gotta see this."

I handed him one of our business cards. Between the hobgoblins and now Bill, I needed to add "contract negotiations" to the job description.

His mouth pursed in thought as he examined the card. I could almost hear the gears working. "Knowledge of Eternity? That mean you know a lot about the Faerie wildlife?"

"Saint George's spell took away a lot of it, but I remember something about most of the major species in my former territory, and I copied a lot of bestiaries as a scribe."

"An' if I asked you to be on the show as an advisor—you gonna be insulted by that?"

I grinned. "Consultant might work. And it depends on the kind of offer you make. To show I'm fair, I can suggest a Mundane for you to consider as well."

Grace snapped her fingers. "Bill Reed?"

I suppressed a grin. Faerie aren't psychic, but some days you wouldn't know that by the way Grace and I operate.

"Bill Reed, indeed. And we'd be glad to help you with arrangements—at a reduced rate, even."

"I'll have my people call you." He tucked the card into his pocket.

Grace stepped forward and slid her hand through his arm. "Sinclair, I'd be glad to escort you to the hotel and introduce you to Mister Reed."

Once they'd gotten out of earshot, Roxanne said, "That was masterful.".

I thought so, too, but all I said was, "Don't feed the dragon's ego."

She laughed. "No, I'm serious. Sinclair is a first-class pain in the tail when it comes to getting what he wants. Speaking of pains, can I get a response to those protestors now?" Her eyes widened and she covered her mouth and spoke through it. "Oops. I didn't say that."

Okay. She's a reporter—but she's my kind of reporter. "Where do you want to set up?"

"Thank you, Dave. This is Roxanne Lewis, and I'm here with Vern, one of the many Faerie races represented here at the Mensa World Gathering. Vern, what brought you to this convention?"

We'd stationed ourselves in front of the hotel where two of the buildings were joined. This allowed the cameraman to get a shot of the building and the pond area, and the naiads were flirting and primping for the cameras. We'd been near the lake originally, but their behavior had proven too much for the cameraman, who hadn't been able to keep himself or his lens focused on me or Roxanne. Some humans have a low tolerance for their kind of magic, and the camera, it seemed, proved too great a temptation for the naiads. That or they were bored now that Sprout Stumpyfoot was happily back in the swamp.

This spot had the advantage of being out of the way from folks entering the hotel while far enough from the naiads that the cameraman had stopped slavering. It also allowed me to watch the entrances of both buildings. Galendor should be coming back soon to pick up Galinda, and I wanted to catch him when he did. In the meantime, I concentrated on not saying anything that made me sound bizarre or dangerous or like something better handled by animal control—or worse, by Gator Louie.

"My associate Sister Grace and I were hired to provide security and prevent magical mishaps."

"Have there been any magical mishaps?"

"Nothing major, but enough to keep us on our toes—or in my case, claws." I flexed my claws one at a time, in part to show off and in part to show my control.

"You've been part of two incidents yourself: the fire alarm yesterday and the protest today."

I shrugged. "Cultural differences? Mundanes routinely make dragons the bad guys. People usually change their minds once they get to know me. Like the Earth, I'm mostly harmless."

Alas, Roxanne didn't get the reference.

"And a bit of a ham," she said. "As viewers saw this morning, you put on quite a show for the protestors. You didn't seem to be taking their accusations very seriously."

"A twelve-foot dragon swims in a 615,000-square-mile body of water for half an hour. Is that significant?"

"What about the possible rare fish you ate?"

"Next time I'll read the labels. How do they plan to warn the sharks, anyway?"

"You're not a shark."

"You're right. I have self-control. I specifically went at night so I wouldn't create a disturbance. I saw three boats in the area; two for fishing and one for the divers who caught me on film. I can guarantee you any of those boats did more damage to the environment than I did with my little dip." As I spoke, I gave the camera my "I can be reasonable if you can" look.

Behind the cameraman, I saw a shiny black limo pull up to the hotel. The driver got out, but before she could circle around, the passenger door opened and Galendor stepped out. He slammed—slammed!—the door and strode into the hotel—our building of the hotel, not the one where his suite was located. That didn't look any better than the grim expression on his face.

"Excuse me a moment," I told Roxanne and waited until she signaled the cameraman to stop filming, then texted Grace: *Irate elf incoming. Be right there.*

She responded: *No hurry. They are High Elves.*

I snorted as I put my phone away.

"Trouble?" Roxanne asked.

"Someone I need to talk to. Business. It can wait a few, if you had any other questions."

She clearly wanted to ask more about what kind of business, but directed the cameraman to resume. "Well, I think a great many of us were surprised to discover that a fire-breathing dragon can swim."

"I love to swim." I waxed poetic about my beloved Medsea, checking to make sure the naiads weren't listening before mentioning the mermaids. She asked a few more questions about my service to God and His creatures and my current assignment. I told her about helping security break up a fight.

While my mouth worked on automatic, my ears focused on the hotel. The way Galendor had stormed into the hotel disturbed me. I'd seen plenty of humans use that fast-paced stride when angry, but never a High Elf, unless they were "running" into battle. No one does battle-frenzied power walk like a High Elf. I didn't care how long Galendor had lived with humans; that was just not right. So out of habit built from years of experience as a PI, I kept my ears peeled for trouble.

Nonetheless, I had to admit I was surprised when I heard Galendor shout Gozon's full name across the crowded convention hall and launch into the Tribal Declaration of War and Individual Challenge of Honor.

"Damsels and Knights!" I shouted, causing Roxanne to give a little shriek in the middle of her question. "Sorry, Miz Lewis, but it sounds like trouble after all!" I took off at a lope, then launched myself at the con café balcony, the quickest way to the hall. Below, I heard Roxanne tell her crew to get moving.

I landed on the railing, trying not to dig into the cement with my claws and startling a couple having tea. "Door!" I shouted, and the guy scrambled to get it open just as I flew through. I like Mensans. They think fast.

In all, it took me less than two minutes to get to the hall. It was going to take about that long to get to the Elves. I couldn't fly in the hall; too low and too narrow. I pushed my way through the crowd, my neck craned to see what was happening. Under normal circumstances, Galendor shouldn't have even finished his challenge; in the current situation, I was expecting to arrive just as Gozon was gearing up with his reply.

I did not expect to find the two Elves shouting obscenities at each other while being physically restrained by two burly Mensans and Siegfried.

Grace stood between them, but they spat insults around her as if she weren't there. Apparently her peace spell had not been enough. She was about to launch a major "Shut Up" spell, when Garn suddenly barreled through the crowd, knocking her down, and punched Galendor in the stomach.

Down the hall, I heard Galinda's screams, and fast as glass slippers could take her—and you'd be surprised how fast a Faerie princess can run; she actually passed me up—she was at her husband's side, crying over him and shouting unprincessy epithets at the dwarf, who was accusing Galendor of theft and issuing challenges of his own. It was beginning to sound like Geraldo during sweeps week.

I heard the elevator bell and guessed Roxanne and her crew were on their way. That or Janey had finally arrived with her Taser.

Time for drastic measures. I opened my mouth and let out a full-throated roar.

By the time the echoes had died and the tables and potted plants had stopped shaking, everyone was silent but for some whimpering. Several people had ducked into corners or under tables. No one was within twenty feet of me.

Better.

I put on my Menace Face and stalked my way to the Elves. People parted before me like the Red

Sea before Moses. Some cautiously removed their hands from their ears as I passed. I reached out with my tail and righted one fake palm tree that leaned over Bill, who was crouched down against the wall. Beside him, Sinclair was looking at me with calculating awe. Even Coyote, who'd found a perch on the registration table, raised his eyebrows and nodded in my direction.

That's right, you'd better respect the dragon.

I got to the small circle that held the quarrelsome quartet. Galinda opened her mouth to complain. I glared at her, and she shrank back.

Grace had stood up and had brushed off her habit, which had gotten damp from a cup of Ping she'd fallen over. She looked frustrated rather than hurt, but I asked anyway, "You okay?"

Once I saw her nod, I stared down each troublemaker in turn. Galendor stood fuming but still, with the Mensans holding him loosely and Galinda tucked under one arm. Gozon, however, was twitching and struggling slightly against Siegfried. Garn had been pulled back by Kent and Brunhilde, and though he looked ready to resume his fight, he was the calmest of the group. I decided I'd start with him.

"All right," I said in a calm, clear voice. "We're going to get to the bottom of this, and we're going to do it like civilized beings. Do I make myself clear?"

Galendor snarled, "You have no right—"

Almost on top of him, Gozon started, "This is the business of the Elves—"

I dragged my claws across the floor, ripping through carpet. I'd probably get a sermon from Aiden when he got that bill, but I was not going to take any fewmets from upstart Elves. "I am an Eighth Day Creation. You're on my turf, and it is my right, and you do not have leave to speak!"

They silenced. I did not have the size or the power of my kind anymore, but I still had millennia of tradition. When a dragon decides to involve itself in the affairs of other sapients on its territory, its authority is second only to God's.

Janey came dashing up then, Taser in hand. She took in the restrained Elves, the rips in the carpet, and my grim expression and wisely let me take the lead.

"Garn." My voice rang in the hallway—quite a feat in a hotel built to muffle and soften noise. He stepped forward.

"Yo," I said, "What is your argument with Ga-lendor?"

"He has stolen my future!"

"What?" I asked.

"What?" Galendor asked, equally puzzled.

"What?" Gozon roared and lunged toward him. Siegfried held him back.

"He knows what I'm talking about," Garn growled. "I don't know how he did it, but when he realized Gozonvabosomofic didn't have the bull, he sent his brownies after me!"

"Bull?" Grace and I both asked.

"You?" Galendor gaped.

"You!" Gozon screamed. "You idiot! Shut up!"

"'Bull?' You've got livestock in this hotel?" Janey asked.

Garn started yelling again. "Don't play stupid, Elf! Your brownies didn't find what they were looking for in Gozon's luggage, so they went after my pickax!"

"You had a bull in your pickax?" Janey's brows knitted together. "With a spell of some kind?"

Galendor was no longer paying attention to Garn. Instead, he yelled at Gozon, "You entrusted the bull to a dwarf? Are you insane?"

"Crazy like a fox! Ha! Didn't know I understood human idioms, did you? Fools, fools all of you! Decades ago, I set this plan in motion—the greatest puck of all! I waited for the perfect time to spring my trap—and you've ruined it!" With a roar, Gozon tore himself out of Siegfried's grasp and lunged after Garn.

I intercepted him, and he swung at me. I wrapped my tail around him, pinning his arms to his sides.

Grace gaped. "You used the bull...in a prank?" She crossed herself.

"Would someone tell me how you can hide an entire bull in a hotel, much less in an ax?" Janey cried.

People were starting to mutter among themselves. The three-way fight was brewing to break out anew, dragon moderation or no. Grace looked ready to take them all on. Janey looked about ready to use the Taser on someone if she didn't get some answers.

In all, the Faerie were putting on a good show but not making a good showing. And somehow, I'd lost control of the room, roars and ripped carpet notwithstanding.

So naturally, the elevator door dinged again, and this time, it really was Roxanne and her camera crew.

I directed my hearing toward the nearest conference room, found it empty and said, "Into that room right now, and that includes you, Kent, Brunhilde, Siegfried...and Coyote."

"What'd I do?" Coyote whined.

"I'll figure it out. Janey, meet Coyote. If he so much as twitches, tase him."

Garn had already stomped into the room with Grace and the others. Grace's friend Eliza, I noticed, also followed Grace. Well, she was a coordinator for the conference.

I looked at Galendor. "Are you going to walk, or shall these guys frog march you in?"

"I'll walk," he snarled.

"May I come, too?" Galinda asked timidly. She'd never seen me in ferocious dragon mode.

I started to say "yes," but Galendor's short answer and Gozon's struggling against my restraint reminded me of something. "First, I want you to find the Mage Frederico SanGermano. Do you know him? He does research for your father."

She nodded and let go of her husband. Immediately, her maids appeared beside her. In thirty seconds, they had her transformed from weeping wife to royalty. She gave them instructions quietly and sent them on their way. Then she saw the camera.

"Galinda, find Fred," I growled as I started to pull Gozon away.

Gozon, however, had seen the reporters as well. He resisted, digging his heels in, literally; his shoes caught in the tears I'd made in the carpet, ripping it further. I struggled to get him to move to the room in a dignified manner. I had started to remind him, in Elvish, that his argument had moved to another room when he stomped on my foot. Gozon may have been wearing his Armani suit, but he'd accessorized it with women's spiked-heeled boots. I let out an undragonlike shriek as my tail loosened in surprise.

"Members of the press!" he shouted, pushing Galinda aside to make sure the camera got a good shot of him. "I have a message for the traitorous state of Florida!"

"Gozon, don't!" I said, but he was beyond reason. For a moment, indecision stalled me. If I dragged him away by force, it was going to look bad for the cameras, no matter how I explained. But if I didn't, would it look worse?

I moved toward him, hoping to pull him away subtly. Maybe I could make it look like his idea. "Don't you think you should wait until after we—"

He punched me in the snout, and while I saw stars, he declared war on Florida.

Chapter Twenty-Nine: How Do You Hide a Papal Bull?

"Is this a joke?" Roxanne asked. Her cameraman had already come to his own conclusion and was laughing into his hand. The stunned Mensans around us were not so sure.

"Roxanne, he's not in his right mind," I said. My voice sounded funny as my nose swelled. Gozon had struck me in the nostril, and thus confirmed my suspicion. His hand smelled like Ping Cola, and I guessed the cup on the floor that Grace had stepped on belonged to him rather than Galendor. I set my paw on Gozon's shoulder, my claw pressing on a nerve that effectively paralyzed his vocal chords. He twitched, and I pressed harder. He glared at me, but otherwise did nothing. Wish I'd thought to do this earlier.

"He's...under the influence. I promise: Give me ten minutes and I'll explain everything, but don't show that tape yet."

"The elves declare war on us, and you don't want me to broadcast?" Roxanne regarded me skeptically, but I could tell she wanted to be convinced. Like I said, my kind of reporter.

"The story is bigger than that," I wheedled.

She bit the side of her lip. "Ten minutes. Turn off the camera."

"Thank you." Why hadn't the Gap formed in Florida? I liked it here.

I turned to Galinda. "Princess, may I escort you inside?"

"But you said—"

"Inside. Your husband awaits you." I knew the minute I was gone, she'd be giving Roxanne an interview. I'd have to trust her maids to find Frederico. I offered her my arm. I don't like walking on my hind legs, but I can do it without looking like a circus act. Besides, I already had one arm occupied with Gozon. She hesitated, clearly wanting to stay and talk to Roxanne, but finally drew herself up into a dignified pose and slipped her hand through my elbow, and we entered the conference room together.

I grinned slightly when I saw the peaceful scene in the room. Grace had settled herself into a conference chair and was humming her calming spell. Eliza sat beside her. Garn brooded in his chair with Kent on one side and a crestfallen Brunhilde on the other. Coyote perched himself on the refreshment table, his legs swinging while he lapped up ice water from a pitcher. Janey sat beside Grace, but with her chair turned partway toward Coyote and her Taser in her lap. She was taking me very seriously. Good.

Galendor was still moving about restlessly, but Galinda went to him and he acquiesced to taking a seat beside her and opposite Garn. I didn't trust Gozon to behave with the state he was in, so I kept a hold of his shoulder and took a position triangular to Garn and Galendor.

"All right. With the exception of security and Eliza Smithing, as representative of the Mensans, it's just us Faerie. We've got curious Mensans and reporters outside, so no one leaves this room until we've got everything figured out and have a good story for the press. Don't make me tear another hole in the nice carpet."

"You're going to have to pay for that," Janey commented.

"We'll put it on the Duke's bill. Galendor, you don't have the bull, do you?"

"Of course ye have it!" Garn snarled. "Ye stole it out of my pickax."

"He stole a bull out of your pickax," Janey restated.

"Aye! And my future with it!"

"But I thought you were taking it to your cousins," Galinda said to her husband. "You took the Lear and everything."

Galendor answered his wife. "I did, my dear, but the bull was counterfeit."

"A counterfeit bull? You mean a clone? Like Dolly?" Eliza asked.

Garn glared at Gozon, "So ye gave me the fake?"

Gozon glared back. "No, you idiot! His brownies stole the fake from me, and your carelessness lost the genuine papal bull."

"The Church has cloned a cow?" Eliza asked, torn between fascinated and horrified.

No one replied.

"My carelessness? I haven't let that pickax out of my sight all week!"

I felt Gozon twitching under my grip, but he merely snarled, "No? And you would have me believe that...creature...did not distract you?" He spat the words toward Brunhilde, who winced guiltily and edged closer to Garn. Kent rose and went to her other side protectively.

"Her? Are you mad?"

"I saw her tickling your beard!"

"I'm sorry!" Brunhilde suddenly cried. "I was not meaning to make trouble. I was just having fun, ja?"

"Yes, quite a bit of fun," Garn said. "but not the kind of fun I was interested in. She was with Kent. Nay, I slept with my pickax under my pillow. 'Twas his brownies!"

"Don't blame the brownies for your incompetence!" Gozon started to lunge toward Garn, and I tightened my claws on his shoulder.

Galendor stood to yell at Gozon. "Don't blame the dwarf for your incompetence. It's pucks like this that only show how slow and senile you've gotten! Now the bull is lost, and we shall both be disgraced!"

"Fine! As long as I take you down with me!"

"Bring it on!"

"All right!" I called over the noise. "Siddown! I think I've got this figured out."

The Elves turned toward me. "You know where the bull is?" they demanded as one.

"Would someone explain to me how you even got a bull into this hotel without anyone noticing?" Janey shouted.

Grace stopped humming to answer. "It's not that kind of bull, Janey. It's a special charter. It's called "bull" after bulla, the seal—and in our case, because it's written on parchment made from the skin of a bull of the purest white. This particular one was penned by Saint Patrick and signed by Saint Leo, the pope of the time. It outlines certain matters of dogma for the High Elves."

"And it's been lost or stolen? And no one reported it? What's it even doing here?"

Grace now turned to me. "That's what I'd like to know."

Coyote spoke for the first time since we got into the room. "Yeah! This should be good!"

I ignored him, but spoke to Janey and to Brunhilde, who sat hand-in-hand with Kent. "You have to understand that even though the House Eternal

Winds is one...nation, if you will...it is divided into tribes."

"Like Bosnia," Janey said, "or Iraq."

I shrugged. "Elves generally get along better, but close enough. And in fact, the tribes do sometimes fight for overall power of the House. Gozon has been Speaker for the Winds for the last 250 years—but in the past century, there's been talk that he's getting too old for the job."

"How old do elves get?" Janey asked.

"I am still in my prime," Gozon said proudly, but Galendor just snorted. I was beginning to wonder how long it would take them to get off their high, but at least it made things go faster.

"He's got a good century yet, but Gozon's always had trouble conforming to human conventions of time. In the past, regents and royalty actually revered the stateliness of Elvish speech, but in the past couple of generations, and especially since the opening of the Gap, humans have less patience with Elvish Longspeech. Gozon hasn't been able to adapt. There's been a move to retire him and put in an Elf who can better relate to humans, and Galendor has been the recent favorite. They want someone more modern, and

Gozon has proven himself too set in the old ways. I'm sorry, Gozonvabosomofic, but that's the hard truth.

"In fact, rather than respond to the threat to his job by trying to modernize his ways, he turned to an ancient tradition—raising his personal stature by pulling a puck. That's a kind of practical joke. That's where the bull comes in. The bull has been in the care of the Keeper of Ages—kind of like a royal librarian. It's a very prestigious position because of the value of the artifacts, and is a step on the ladder to Speaker. Galendor, a member of the Forests tribe, held that position seventy-five years ago. Gozon stole the bull from him."

Gozon snickered. "It was not hard. I spent a mere year in the planning."

Galendor spat at him and the two started for each other. I interposed myself between them. "I have the floor, thank you."

Once they had returned to their ides of the room, I continued, "The Forests tribe gets disgraced and Galendor loses his position. But hey, he's young and adaptable, even married a human. He's back on his way up. Gozon, meanwhile, never revealed that he'd taken the bull, waiting until the perfect time to spring his trick, force Galendor into demanding a public explanation, and thus elevate himself in the eyes of his chosen audience— you the Mensans, the most intelligent of the Mundanes."

"I'm sorry. Why would this impress us?" Eliza asked.

I just shrugged. "Yeah, that was a flaw in his logic."

Galendor snorted. "Just more proof that you're no longer fit for the job, old one."

"Don't reply to that, Gozon," I warned before they could start a fight again. "Galendor, you're not much better. When you learned of Gozon's plan, you decided to play a puck of your own and steal back the bull before Gozon could reveal his trick. He snuck the brownies onboard the airship with the mission to search the luggage and take the bull."

"How?" Janey asked. "I thought you couldn't force them to do anything."

"He didn't. He used magic to contact them and bribed them with Ping. Probably as much as they could find while here and a supply when they got back to Faerie. His and Galinda's friend Kevin is actually Kevin Olson, owner of Ping Cola. That's why the trip to the bottling plant, right?"

Galinda shook her head. "Daddy just wants to start a business."

"We'll discuss that later," I told her. "Gozon, for all that he has a problem adapting to human customs, has no trouble anticipating intrigue. So he took steps. No one would ever expect a High Elf to conspire with a dwarf, so he gave the bull to Garn to store in his pickax, promising him his greatest desire if he kept it safe. A faerimet mine in Australia, right?"

Miserably, Garn nodded.

"Gozon, meanwhile, carried a counterfeit in his briefcase, a briefcase that while expensive, was common enough to ensure there would be a few at the convention. Then, he arranged for the room mix-up, didn't you?" The Elf glared at me, confirming my guess.

"And when did he learn to manipulate computers?" Galendor demanded.

"He didn't, and don't insult him. That would have been too direct an action for an Elf of his stature. He found someone who was willing to...persuade...the guy who works the reservations to make a hash of them." I saw Brunhilde flinch and took a guess. "What'd he offer you, Brunhilde?"

She sighed. "He said he'd help me market Valkyrie's Whisper; he said he had connections if I helped him—"

"Valkyrie's Whisper? The lingerie?" I blurted. Yes, even a dragon could be surprised.

Brunhilde brightened. "Oh? You've heard of it, ja? I brought some with me, you know. I show some people here. Coyote bought some for his girly-friends."

"We really like them!" Coyote interjected, smiling so big his tongue was practically lolling out of his mouth. Mick Jagger would have been jealous.

"Ja. And Cambridge said he had a client who might be interested in starting a Mundane line. He set up a video conference with a buyer. I modeled. It was fun, ja?"

"I thought you said you were in the shower with Cambridge?" I blurted.

Grace gave me a hard look, but now I was getting confused. Just what was Ramada's role in all this?

"No. The bath. He was teaching me—"

"Teaching you what?" Janey exclaimed, a disgusted twist in her voice. Grace, meanwhile, looked ready to do the magical equivalent of sticking her fingers in her ears and singing "Lalalalala." Some things a nun did not need to know. Come to think of it, the dragon didn't need that mental picture, either.

"Well, the manicuring and the pedicuring! What did you think?"

"Pedicures?"

"Have you ever seen a Viking's toenails? Everyone says, 'Vikings, they are so hygienic.'" She rolled her eyes.

"Weren't they?" Eliza asked.

I answered, "Sure—by eleventh-century standards."

Brunhilde shrugged, pleading with her eyes for people to understand. "I want more. Cleaner. But they fight me and say it's sissy stuff. So Cambridge, he tells me, 'Make it fun, my dear,' but what do I know of this? So he teaches me. Cambridge, he's so nice to help."

"But you said you were sudsy," I protested.

"Sure. Sudsy feet. And we had those little foamy things between our toes—"

"So you couldn't run just then—or he didn't want to embarrass himself. Fine." Just to make sure I had it all straight, I asked, "So there wasn't anything going on that..." My voice trailed off.

Fortunately, she picked up the innuendo. Maybe unfortunately, because she drew herself up. "Cambridge is a gentleman, ja!"

"And SkinnyZits?"

Grace glowered at me, but I couldn't let it go.

"He changed the reservations. I tell him thank you, and he was so sweet—"

"'—and minty, and all you did was kiss him,'" I muttered. This was embarrassing. Grace pinched the bridge of her nose and shook her head at me.

At least Brunhilde looked a little chagrined. "I just thought it was a joke, ja? A funny puck. Gozon said he would straighten it all out, be the hero, ja?"

"He may have told you that, but the puck didn't stop there." Now we'd returned to ground I was sure of. Everyone continued to listen quietly, and I sat down to really finish the story.

"The brownies, as Gozon planned, searched the wrong room; and when they didn't find anything, they went a little nuts and started cleaning and searching at random. They couldn't get into

Gozon's room because of all the wards, and Gozon made sure he kept his briefcase always within sight so they could not get at it. I'm sure he planned to set it aside eventually so they could steal it once it was too late for Galendor to realize he'd stolen a fake. However, Galendor decided to make his own opportunity. He picked a time when Gozon would have his briefcase out of the room, then arranged for the pixies to play their little puck on me, figuring the humans around me would panic, set off the fire alarms and force an evacuation. In the ensuing confusion, they could get at the briefcase. Gozon went along with it, trusting that Galendor would believe the copy was genuine long enough for all to continue according to plan."

"And it nearly did, if not for this fool of a dwarf losing the real one!" Gozon snapped.

"It's not lost, is it, Brunhilde?"

Clutching Kent's hand, she looked at me with wide-eyed innocence. In this case, I wasn't going to buy it. "Bruni, you got some 'splainin' to do."

She sighed and released his hands. "Ja, all right. I'm sorry, Kent. I took it. I didn't know what it was. Garn, I am sorry. I didn't know. I didn't mean to hurt you, either of you."

"Why?" Kent asked with a gentleness that seemed out of place. He took her hands again.

She tossed her blonde hair and shrugged. "I was just having fun, ja? It was a joke. I never pucked with an Elf, so when Gozonvabosomofic asked me, I said, 'Ja,' ja?"

Brunhilde batted her eyes at the dwarves pleadingly, and they melted. Who said Valkyrie didn't have feminine wiles?

Still, *I* wasn't going to let her off the hook. "You didn't stop with that, did you? You thought it was so funny, you told the one creature you figured would appreciate it. Someone with good ears to overhear about Garn's odd attachment to his pickax and his strange 'bull.' He put two and two together and convinced you to steal the bull."

"No!" Brunhilde said. "I didn't know about the bull. He said he wanted to see the pickax. He made me a bet that I couldn't get the pickax away from Garn. So I played the loving games, and when they were asleep, I bring him the pickax. He took it to another room. I thought he was showing it to his friends. Then I took it back. I didn't know he stole anything from it."

"Who has it?" Garn demanded, but really, there was only one good suspect left, someone who's also spent time with Brunhilde and had a penchant for trouble on general principles.

Grace had figured it out, too. Together, we turned to glare at Coyote.

Janey, smart woman, followed up by aiming her Taser at him.

The Legendary Trickster just laughed and pulled the scroll out of the inside pocket of his tweed jacket. "Well done, Vern! I wondered how long it would take you to figure it out!"

"I'd have figured it out sooner if the brownies hadn't shown up in Garn's room after Brunhilde returned the pickax. You peed on the ax before you left, didn't you?"

"Well, sure! How else would anyone know it was my trick? Besides, a hollow handle? How could I resist the challenge? You mean they cleaned it up? Aww. Guess I got pucked!"

"Coyote!" Grace remonstrated.

"Frankly," I said, "this whole thing has been a big cluster—"

"Don't say it!" Grace snapped, Eliza and Janey echoing her.

Janey used her speed dial to call the police, but since Coyote returned the bull willingly and neither Elf wanted to admit they'd been tricked by a mischievous Native American Spirit, the best they could do was cite him for causing a disturbance. Nonetheless, it was enough to get him hauled back to Montana for breaking parole.

"It was worth it!" he said as Janey handcuffed him to take him down to her office to await the authorities. He stopped in front of Gozon before he left.

"No hard feelings?" he said and moved in for a hug.

Gozon kneed him in a part of his anatomy I was glad dragons did not have.

"Guess so," he squeaked, and Grace put her arms around him to help him straighten up and walk. At the door, however, she let Janey drag him away. Kent and Garn followed with a remorseful Brunhilde between them.

Galinda started to rise, but I told her to sit. "We've still got some business," I said, and with perfect timing, the maids showed up with Frederico.

Gotta love the Faerie. They never miss a cliché or a cue.

"Frederico, why don't you tell us all about the effects of scanatine on Elvish metabolism."

He looked nervously at Princess Galinda Tavendor, his boss's daughter. "It's just theoretical..." he started.

"Bull," I said. Okay, it was a cheap shot. Sue me. "We've got two Elves, both holding dignified positions in the House Eternal Winds, who have spent the last half hour swapping insults in choppy sentences and trying to start a war on behalf of their tribes. In fact, the Great Diplomat here just issued a declaration of war against Florida."

"Surely, you're overstating—"

"Gozon, say something," I ordered.

"Get to the point, dragon," the High Elf snapped.

Frederico gasped and immediately went to Gozon, looking into his eyes and grabbing his wrist to take his pulse.

"Gozon's been chugging Ping for at least the last twelve hours, haven't you?" I asked.

Suddenly—and how else would he do anything at the moment?—Gozon crumpled into a ball of shame. "It's true. After the incident at the governor's luncheon, I began to realize the truth in what you had told me, O wise dragon and my friend. So I determined to attempt some of their customs, to assimilate myself into their social order as Galendoropynphordaladys had done."

"In other words, you were drinking to fit in." See what I meant about cliché? At least his speech had started to lengthen out.

"It tasted vile, oversweet and with an aftertaste that coated the tongue. But then, it was...wonderful. Things became so sudden and clear and exciting. And, and when it was over, everything seemed so long and pointless. So I had another can. And another. And whenever the effect seemed to fade, I just had another can. Everything seemed so obvious. But now, it's a horrible blur. This is your fault!" he shouted at Galendor.

"Take it easy. Galendor's worse off than you. Aren't you, Galendor?"

"I'm fine." He crossed his arms and glared at me.

"Are you?" I asked softly. "Why don't you ask your wife about that?"

Galendor spun toward Galinda. "What did you say?"

"I was upset. I needed someone to talk to, and, and whenever I tried, you have been so rushed and abrupt."

"Abrupt?" he said, his face reddening. Calling a High Elf "abrupt" was like accusing the Pope of adultery.

"I tried to talk to you about it; you know I have. You kept insisting you were fine, and Betanna kept telling me I was being oversensitive, but I knew there was something wrong. I just knew."

"You talked to Betanna?"

"She's my best friend!"

"And a notorious gossip! Why didn't you just broadcast it to the entire Five Kingdoms? You may as well have told Maurena on her show!"

Galinda wrang her newly manicured hands. "Galendor, my love, you know I'd never—"

He spoke atop her protests. "Then you go blabbering to a dragon? Like it's a qualified marriage counselor?"

"Well, at least he figured out what was wrong!"

"There's nothing wrong with me, you traitorous wench!" Galendor raised his hand to strike her.

Galinda squealed and shrank back. I readied my tail to grab his arm and sensed Grace preparing a quick protection spell, but we didn't need either. Galendor looked at the fear in his wife's tear-filled eyes and slowly lowered his arm. For a moment, he simply gazed at her, trembling almost as much as she did.

Then he fell to his knee. "Galinda, oh my faithful bride whose beauty blooms like the faspella in the meadows of the forests of Eldenafarandoria, rare and far too fleeting when compared to an Elf's life. If I have hurt you, I—" He choked up then, something else unheard of in an Elf, but Galinda threw her arms around him and whispered reassurances.

After a moment, she pulled away, wiped her eyes, and addressed Frederico like a princess of Tavendor. "What exactly is scanatine, and how did my husband and this worthy Elf become so poisoned by it?"

"My lady, my studies aren't complete, and I only suspect it's the scanatine because it is a Mundane creation. I could be completely wrong—"

"I am not my father, Researcher, and my husband's health suffers. You may speak fully and frankly. In fact, I demand it."

Frederico must have been waiting for those words, because he relaxed visibly. "Scanatine is an artificially created flavoring, mostly used in beverages because of its unique taste, although some Mundane candies and snack foods use it."

"Junk food," I said.

"Exactly. The overall research seems to indicate that it's essentially safe for most humans, which includes Faerie because the body chemistry is the same, of course. Elvish biology, however... It's rather technical, and I can't give you too many details because I've not been able to do the research—"

"Then just tell me the effects," she demanded.

"Essentially, your Highness, the scanatine impacts the brain chemistry, affecting Elvish perception of time. As well, as I'm sure you've seen, the effect is widespread, impacting speech and emotions, certainly. As I've said, I have not been able to fully study the phenomenon, but I would conjecture physical symptoms might eventually manifest, as well."

Galendor shifted uncomfortably, but Galinda merely set her hand on her husband's shoulder and nodded. "So what do we do, Researcher?"

"Well, most obviously, they must stop imbibing scanatine-containing beverages. If what Gozonvabosomofic said is any indication, the effects do wear off eventually, but I cannot predict when or how fully, or how easy the process will be. I think it goes without saying that we should get you to Los Lagos as quickly as possible. The university hospital there will have the resources we need to do some tests that may help us to make things easier on you, and we can bring a healer across the Gap."

Again Galinda nodded and turned to her maid to give her instructions.

Meanwhile Gozon moaned, "My speech. My career is ruined. No longer shall I be renowned among the House Eternal Winds as a paragon of dignity and a beacon of the old ways. Nay, now I shall be known as—"

"—the brave warrior who risked his own life to expose a threat to all Elves," Galendor finished. "You tried to warn me, Gozonvabosomofic; I see that now. 'Do not be so quick to embrace the new, the radical,' you said. 'That is for humans. They are the swift-flowing stream, while we are the land. It is our duty to stand for the traditional, the patient, the enduring.' I failed our people, and had I been allowed to continue my role in the plans of the father of my wife, the King of Tavendor, who would be the Czar of Soda as well; yea, I would have brought our people to peril and ruin. You were right—and I am ashamed." He buried his head in his hands, and Galinda left her maid to wrap her arms around him.

"Nay, Galendoropynphordaladys." Gozon knelt in front of him. "You have been impulsive, it is true, quick-acting like the dareta mouse who moves from place to place, and task to task, never stilling lest it fall into paralysis until pressed into motion again. Yet, though you have indeed fallen too well to the influence of the humans whom you have chosen to love, for long have you loved these fleeting lives, these—"

"Cut to the chase. My head hurts," Galendor complained.

And, miracle of miracles, Gozon did. "You were also right. The Faerie humans have long understood our people and our ways, but Mundanes do not. Nor are they willing to alter themselves to our customs. Perhaps they simply cannot. Verily, then, we must be the ones to adapt. I cannot do that alone. I would keep my position if it is so determined by the House, but I need an advisor, a...mentor in the ways of humans."

Galendor dropped his hands to look at Gozon disbelievingly. "Are you suggesting a partnership?"

"The universes are too big for one Speaker. I am coming to see that—and it has only taken a few years." Gozon quirked his mouth in a grin. "Let us go to Los Lagos. Then let us go home and together present the House with the—" His eyes went wide, and he began to pat his pockets. "The bull—it's gone!"

"Coyote!" I moaned.

Grace laughed, however, and pulled the parchment out of her robe. "Well, he did try," she said, "but he's not the only one who can pick a pocket."

I could only smile with pride. Grace had come a long way since we'd first met, though I wasn't quite sure whether Bishop Aiden would agree. "Well, that's two problems solved. Now for Number Three: King Daddy's gonna want his soda factory, and he's not going to be happy. He's already tried to suppress Frederico's findings."

Frederico nodded.

Galinda released the cuddly stranglehold she had on her husband's arm. "I'll handle Daddy. And is that reporter still out there? I'm going to give her a nice little scoop on scanatine and how it almost poisoned an entire race. If that isn't enough to get it on the banned export list, I'll take it to Maurena."

I grinned wider. I love it when a plan comes together.

Eliza spoke up. "You don't have to make soda with scanatine. It's a cheap flavoring and unique, but plenty of other sodas don't use it."

"Still," Grace said, "I think we're going to have to be more careful about foods that get carried across the Gap from now on."

"Yeah, but that's a job for the governments, not us," I told her. I was already doing too much gratis work. "Galinda, would you like me to introduce you to Miz Roxanne Lewis?"

Her maids quickly attended to her dress and make up while she instructed them to escort the Elves to her room where Jeeves would start making travel arrangements. She kissed her husband and told Frederico to accompany her. Then she settled her hand on my flank and we headed into the hall and the afternoon news.

Chapter Thirty: Another Fine Mensa

"Well, you didn't end up just a sidekick after all," Grace said as she leaned back in her seat onboard the *Cloudskater*.

"I guess you could say that was another fine Mensa I'd gotten us out of."

Grace groaned. "How long have you been waiting to say that?"

I grunted and stretched, walked a tight circle on the padded floor and flopped down. Things had turned out rather well, considering. Galinda gave Roxanne a terrific interview, with Frederico providing what facts he knew and what conjectures he'd made. The declaration of war became merely an example of the harmful effects of scanatine on Elvish metabolisms. I got the feeling once Roxanne was done with this story and the big news networks picked it up, scanatine was going to be a thing of the past. Except on the black market, of course, but fortunately, illegal drug use was not the problem in Faerie that it was in Mundane.

Roxanne, of course, had been thrilled, as had been her network. By the time we were leaving, she'd already made arrangements to do a follow-up story in Los Lagos, and made me promise to give her an in-depth interview then, too. The scanatine scandal would get played, I knew, again and again, but I also knew that Gozon and Galendor would spin it to their benefit. Our interview had been overcome by events, of course. I didn't mind.

The ever-efficient Jeeves had shown up just as Galinda was finishing. He informed her that the flight plans were filed, everyone's bags, including Gozon's, had been packed, and her car awaited her. Galinda instructed him to make her apologies to whomever it was princesses apologize to, and left to take Galendor and Gozon back to Los Lagos.

Eliza approached me to give the farewell speech in Gozon's stead. I kept it light, recapping some of our adventures of the week and cracking jokes. They loved me. For a change, the dragon slew the humans.

Nick (the color-blind Magic Squares Man) came to thank us. He'd cracked the shoemaker math code with some help from the InterdimNet and was negotiating with Mensa Market on a whole new line of game books based on the "New Faerie Math."

Melchior pranced up to us as we were leaving our room. Even in jeans and a T-shirt declaring "Art is for Everyone!" he looked like a fop—but a happy fop, at least.

"I'm saved!" he declared. "My art is rejuvenated! And it's all thanks to this fabulous conference and you!" He showed us a note: *Pretty people need clothes. Fun to draw. I stay?*

He actually fanned himself like Galinda drying her nails. We wished him luck and warned him that a Brownie might not stay for too long so far from the Gap.

"What?" he shrieked.

"Deep breaths! Inspiration is fleeting, yet its effects span infinity. Soak in the process. Oh, and avoid Ping for the brownie's sake."

Ray caught us at the bus to say good-bye, as had Heather, dressed in full Rhoda Dakota costume. In a fun turn-around, she asked us to pose for photos. She signed a bunch of headshots for some of the Faerie who recognized her and double-checked that we still had the one for Charlie. Templegrass cooed over her and insisted that she visit the studio for a fitting. The sparkle in Heather's eyes said she just might—if a certain herald might also be in town that day.

Through some miracle, getting the Faerie to leave went smoothly, with a few surprises. Brunhilde sat on the bus, holding hands with Kent while Garn sat on her other side. I overheard them talking about the future: joining Garn in his mines until they made enough money to open their own acting school/dinner theater. Siegfried, meanwhile, had elected to change his flight plans and go to Mundane Norway with his new lady friend. Coyote was heading back to the reservation in chains. I hoped his trailer/doghouse had a nice strong leash.

Grace left amid hugs and promises to email soon. Despite all the craziness, Faerie tricks, mystery, and even declaration of war, she had thoroughly enjoyed the convention and looked more refreshed than I'd seen her in nearly a year.

"Still, it'll be good to be home," she said when I commented on it.

I snorted. "Oh, you think chaos does not await? I've not heard from my padawan all day."

Grace glanced at her phone. "He passed on a message from Sister Eloise to me. She got the containment field set up around the amusement park and thirty feet into the ground—well above the restaurant level but deep enough for the MOUSs to burrow. She wants to wait until we get there so they can explain."

"'Explain'?" I asked. If I had hackles, they'd be rising.

Grace, however, seemed unconcerned. "The spell, I suppose. Or maybe the setup?"

"Maybe."

It was neither the spell nor the setup that needed explaining. At least, those weren't the only things.

"How could you let a live MOUS into our house?" I demanded of the chagrined group that stood shame-faced in front of us. They were a motley bunch: Sister Eloise's habit was rumpled and dirty, and she had a bruise and a scratch on one cheek. Kenjo and Pinjal were covered in sawdust, dirt, blood, and sweat; rather than a sword, Pinjal had a mop. Even Gapman looked worse for wear. His bespelled supersuit might deflect dirt as well as bullets, but that didn't stop the sawdust and MOUS dander from resting on his shoulders. His gloves and knees were wet.

Around us, the house gave witness to their shenanigans and attempts to rectify the destruction. We stood in the entryway, the side cabinet where Grace kept her hiking shoes and snow boots now busted and titling at a forty-degree angle sideways, the bowl that sat on it a neat pile of ceramic on the floor beside it. The walls had scratches and, despite the cleaning efforts of the hobgoblins, fur and blood. I wasn't sure all the blood had been the MOUS's, either.

"Pinjal said it was dead!" Kenjo started.

Pinjal immediately added, "Gapman did, too!"

I saw my padawan's jaw clench as he fought his inner-Ronnie's urge to protest being tossed under the bus. He replied curtly, "Mistakes were made."

"So we see," Grace said with all the sweetness of a nun with a ruler behind her back, just aching for some knuckles to smack.

To the right, the kitchen entrance had a MOUS-sized hole in the door and adjoining wall. I could almost fit through it. Why had Kenjo let the MOUSs get so big?

"It's my fault," Sister Eloise said miserably. "They locked it in the freezer, but when I came home, I heard noises and I opened it—"

"It is not your fault, Sister," Gapman said. "I should have escorted you home."

"But you were busy with the park. The MOUSs are so happy there, Sister Grace—you have to go see! Besides, Gapman was here moments after I screamed!"

"When I got here, the MOUS was thrashing about the kitchen. Sister Eloise had wisely climbed onto a counter and out of the way. It crashed through the door. I tried to chase it out the front door but Pinjal and Kenjo were blocking the way, brandishing swords." Despite his smooth, nothing-to-see-here reporting tone, it was obvious Gapman wanted it known why the rest of our house was a mess and who deserved the blame.

"We came to rescue Sister!" Kenjo declared with no remorse at all. "This is the business we've chosen."

Grace crossed her arms. "I don't like violence, Kenjo. Blood is a big expense."

Gapman whistled. "Good one, Sister!"

"Focus!" I told them. Godfather quotes were not going to lighten my mood, even from my nun. "Is that when it tried to tunnel through my wall?"

With a jerk of my head, I pointed toward the MOUS-sized dent in the otherwise beautifully hewn stone hallway that led to my lair.

Kenjo continued, "Would have, too, but Gapman grab MOUS by the haunches. He swung it around—"

"—breaking the cabinet!—" Pinjal interjected.

Gapman grimaced in apology. "I'm glad to replace it, Sister."

"—and then we chopped off its head!" Kenjo concluded proudly.

Pinjal reenacted the fatal blow. "MOUS wiggled and jerked! Gapman dropped it. Screamed like pixie, he did!"

"I was surprised!" Gapman finally lost enough of his cool to snap—or would have snapped, if his voice hadn't risen. He cleared his throat. "Be that as it may, the MOUS is well and truly an ex-MOUS now and resting safely in the freezer, most of the mess is cleaned up, and I'll arrange to replace any damaged property."

"We fix," Kenjo said. "Vern good to us. We come to him in friendship, he treat us good. Now we return friendship. We fix good."

Then he turned and regarded my wall.

"But not wall. No fix wall. Get dwarf. Pay dwarf MOUS, dwarf fix wall. Make him offer he can't re-fuse. Dead MOUS. Chop head. No doubt."

Gapman rubbed his temples through his mask. Sister Eloise still looked like she might cry from guilt.

Grace took pity on them all. "Alright. I think things are settled enough for today, and we've all had enough excitement for one evening. Is the kitchen clean enough that we can make some din-ner?"

"No, Sister, no!" Kenjo protested. "Come to camp. Big party to celebrate hunt. Much MOUS meat."

Twenty minutes later, we were sitting on the ground in the middle of the hobgoblin camp. The sun had set; the mountain air was dry and cool, but the bonfire warmed us and sent delectable smells of roasting MOUS our way. I felt a comforting tickle over my scales that penetrated into my muscles and realized it was the flow of magic from the Gap seeping into my body. It felt good.

The hobgoblins danced and sang, cajoling Sister Eloise to join in. Apparently, they'd taught her a couple of tunes while building the MOUS ranch. Then they reenacted highlights of the hunt, with one of them wearing a torn napkin around his neck to mark himself as Gapman. Kenjo made a speech praising Gapman's role and declaring him one of the tribe. "And may his first child be masculine child!"

Gapman raised his kebab in salute, and the festivities once again commenced. The hobgoblinettes grabbed Grace's hands and pulled her into the dancing circle. Sister Eloise, clapping, jumped up to join them.

Gapman took a seat next to me. "Thanks for trusting me to go solo. Sorry you had to come back to such chaos," he said. "Did you have fun?"

"Chaos is our natural state, but yes, I did have fun." I'd met some interesting people—people who'd appreciated me. I'd basked in the heat and humidity. Even reconnected with old friends and made new ones.

Still, as I sat there, the heat of the fire contrasting with the chill, my padawan beside me and my partner dancing with our own little mob of hobs, I realized that, although the travel had been fun, it did not compare with being home.

Do you love Vern?

Coming in 2026: *Live and Let Fly*—a spy spoof. I'm revising it from its original version.

You can also follow the series on Amazon. There, you'll find all the stories published thus far. I'm working hard to keep a regular stream, so check back often!

Also, if you love Shogzallie, I have coloring pages! Contact me through my website.

Keep in Touch

If you want to learn about future books, please

- Sign up for my newsletter. https://fabianspace.substack.com/subscribe for extra Vern stories, updates and a free book!
- Visit my website (https://karinafabian.com)
- Follow me on Facebook: https://www.facebook.com/Karina-Fabian-Speculative-Fiction-with-a-Grin-2233839790277963
- Follow **Vern** on Facebook: https://www.facebook.com/DragonEyePI

Acknowledgements

New Edition:

I've been anxiously awaiting the time I could bring this story back into the Vernverse. So much has changed! Thanks to everyone who has supported me in my writing. For this version, I have to thank:

Suzanna Linton for the mole idea. She's the one who told me her experience with moles where the ground opened up and "accepted" them.

Nikos Lambdin for requesting some old characters return. That's why Ray is here. In If Wishes Were Dragons, he was moving to Florida, anyway.

Critiquers: Matthew Schmidt, Nikos Lambdin, Corinna Turner, Suzanna Linton, Jacqueline Casasnovas, Joshua Higginbotham

Omgitswicks is never listed by name, he's the guy holding the flip phone. He's an actual comedian in Florida, and I love his videos of crazy things that happen in our state, so when I was going over the scene where Vern's mistaken for animatronics, it seemed perfect to add him. He graciously gave me permission. Check out his stuff on Facebook.

Old Edition:

It all started with an idea.

Yeah, right. Actually, it all started with the *lack* of an idea. I'd heard about an anthology, *Firestorm of Dragons*. They wanted—duh—dragon stories. I wanted to write them one, but first, I needed a dragon. Not just any dragon. Something unique. Something a dragon had not done.

Well, I thought about it, then discussed it with my husband, who in college read the entire USAF Academy library of Fantasy/SF and had done a fair job of keeping up with the market even to that day. Needless to say, every idea we had, he'd seen. So I gave up, let the ideas rattle in my mind, and went to watch *Whose Line is it, Anyway?* with the kids.

You have to see this show. You will not stop laughing. Drew Carey hosts, leading a team of four comedians through improvisational skits according to the directions on a card. That night Colin Mochrie and Ryan Stiles were instructed to do a film noir skit. I think it had to do with a dead parrot, but that didn't matter. There was something about the clichéd lines delivered in mildly sarcastic tones, the first person narration that followed the beat of moody jazz. The fun they had. I wanted to jump in the skit with them. I could do it.

Hey, I could do it. *With a dragon!*

Thus came Vern, a cynical dragon on the wrong side of the tracks (or in this case, the Interdimensional Gap), working off a geas by St. George by being a professional problem solver for the particularly desperate. **Lost treasures found. Virginity verified. Wisdom of the Ages, Knowledge of Eternity. Rides extra.**

"DragonEye, PI" appears in Firestorm of Dragons by Dragon Moon Press.

Vern was too much fun to write, so as I heard about anthologies (which inspire me), I started writing other stories and making up more adventures than I could write. Vern has solved the mystery of a murderous crop of chili peppers, defeated a Cthulhu-wanna-be and has even had a horrifying experience as a human. He picked up a partner, Sister Grace McCarthy, a nun and mage for the Faerie Catholic Church. I've built a brave new world—or at least a sarcastic but fun new world, developed with clichés stretched to the limit and legends old and new getting shoehorned into a noir style and Vern's own special point of view.

When an anthology based on the Ten Plagues of Egypt came along, I decided to play on a Gaelic legend of the fairies having a war in the form of insects. "War of insects" sounds phenomenally stupid, however, so I decided to dress it up by changing it to Gaelic. A friend from the Catholic Writers Online (Deal Matthews) introduced me to Shirley Stark, a Mensan in North Dakota and an expert in ancient Gaelic. She gave me the translation; I sent her "Amateurs" as thanks. And as it turned out, she was editor of her regional Mensa Magazine, *The Prairie Dawg,* and asked if she could publish it.

Since I'd planned "Amateurs" for the *Ten Plagues* anthology, I declined, but the idea was so fun, I suggested we make up another mystery—a serial with Mensans. Florida hosted the Mensa World Gathering that year; what better place for magical mayhem than the Magic Kingdom itself? "Magic, Mensa and Mayhem," a fantasy noir comedy, made its debut in *The Prairie Dawg* in June 2006.

In October that year, I attended the Muse Online Conference, where Dindy, publisher of Swimming Kangaroo, offered to critique first chapters and stories. I sent her "Amateurs" to see if she had any ideas for improving it. She liked the story and asked if I had a book's worth. Alas, I didn't—but I did have this rather funny serial that would novelize easily...

And it did, for the most part. The not-most part gave me fits, however. Suddenly, characters from other stories wanted to make an appearance: Cambridge Ramada, a private investigator specializing in rare objects who nearly cost Grace her life in *Greater Treasures*. And Coyote! How did he become a Mensan? (Well, OK. He cheated on the test, but only because he could.) Then characters started doing un-characteristic things. Brunhilde the Valkyrie, in frilly lingerie? The dwarf wants to be an actor? And Rhoda Dakota? She came out of the blue. (Or maybe not; my kids were watching *Hannah Montana* at the time.) Oh, what fun to write though—once my characters told me what was going on!

A lot of other things came up—like what was this weird tension between Vern and Sister Grace?

I've also planted the seeds of at least a half-dozen other past cases. Hope that's not bad. I'll write them, promise!

When I'd finished, I passed it around for critique. Most folks were too busy laughing to say anything—music to my ears—but my best friend and writing partner, Ann Lewis, zeroed in on the fatal flaw. I'd flown to New York City to meet her and another writing friend for the very first time. Heading down the interstate to our friend's crit group, AAA Writers of Huntington, she told me, "It's very funny, but nothing happens to make me care. The crisis only concerns the Faerie. What danger is there to humans?"

Well, oops!

We took the problem to the crit group, and after letting me take more than my fair share of time explaining the Faerie world and all the crazy creatures in it, they helped me discover a crisis that made you care, was topical and fun. I won't spoil it except to apologize to the State of Florida in advance. I'm forever grateful for the group's input.

Oh, what happened to "Amateurs"? *Ten Plagues* rejected it, but *The Sword Review* published it in October 2007.

There's More Fun in FabianSpace!

Thank you for buying this book. If you enjoyed it, click to see the others in this series or discover one of the other worlds of FabianSpace.

Science Fiction

Space Traipse: Hold My Beer: Redneck ingenuity and common sense in a Star Trek-ish universe. Enjoy the adventures of the *HMB Impulsive.*

The Rescue Sisters: Intrepid women doing dangerous missions in space for the love of God and humankind.

The Old Man and the Void: Dex is a relic hunter on the edge of the black hole, desperate for the catch of a lifetime.

Jovian Heat: As the next Great Storm of Jupiter rises, Cass must find the father of a baby in peril—but the father died before the child was conceived.

Fantasy

DragonEye Story: Vern's a snarky dragon on the wrong side of the Interdimensional Gap, solving crimes, battling evil, and saving the universes on an all-too-regular basis.

Madness of Kanaan: Deryl isn't crazy; he's psychic, and aliens of two worlds thinks he can save them. Maybe he can—but can he regain his sanity in the process?

Horror

Neeta Lyffe, Zombie Exterminator: Neeta's an average exterminator, taking out bugs, rodents, and the undead. Can she keep her friends alive, pay her bills, and find romance?

Frightliner and Other Tales of the Supernatural (with Colleen Drippé): Truck-driving vampires terrorizing the road, Southern women doing what needs doing, a zombie wedding—a great story collection for horror lovers.